HKac

AUG   2014

GUILTY PARTIES

GUILTY PARTIES

A Crime Writers' Association Anthology

Edited by
Martin Edwards

This first world edition published 2014
in Great Britain and the USA by
SEVERN HOUSE PUBLISHERS LTD of
19 Cedar Road, Sutton, Surrey, England, SM2 5DA.

Trade paperback edition first published 2014
in Great Britain and the USA by SEVERN HOUSE PUBLISHERS LTD.

British Library Cataloguing in Publication Data

Guilty parties : a Crime Writers' Association anthology.
1. Detective and mystery stories, English.
I. Edwards, Martin, 1955- editor of compilation.
823'.087208092-dc23

ISBN-13: 978-07278-8387-2 (cased)
ISBN-13: 978-1-84751-516-2 (trade paper)

All Severn House titles are printed on acid-free paper.

Severn House Publishers support the Forest Stewardship Council™ [FSC™],
the leading international forest certification organisation. All our titles that
are printed on FSC certified paper carry the FSC logo.

MIX
Paper from
responsible sources
FSC
www.fsc.org   FSC® C013056

Typeset by Palimpsest Book Production Ltd.,
Falkirk, Stirlingshire, Scotland.
Printed and bound in Great Britain by
TJ International, Padstow, Cornwall

CONTENTS

FOREWORD

Rather like letter writing, or music on vinyl, the death of the short story seems to be constantly anticipated. 'Oh, people don't read short stories,' it is said, in publishing circles, or by magazine editors. 'The days of the short story are numbered.' Well, if this volume is anything to go by, the short story, on the contrary, has a very healthy future.

The short story is in the DNA of crime fiction. One only has to glance at the eminent history of the genre to see that short stories were absolutely central to the work of some of our greatest crime writers. There is the work of Conan Doyle, of course, but also the likes of Allingham, Christie, Chesterton and Simenon all knew that some tales demand the brevity and elegance that only a short story can give.

This CWA Anthology continues that proud tradition. Since our foundation in 1953, the nature of crime writing has evolved and broadened, the characterization ever richer, the story-telling more exploratory, experimental, surprising. The genre continues to be popular because people love being told a proper story. A reader reaching for a crime story knows that they will be given a page-turning narrative and a real resolution.

And the popularity of the short form of our genre reflects that. A crime short story can be writ large or small. It can describe the culmination of a lifetime in one moment of change; or, it can be a little tale of neat resolution. It can chart unimaginable evil, or quiet homicide, or just a dull day in a copper's life. It can talk of death, of love, of vengeance. It can describe psychological torment, or the orderly processes of a detective's puzzle-solving. Sometimes it doesn't even need to have a crime.

The CWA Anthology is always an opportunity to showcase the huge range of talent within the genre and the writers represented here are no exception. Some are familiar names, some are people who have never contributed before; some British, some from overseas. As a collection of work it proves the continued importance of short stories, an importance which I am sure will continue to grow, not only in print form, but also within the proliferations of web-based and electronic forms, so that a bite-sized chunk of narrative is just the thing for a short train journey, or a moment between meetings.

I am delighted to introduce this collection and to celebrate the work of the featured authors. I also wish to thank, once again, our publishers, Severn House, and our wonderful editor, Martin Edwards. And as even a cursory dipping-in will demonstrate, the crime short story is in robust form, and all set to continue the rich tradition of the genre.

Alison Joseph
CWA Chair

INTRODUCTION

The number of members of the Crime Writers' Association, which celebrated its Diamond Jubilee last year, is now higher than ever, and this reflects the relentless (and very welcome) rise in interest in crime fiction across the world. The CWA may be primarily a British organisation, but its members come from many different countries. An Icelandic chapter was formed not long ago, and there are plans for a chapter based in France. This international dimension is reflected in the fact that two contributors to this book hail from Iceland and New Zealand, while others live in Greece and Abu Dhabi.

In putting this book together, I was keen to offer a flavour of the remarkable and fascinating diversity of the crime genre, as well as of the people who write it. Only four of those authors who featured in last year's anthology, *Deadly Pleasures*, return this time, but I am confident that readers will find that the quality of the stories is as high as ever. Several contributors have never previously featured in a CWA anthology, and they range from relative newcomers such as Ricki Thomas to very well-established authors like Aline Templeton and Paul Johnston. From the many submissions I received, I have chosen a few very short, but I think highly effective, stories, and even a contribution in verse.

I am optimistic about the future of the short story, an optimism fired in part by the quality of the submissions, in part by broader trends. Markets in print magazines may be in short supply, but the opportunities for online and digital publication seem to be encouraging more and more writers to try their hand at the form, and sometimes in daring fashion – at least one CWA member has produced a short story via Twitter. As for the CWA Anthology, it has a long and proud history of showcasing splendid work by writers both famous and new to the genre, and I am confident that, changes in the publishing world notwithstanding, it will continue to go from strength to strength.

As usual, I must express my thanks to all the contributors, the publishers, and my colleagues on the CWA committee who have given this project their support. And now, without any more ado, on with the stories!

Martin Edwards

HEY JUDE
Frances Brody

Frances Brody writes the 1920s Yorkshire-based mystery series featuring war widow turned sleuth, Kate Shackleton. Before turning to crime, Frances wrote radio and theatre plays, TV scripts and sagas, winning the HarperCollins Elizabeth Elgin debut award for the most regionally evocative family saga of the millennium.

Why does a police car look so much like a police car, like it couldn't be anything else? It couldn't be any more noticeable if it came onto the estate sirens blazing.

'It's there,' I said, 'past the lamppost.' She stopped the car. She got out, I got out. Our house is the corner one in this squared off bit of street so you have to walk across the stretch of grass where you're not supposed to play football or cricket, and everyone does. I'd heard them as we came round the corner. The Patel kids and our Anthony. They play cricket like World War Three. When the car stopped and I got out it went quiet. Desperately, impressively quiet, like someone had said, 'Freeze!'

We went through the gate and she was going to knock on the front door.

'Back way,' I said and we walked round.

Just for a second it crossed my mind that I could run for it. But where could I go? Besides, she was dead close. Breathing down my neck. I went in. As usual, Mum and Dad were at the table, drinking tea. Smoking. They looked across – and then they saw her. Miss Bluebottle.

'Hi,' I said. And my voice was real normal, as if I wasn't being brought home by the busies.

She said, 'Hello, Mrs Markham, Mr Markham.'

They just sat there. Looking. Like they were seeing a scene on telly and waiting for it to change. They're not exactly action packers at the best of times.

'Are you going to tell them, Rachel, or shall I?'

Mum and Dad just sat there. Like, What's this? What's going on?

'I got picked up for shoplifting,' I said.

'What?' said Mum.

Dad didn't say anything. He forgot to smoke. His mouth kind of opened, like it was waiting for his cig. Then he closed it, and his head kind of nodded, as if it didn't have anything to do with him.

'Can I sit down?' the copper asked.

'You better come in the front room,' said Mum.

'Hang on a minute.' Dad looked at me. 'Did you do it? Were you shoplifting?'

And I knew if I said no, he would shove her out the door, copper or no copper.

'Yeah.'

We went in the front room.

We all sat down. Somehow the copper ended up sitting next to me on the settee. Mum and Dad in the chairs, looking . . . separate.

'A colleague and I responded to a call from Meredith's Bookshop at four thirty,' said the copper, like she'd learned the lines. 'There were several girls together, seen behaving suspiciously, and suspected of shoplifting. The manager had apprehended Rachel.'

Mum said, 'What were you doing in Meredith's?'

Dad said, 'Who were you with?'

'That's what I'd like to know,' said the copper. 'The other girls got away.'

I said nothing.

'Meredith's?' said Mum. 'What did you take?'

'*Jude the Obscure.*'

'Who?'

I really appreciated Dad making one of his stupid jokes. It was almost like he couldn't help it, even when I was on the point of being hung, drawn and quartered. Then I realised, he wasn't joking. He'd gone senile. I always knew he would. He always said I'd send him round the twist one of these days.

The copper said, 'Rachel had four copies of *Jude the Obscure* in her bag. We have reason to believe one of her friends took multiple copies of *Twelfth Night* and another girl took . . . some poetry.'

I nearly said the set anthology, but that would have given the game away.

'Is this true?' said Mum.

I wished I could think of some way of denying it. Like claiming Jude had just kind of made a rush at me and leapt into my bag, like someone was after him, *Tess of the d'Ubervilles* or *The Mayor of Casterbridge*.

'Yeah.'

'Why?' said Mum.

'Because they're on my book list.'

'Why four?' said Mum.

That was when I decided to shut up altogether.

'Were you taking them to re-sell at school?' the copper asked. As if she hadn't asked me before.

Dad was looking at his feet. I expect he was remembering how when I was little and looking through his books he'd told me which ones he'd liberated and when I asked him what liberated meant Mum had nearly started to beat him up.

I wanted to tell him it wasn't his fault. It wasn't even my idea. I said nothing.

'So what happens now?' said Mum.

'I have to write a report. The inspector needs to see it. Then it's up to the inspector. And Meredith's.'

'Is she going to be prosecuted?' said Mum.

'You're an idiot,' said Dad. 'What are you?'

I didn't think I needed to answer.

'Possibly,' said the copper to Mum. 'It would help if she'd give a full account.'

Shop my mates, she meant.

'Can you leave us to talk to her?' said Mum, thinking she could get it out of me.

'I'd prefer it if we could have a statement now,' said the copper.

I said nothing. Why was I so slow? By the time I'd got to the door at Meredith's, everyone else had gone and they'd done this clever blocking me thing so I couldn't get out. I mean, four copies of *Jude the Obscure*. I wouldn't have minded getting nicked if I'd gone for a big one. Post Office job. I wished I didn't feel sick.

'Well?' said Mum. 'Who was with you? Whose idea was it? Have you done this kind of thing before?'

Say nothing.

'What was wrong with the library?'

'I told you. I told you I needed the books.'

Dad leapt off his chair and came yelling and screeching towards me like he was king of the apes.

'I was gettin' 'em. I was gettin' 'em for you. I gave you one. I gave you *Jude the* bloody *Obscure*.'

Mum glared at him and I could hear her thoughts saying, Sit down, you. Stop making a show!

He sat down, but like he couldn't keep still. He was bashing his hands up and down on the chair arm.

'They were captured on camera,' said the copper. 'We will identify them. It would be simpler for us and easier for you if you'd make a full statement.'

'Come on,' said Dad to me. 'Come in the kitchen.'

I got up and followed him in.

He put the kettle on. Tea and cigarettes. That's what he lives on. Cigarettes and tea.

'Why? Why? Why bring one of them in the house? We can do without the law. Isn't it bad enough?'

'Yes, it's bad enough.'

He sent me back in, to ask if the policewoman took sugar.

In the kitchen, he said, '*Jude the Obscure, Jude the Obscure*. What was wrong with my copy of *Jude the Obscure*?'

'It was scribbled in.'

'Annotated. The word is annotated.'

It was like he was dragging the word from somewhere a long way off.

'You're an idiot? What are you?'

There are always three choices when you get a remark like that. You can say, All right. So I'm an idiot. You can say nothing, maybe include a sigh. Usually a good option. Or you can say something else. I said, 'Property is theft.'

He banged his hand on the table and at the same moment looked out of the window and saw the police car. He said, 'And theft is a criminal record. For the rest of your life. We don't do that. We pay for what we want or we go without, all right?'

'I'm sick of going without.'

'And do you think I'm not?'

He put teabags in three cups. I poured myself an orangeade.

'Before this tea mashes, I want to know.'

'What?'

'Everything.'

I closed my lips.

'Not her. Me. I want to know. Why four copies of *Jude the Obscure*?'

'Me and my mates.'

'Most kids don't care. Most kids play truant. Couldn't you just have played truant during English?'

'We like English.'

I shouldn't have said that. It narrowed it down. He pretended I hadn't given anything away. He said, 'Good. You can study for a degree in jail.'

I started to drink my orangeade. He snatched the glass off me.

'Who? Name names.'

'No.'

'They've got them on camera.'

'So they don't need me to tell.'

'Holly Gill, Emma Wilson, Lucy O'Hara . . .?'

He should have been a detective. He should have been something. Then he wouldn't have been here. Spending his life at the kitchen table in a puff of smoke. Offering me his scraggy old books. I wanted something new. Mine. I kept remembering that time I'd spread his books on the carpet, and he'd said, These were the ones. The ones I liberated.

'What about you? You used to liberate books.'

'That was then. This is now.'

'So?'

'Liberated. The word's . . . gone from the language.

And . . . it was different. We thought we were on the edge of something, something better. We thought the world was going to be a better place. New . . . social arrangements.'

He bashed a teabag round the cup.

'You could be expelled.'

I cared and I didn't care. I cared when I got caught. I cared in the car. I cared when I saw Mum's and Dad's stupid pathetic faces. But now, I was only sorry I was an unsuccessful liberator. I was only sorry it was just books. I hated him for ever liberating books. I hated him for stopping.

He squeezed the teabags. I passed him the milk.

'You make a statement. You've got no choice now. You were caught red-handed.'

Cliché. I didn't say it, but I looked it.

'You tell her what you told me. And . . . if they were your friends they wouldn't have left you. You're an idiot.'

'You keep saying that.'

'I know one when I see one.'

It should have been, like heightened experience. Like, this is happening to me. This is happening to me, now.

But it wasn't. This rhyme kept coming back to me. Dad had pinned it on the back of the kitchen door and now I didn't just know it, I Knew It. The look of it, the curly scrawl of it.

> The law condemns the man or woman
> Who steals the goose from off the common,
> But lets the greater villain loose
> Who steals the common from the goose.

'You shouldn't steal from bookshops,' he said. 'Like you shouldn't steal from . . . You shouldn't steal from bookshops.'

'You did.'

'I was wrong. You're supposed to be smarter.'

'Says who? And anyway . . . if I'd come home with a diamond ring that would have been all right, would it?'

'No! Are you determined to throw your chances away?'

'I'm not supposed to have chances. I'm not supposed to do well. I'm supposed to play truant. I'm supposed to fail.'

'What?'

Mum came in, looking to see what had happened to the tea. She made me carry the cup of tea to the policewoman. As if that was gonna make some difference. As if she's gonna say, Oh thanks for the tea. It's such a good cup of tea that we'll leave it at that, shall we?

The copper took a sip from the tea. It was too strong for her. She said, 'Right, Rachel. I'll take your statement now.'

They both looked at me. They all looked at me. Waiting.

'I needed books for school. I needed *Jude the Obscure*, *Twelfth Night* and that anthology. I needed to be able to read them. Learn them.'

It was supposed to be my statement, but Mum butted in, saying how I'd always been a reader and they'd never had the money for electronic stuff and computer games. That I was in the junior library, and how upset I was that time I got butter on *Haddock 'n' Chips*.

The policewoman waited till Mum had finished.

'And had you planned this, Rachel? You and your friends. Or was it spur of the moment? You had £2.50 on you.'

'I knew what they cost. I'd already checked the price. I didn't have enough money.'

'So you planned it?'

I said, 'It was premeditated.'

Dad looked as if he was gonna do his jungle act. Mum put her head in her hands. Visual cliché.

'Premeditated, between you? You and the other girls?'

I suddenly thought that maybe I should use all sorts of words that I could later claim weren't my vocabulary and then I could say the statement was fabricated. Or maybe I could just leave the country. I said nothing.

'Will you tell me who the other girls were? Are they girls from your school? Your class?'

'What other girls?'

Mum said, 'Rachel!'

'Have you taken other things . . . before?'

We'd planned to. Often enough. We'd planned to form a ring: clothes, jewellery, credit cards. We'd sometimes imagine what we'd do if someone approached us like you saw on telly.

I mean people usually thieved it to support a habit. If you didn't have a habit, you could be quids in.

'No.'

'Are you sure?'

'Yes.'

'So why today? Why these books?'

'Couldn't afford them. Needed them.'

She stopped writing. 'It's unusual,' she said. 'Teenagers don't usually steal books. Not even university students steal books.'

'I want a good education,' I said. I glared at Dad.

She wrote that down. Was she going to write everything down? Like the jurors in *Alice in Wonderland*?

'You're refusing to name the other girls?'

'Yes.'

'Is there anything else you'd like to add to this statement?'

'Yes.'

They all waited. Actually, there wasn't, but then I had to think of something.

I said, 'Education is something they can't take away from you. That's why they don't want us to have it.'

I thought Dad was smiling, but he was crying. Like really crying.

DEADLINE

N.J. Cooper

N. J. Cooper is an ex-publisher and former chair of the CWA. She writes for a variety of newspapers and magazines and is a regular contributor to BBC Radio. As Natasha Cooper, she has written many novels, including the Willow King series and the Trish Maguire novels. Four more recent books feature the forensic psychologist Karen Taylor.

You think I'd be angry, wouldn't you? Or terrified? But I wasn't. Even I was surprised that the only sentence in my mind when they told me was: I thought so.

I hadn't exactly felt ill, but I had known something was wrong. At first, when I realised my jeans didn't feel so snug and I got on the scales and saw I'd lost nearly a stone, I was pleased. Who wouldn't be? But over the next few months, as I forgot what hunger felt like and realised how tired simply leaving the house made me, I knew.

It's not as though there was no guide. My mother had had it and so had hers, which made it more or less inevitable for me. It's one of those that creeps up on you unawares until it's got so big that it starts to press on other bits, and only then does it hurt enough to make you understand there's something wrong. At first I thought it was wind. Then I knew. But you still have to go through all the hoops – tests, and more tests – before it becomes real and public. Ovarian cancer.

I was luckier than my mum; she was only 56 when it got her. I'm past 70; not much past and it's not exactly your business how much past. In every other way I'm incredibly lucky. I've had a fantastic career, doing precisely what I wanted; I had a kind and funny husband for forty years before his heart attack (and mercifully that was instant so he didn't have the long slow slide into death we all dread), and two gorgeous daughters. They're well away into their own lives, as they should be, and know nothing about this.

I've written formal letters to the police and the coroner, explaining everything, but this is a fuller version for anyone who needs to read it.

I had to watch my poor mother stagger through four awful years, full of chemo and radio, only to feel the tumour come back, so that she had to have more treatment, feel it come back again, and be faced with yet more treatment before they gave her the verdict: nothing more we can do. Why did she have to go through so much misery and pain and exhaustion when the ending was inevitable?

I don't want that. I don't want to go to Switzerland either. Why should I? It's inhumane that a sentient adult, who has had control of every other aspect of her life, should not be allowed to deal with this in whatever way she chooses.

Again I'm luckier than lots of people. My mobility isn't impaired. Nor my mind. I can find out how much of what to take, open my own bottles as I choose and mash things up and swallow the resulting brew on my own. I don't need any help.

But I've discovered I do want to have company when I do it. Without friends, it might be like standing in an empty desert, with howling winds and sand blowing into my eyes. I just don't know. So I'm not going to risk it.

There's peace afterwards. I do know that. Once my brain has shut down – been shut down by the mashed-up brew I'll make – I know there'll be nothing: no more pain; no fear; none of the terrors invented by the powerful to keep the powerless at bay.

All that will be left of the person who is me will be memories in other people's brains. And that's the only monument I want: good memories for my family and friends; not memories of me ill, muddled up with their own anxieties about whether they did enough for me.

But in the actual moment of swallowing and then waiting for the brew to work, I think I may need my beloved friends around me. Hence the party.

One of the most comforting things I've found is re-reading John Buchan's *Sick Heart River*, in which Sir Edward Leithen, another lawyer funnily enough, faces up to what's coming to him and thinks that he wants to die on his feet, 'as Vespasian said an emperor should'. I've always liked that and now I'm ill too I like it still more, even though it's a bit sexist. Vespasian's thought, I mean. If a man should die on his feet, why shouldn't a woman?

You may be thinking that it's got to my brain already and I'm rambling unnecessarily, but it hasn't. I just want you to understand exactly why I'm doing it like this, why I'm not giving any of my friends any warning. I don't want them trying to persuade me out of it and I don't want them to be found guilty of any kind of complicity. That's in the letters to the police and the coroner too. My beloved friends won't know anything about it until it's too late.

I've always liked planning parties, and this is just a slightly different kind of party. There'll be CCTV cameras throughout the house so that when the police investigate, as they're supposed to, they'll see me doing it all on my own.

So, back to the arrangements. The party's going to be pretty lavish, with all the kind of things I've most liked in my life. After all, what's the point of spending a vast amount of money on a funeral, when I won't be there to enjoy it? My instructions are perfectly clear: my body will go to a school of anatomy, and that's it. No service of any kind and no gravestone or plaque or anything like that. The celebration of my life will take place while I still have possession of it and can order things as I want them to be. And I hope my daughters will forgive me for not letting them come. It's only to protect them.

We'll have had our own goodbyes in advance: they just won't know at the time that they're goodbyes. But when it's all over they'll understand, my Georgie and Josie.

So, the arrangements for the party: the flowers are going to be my favourite, old-fashioned, mix of pink-scented roses, pink and white peonies of the blousiest kind, and regale lilies, which is why it has to take place in June. I was glad to have a deadline. Deadlines have always helped me when

I've had any kind of fear about anything. They make me concentrate on what I can control; not on what I can't. There'll be huge great Chinese bowlfuls of flowers all over the house, and hang the expense!

The drinks will be what the caterers call a full bar, along with champagne because so many people still like it. I'm having the fizz sent up from my favourite wine merchant in Monmouth, who has a particularly delicious apple-y kind. I hope it'll be sunny so that we can spill out, as they say, on to the terrace. The canapés are being provided by the daughter of an old friend, who has a wonderfully imaginative mixture of hot and cold, meat, fish, veg and sweet stuff, and who is sensible enough not to get in a frenzy when she understands what I've done. I've picked her most expensive range and paid everything in advance so that she won't have to wait until probate's been granted. You have to think of practicalities like that when people are self-employed.

My speech is almost ready. All that's left is a final check to make sure I've hit the right note of celebration, explanation and apology, and gratitude for them being there.

An apology is necessary because in a way it's quite a shocking thing to be doing. I do see that. Inviting all the friends you love most and then killing yourself in their company is pretty extreme. I'm not sure quite how long the twenty pills (that's what I've been told will be enough) will take to work, which means that the timing of my speech will be quite tricky: late enough to ensure there's nothing anyone can do to stop me; but not so late that my speech is affected. I mean my ability to speak, obviously, not the piece I'm writing now. I don't want any officious medical bod to whisk me off to hospital to have my stomach pumped – if that's what they do these days.

I think I can trust my friends. They have all been carefully picked. And because there will be about sixty of them, I don't see how any one of them could be found guilty of complicity in my death. I wish I knew the current DPP. Inviting her would be a good way of ensuring safety.

So the plans are in place and I've exhumed my most ravishing evening dress from years ago. Who'd have thought one spin-off from this horrible disease would be that I could get back into the astonishing dress my mother had made for me from a Dior toile the year I was seventeen. The hairdresser is going to come here, and she'll bring a make-up artist with her. I need to look what I am: a fully functioning, celebratory human being. I dread looking like a clown, but they've promised the make-up will be discreet. And the dress definitely is. My mama would never have allowed anything that wasn't, even once I was seventeen.

And I must remember to wait for my share of the lovely champagne until after I've said my piece. Then, of course, it won't matter how much I have, for the first and last time in my life. I can't wait.

There's no peace. Noise is all around. My throat aches like buggery and my eyes are gluey. My joints are tight and sore, all of them, as though someone's been hitting them with a mallet.

If I were a sentimentalist, I might think this was hell and I'd been wrong all along, that this is the punishment for self-slaughter. But I know it isn't. As soon as I can control my temper I'll open my gluey eyes and find out what they've done to me.

Smells assault my brain. How many of them are real and how many the products of my own disordered mind? Have I done damage that can't be undone?

That would be punishment, real punishment, to have been brought back no longer able to do what must be done.

Fury ices me inside. People always talk of fury as being hot. Not mine. I feel as though steel rods have been driven through me and are acting like the element in a deep freeze. I have to know who and where and what and why.

Forcing my sticky eyelids apart is difficult, and even when the lids are open my eyes aren't good at seeing. Have I made myself blind as well? Oh, God forbid!

That was a manner of speaking only. No more than that. No supernatural being is here, tormenting me with fears and hopes and dreams of punishment. This is my mind doing it to itself.

A shape quivers at the end of my bed. I know it's a bed now, and a hospital one, with the usual tears in the thin white cellular blanket. I know those blankets all too well. Behind the quivering figure is someone in scrubs. Nurse or doctor or health-care assistant. You can't tell any more, and that may be a good thing.

I roll my head to the side and see a drip bag, hung on a pedestal, with its nasty yellowish plastic tube wiggling down towards my arm. There's a bubble in it, but that kind of air-in-the-vein promise is a chimera. I once asked a nurse if it would kill me and she just laughed, before flicking the big bubble into lots of tiny ones. No hope there then.

My head rolls back so that it's straight again. My eyes are working now. There's Josie, my younger daughter, clinging to the end of the bed. Her eyes are red-rimmed and her lips look swollen, as though she's been biting them.

'Hello,' I say, or rather croak.

'Oh, Mum, I'm so sorry.'

'Sorry?'

'I couldn't . . . if I'd known . . . How . . .?'

'What couldn't you do, Jo?' Less croaky now and full of gentleness stiffened by confidence. I know my gorgeous Jo wouldn't have been cruel enough to do this to me.

'I couldn't stop them. By the time they rang me and I realised what had been going on, it was too late. They'd pumped you and dripped you.' Tears fill her eyes and spill over. 'I know why you didn't tell us, but if you had I could've protected you from this.'

My mouth smiles. I didn't plan it, but the joy of seeing my Jo being herself was enough to flood me with endorphins and make me grin from here to eternity. My eternity anyway.

'But then I couldn't have protected you, Josie-Jo. And that would have mattered more than any of this.'

'I know.' She wipes the back of her hand against her eyes and smiles back at me. She's tough that girl and I'll always love her for it.

'Who was it?' I say in a conversational kind of way, but my Jo isn't deceived.

'The way you set it up meant collective guilt for all sixty

of your best friends. Can't you look at this the same way and blame them all?'

I think for a moment and know the smile has quite gone from my mouth.

'No. But whoever it was has given me something to live for.'

Jo, my Josie-Jo, my clever, gorgeous, lovely daughter, who knows me better than anyone else has ever known me because we're so alike, laughs.

'Tracking down the guilty party, you mean?' she says.

'And when I've found him, I'll make sure he's miles away when I put the dress rehearsal to good use.'

THE DEATH OF SPIDERS
Bernie Crosthwaite

Bernie Crosthwaite has written plays for radio and stage as well as a crime novel, *If It Bleeds*, featuring press photographer Jude Baxendale. She has been a journalist, tour guide and teacher, and lives in Yorkshire.

I was peering down the microscope at the spinneret of the arrowhead spider, *Micrathena sagittata*, when the telephone rang. I picked it up reluctantly.

'Professor Hannah Staples,' I said, feeling the strangeness of that title, conferred on me at the end of the last academic year. It still made me feel both powerful and terrified.

'My name's Detective Inspector Croft. I'm in need of your expertise, professor.'

'Concerning what?'

'Concerning a suspicious death.'

'I don't see how I can help you.'

'You're an expert on bugs, aren't you? There was that thing about you in the local paper recently.'

I grimaced slightly, recalling the headline 'Spider Woman Made Top Prof'.

'It depends what you mean by "bugs". If you mean insects, then no, I'm not an entomologist. I specialise in arachnids, with a particular interest in—'

'Apparently you're the go-to person, so I need you here straightaway – before they remove the body.'

I was silent. I glanced along the cluttered bench to the tower of wooden racks containing specimens of every type of arachnid. In the corner a sweep net stuck out of a rucksack that I hadn't had a chance to unpack after a recent field trip. The shelves above me were badly bowed with the weight of textbooks and files. The first semester, with its influx of new students and the creation of new courses, was always intensely busy. How could I possibly take time off? After all, I had lectures to write, a failing PhD student to deal with, not to mention my own research into the medical uses of spider silk that had reached a crucial stage.

'Time's passing, professor. Every minute counts in a case like this.'

'I understand that.' I thought about it. I'd never been part of a police investigation before. It might be interesting. I took a deep breath and plunged in. 'All right,' I said. 'I'll come.'

Blue and white plastic tape had been strung across the alleyway behind the row of shops on Victoria Road. When I gave my name, the WPC on guard lifted the barrier and I ducked under it.

'Down the end,' she said. 'Back of the Turkish takeaway.'

I picked my way around discarded packaging, overflowing refuse bins and piles of rotting rubbish, trying not to stain the hems of my trousers. A man in white paper overalls came towards me. He was squarely built, with unruly blond hair. His forehead was furrowed into creases.

'Professor Staples?'

'Yes.'

'I'm DI Croft. This way.'

At the end of the alleyway there was more tape. This time it said 'Crime Scene – Do Not Enter'. I was handed an anti-contamination suit, overshoes and gloves. I put them on and was allowed to pass through.

I could just see, sticking out from the space between a parked Vespa scooter and a crumbling stone wall, a pair of feet in trainers. As we drew level I saw the body of a man lying on the ground, his upper body in shadow. I thought fleetingly, inappropriately, that he had adopted the Pose of the Corpse, a yoga position I used for relaxation. Then I noticed the dark pool of congealed blood that had leaked from under him. A cigarette stub and a tiny pile of ash lay near his left hand.

'Looks like he came out here for a smoke,' said Croft.

'Who is he?' I asked.

'Demir Kemal. He worked here. The last time the owner saw him was at the end of his shift last night, around midnight. He must have come out the back door to collect his scooter, stopped to light up a fag, and—'

'And then he was attacked.'

'Looks like it. The owner arrived mid morning, came out here with a bag of rubbish and there he was.' Croft nodded towards a woman with a clipboard taking notes. 'The MO reckons he was stabbed from behind. It's like someone was lying in wait for him. We'll know more when we do the post-mortem.'

'Poor Demir.'

'You knew him?'

'No, not at all. It's just that I use this takeaway occasionally – it's on my way home. I had a very good lamb souvlaki only the other night – but I never knew any of them by name.' This was all very interesting but I was growing impatient. 'Why did you ask me to . . .?'

'Take a closer look.' He pointed to where the upper part of the body lay in shadow.

I edged my way around the scooter and squatted down. I recognised him. It had been a handsome face, olive skin, black hair. Late twenties, always ready with a flirtatious wink, a charming smile. But now his face was as pale as marble. Glancing down the body I saw that his heart was impaled by a thin spike like an old-fashioned hatpin, and under the pin lay a spider.

'What is it?' asked Croft.

I peered closely, not touching. A hairy long-legged specimen, yellowish-brown in colour. It was in a sorry state. The cephalothorax and abdomen looked flat and misshapen. Two of its legs were missing. 'It's *Phoneutria nigriventer*. Also known as the Brazilian wandering spider.'

'Sounds exotic.'

'They're not uncommon in this country. They arrive in container ships, usually in crates of bananas. Extremely venomous, actually.'

'The way it's pinned to the body – what's the significance of that?'

'I'm not an anthropologist, I'm afraid. You could try the School of Social Sciences.' I stood up, feeling dizzy. 'Unless there's anything else, I really must get back to work.'

'That's it for now. At least we know the species.'

'Glad to help.'

'Thank you, professor. I'll be in touch.'

I've always loved spiders.

No, that's not quite true. As a small child I was terrified of them – the plump bodies with their oddly human waists, the many legs bent like prongs, their rapid scuttling movements.

One day, when I was six, I was lying on my bed reading. Somewhere in the house Simon, my older brother, was playing his guitar, loudly and tunelessly. I looked up from my book and saw a large black spider working its way in around the skirting board. I started screaming and Simon burst in.

'What the hell's the matter?'

I pointed. He smiled, and bending down, deftly scooped the spider up in his bare hands and released it through the open window.

'You've saved my life!' I threw myself at him, clutching at his knees.

'Don't be so soft, Hannah.' He prised my arms away. 'It's stupid to be frightened of spiders. They spin webs to catch their favourite food – *flies*.' He put on a monster face and chased me round the room. I remember the delicious terror of it, the relief when he stopped, picked me up and swung me round, my legs flying out. 'Flies are the nasty ones, not spiders.'

'But flies are harmless,' I panted.

'What? They vomit on your food and give you diarrhoea.'

'Yuk! Why did you have to tell me that?'

He plonked me on the bed, ruffled my hair, and went out grinning, back to his guitar. It was a shame he never made

it as a musician. I regretted that we hardly ever saw each
other these days, not since that last awkward occasion when
he got drunk and asked me for money.

But I'll always be grateful for the precious gift he gave
me when I was six. The next time I saw a spider I remembered what he'd said and my panic disappeared. I became
fascinated by these crafty industrious creatures. At that stage
I still couldn't touch a spider, but with the help of an empty
yogurt pot and a postcard I could remove them to safety,
hating the thought of them being trodden on.

As I learnt more and more about them I became hooked.
Who wouldn't be? There are over forty thousand different
species and every one of them is extraordinary. The more
bizarre they are, the better I like them. I have great affection
for the bird dung crab spider that looks and smells like
excrement to attract insects, and the Saharan rolling spider
that cartwheels across the desert. I even admire the species
where the young hatched spiderlings eat the mother; a prac-
tical and efficient use of resources. Perhaps my favourite is
the Bolas spider that spins a line with a sticky ball at the
end which it twirls to attract moths, then reels them in to
enjoy them for dinner. Genius.

Then there's my own area of expertise – spider silk. It's
a thin, tough polymer made up of the same three building
blocks as human tissue. Already knee cartilage has been
created from it and not rejected. We can't be far off the next
target – replacing damaged spinal cord.

Captivated when young, I've never faltered in my passion
for spiders. What other creature is so useful or so amazing?
A few years ago, in a museum, I saw a coat woven from
the silk pulled from the abdomen of the golden orb-weaver
spider, and stood for hours in front of the glass case, enrap-
tured by its beauty. I heard a woman ask her husband why
there wasn't a spider silk industry, and I interrupted to
explain that these creatures weren't like silkworms: in
captivity they eat each other – they're cannibals. The couple
didn't stay long after that.

Early on in my studies I came across the idea that spiders
cannot die. The theory is that they can be killed – crushed,

drowned, starved. But if protected from outside dangers, they can, theoretically, live forever. Some say there are spiders in Chinese temples that are nearly three thousand years old. It's a myth of course. Most spiders live less than a year, others take a couple of years to mature then die soon after producing young. A few, such as tarantulas in the family *Theraphosidae,* can live for several decades in captivity, but that's it. It took me a long time and a lot of research before I finally accepted the truth. But there is still something in me that longs to believe that spiders are immortal.

When I got back to the lab after helping DI Croft, there was a student waiting for me. It was Jack Lomax, whose PhD thesis on spiders' fangs – *chelicerae* – I was extremely concerned about. It was already overdue and of poor quality, and I was convinced that even if he completed it he would fail to gain his doctorate. I'd warned him on several occasions that I was unhappy with his work. Now I had made the difficult decision to advise him to drop out, saving him – and the department – the embarrassment of failure.

'Professor Staples . . .' He stood up from where he was slumped at the bench. Long straight hair hung in an untidy curtain down both sides of his face, giving him a mournful look.

He took the news with an increasingly resentful expression on his face. 'No, no . . .' he muttered when I'd finished. His red-rimmed eyes burned at me. 'You can't do this.'

'I can't force you to stop, it's true. But I've spoken to your second supervisor, and he agrees with me. Think about it, Jack – it's for your own good. At our last meeting I gave you a detailed list of changes you needed to make to bring your thesis up to standard and you've merely tinkered with it. In its present state it has no chance of passing.'

'I've worked so hard,' he whined.

'On the contrary, your research is derivative and lazy.'

He banged his hand down on the wooden bench. I flinched at the sharp sound but stood firm.

'Don't try to intimidate me, Jack. It won't work. Now if you don't mind . . .'

The look in his wild eyes narrowed into a beam of hatred.

'You'll be sorry, professor.' He kicked stools aside as he stormed out, making a clattering sound that nearly deafened me. I waited until I heard his footsteps recede along the corridor, righted the stools, made myself a cup of coffee and got back to work.

A few weeks later I had another call from Detective Inspector Croft.

This time it was a middle-aged woman, a dental receptionist, murdered in Jubilee Park. Could I come at once?

Once again I hesitated. On top of my normal workload I was staying up late every night writing articles for science journals, and when I finally put my head down I was plagued by thoughts of Jack Lomax whose barrage of emails veered from pleading to vengeful. My sleep had been thin and broken for many days. I closed my eyes.

'Professor? Are you still there?'

I snapped to attention. 'I'm sorry, I was distracted for a moment. Can I ask if you've made any headway with the Kemal case?'

'The investigation is ongoing. But now there's another one . . .' Croft's voice dropped, almost as if he was speaking to himself. 'God knows what we're dealing with.'

How could I refuse?

Just as I was about to go my laptop bleeped. Another email from Jack. I skimmed it rapidly. The words 'cow' and 'dictator' leapt out. I shook my head. He seemed to be losing all self-control. I was about to delete it, as I'd done with all the others, then stopped. No. It was evidence. I might need it if this came to a bare-knuckle fight in front of the Dean of School. I shut my laptop and left the office, locking the door behind me.

She was lying behind the bandstand in the same supine position as the first. And just like the other one, a spider was impaled on a spike driven into the heart. Croft stared at the body intently as if willing it to give up its secrets.

'Carolyn James,' he said. 'Divorced, lived alone. Wasn't missed until she didn't show up for work this morning.'

'At the dental practice on Queen Street.'

He looked at me sharply. 'Friend of yours?'

'No. I'm just a patient there. I had an emergency appointment recently – an abscess – and she was on the desk. She was very . . . chatty.' I looked away, remembering how she told me she'd seen the article in the local paper.

'A professor – fancy that! Congratulations. What exactly do you study?' she'd asked. I'd explained that I specialised in arachnids, creatures with eight legs and two body parts, like scorpions, ticks and mites, but my chief area of expertise was spiders. 'Creepy crawlies, you mean? Yeuch!'

She'd shuddered so violently I didn't go on. It was a reaction I was used to.

'I'm sorry,' Croft said quietly.

'No, really . . . she wasn't . . . I didn't even know her name.'

'And the spider?'

I knelt down on the cold flagstones and examined it. Dark brown body with pale brown lateral bands, squashed almost flat. Its once long slim legs had curled inwards; when spiders die it causes a drop in the pneumatic pressure in their leg joints, making them into shrivelled versions of their former selves. It was a sight that always filled me with sadness. 'It's a common house spider – *Tengenaria domestica*.'

'Nothing special, then?'

I stood up. 'All spiders are special.'

'If you say so.' He glanced around the park, at the iron-work bandstand, the rolling stretch of grass, the pond in the distance. 'I can't work out any connection between a man working in a Turkish takeaway and a dental receptionist. Why these two? It seems so random.'

I shook my head. 'I'm afraid I can't help you there. I only know about spiders.'

When I accepted a Chair in the Faculty of Natural Sciences I hadn't quite realised how much my workload would increase. I was now responsible for making important departmental decisions, as well as the vital business of submitting grant proposals to funding bodies. A lot of time, thought and effort went into every aspect of my duties. It was hard work, but I was beginning to enjoy it. At the same time I was on the verge of an exciting breakthrough in my own research – the creation of artificial human nerves from spider silk.

The only downside was the constant stream of Jack Lomax's emails, growing steadily more offensive and menacing. Now he had lodged a complaint with the Dean of School about my behaviour and a date had been set for a preliminary hearing.

I was fully stretched. Perhaps that was why my heart sank when I heard DI Croft's voice on my office phone.

'There's been another one.'

It felt odd to be driving along my own street in the early afternoon. Even odder to see police cars and crime scene officers in white overalls clustered round a dense copse of trees fifty metres from my house. Tape barriers had been erected, and when I'd covered up, Croft ushered me through.

'It's a bad one,' he said, staring at the body lying on the ground, almost hidden in the undergrowth.

I reluctantly followed his gaze. A young boy. The Pose of the Corpse. A spider impaled on his heart. I leaned over to inspect it.

'Family *Lycosidae*. A wolf spider. Female.' It was easy to identify from the egg case attached to its spinneret. It had lost all eight of its legs.

'You live on this street, don't you?'

I nodded.

'I expect you know the child?'

'By sight, yes. Not by name.'

'He's called Scott. Aged ten. He was supposed to be sleeping over at a friend's house around the corner last night. The other boy says they argued and Scott came home before bedtime. But he never made it. His parents went off to work this morning, thinking the boys had gone to school together. Mum texted him at lunchtime, got no reply, spoke to the school. He'd been marked absent. She rushed home, started searching. Found him here.'

'That's terrible.'

'Have you ever met him, spoken to him?'

'Once or twice.'

'Recently?'

'No. The last time was weeks ago. He wanted me to identify a spider he'd found. I thought he was taking a real interest but I don't think it was genuine. To be honest he was a bit wild, noisy. I avoided him.'

Croft massaged his creased forehead. 'Why are they doing this – this – spider thing?'

'I suppose it's a way of leaving a mark, a signature.'

'But what does it mean?'

I shrugged.

He looked at me intently. 'I'm beginning to see a link.'

'What link?'

'You.'

I almost laughed. 'You think I . . .?'

'What I'm saying is that you knew all of them. They're all in some way associated with you.'

'Very tenuously.'

'Then how do you explain the spiders?'

'I can't.'

Croft turned, walked a few paces away from me, strode back.

'You bought a takeaway from Demir a few days before he was murdered. You saw Carolyn at the dentist's, then shortly after that, she was killed. And now this poor little boy . . . OK, you haven't spoken to him recently, but you have done in the past. And then there are the spiders . . .' He began pacing again. 'I've checked the distances. Prestige Takeaway is about three-quarters of a mile from here. Jubilee Park no more than half a mile. And here we are on Langley Road – the street where you live.'

'What are you implying?'

'These murders . . . it's almost as if they're closing in on something . . . or someone.'

'On me?'

'I think that's the meaning of the spiders left at the scene. A warning.'

'Of what?'

He looked at me thoughtfully. 'I think you're next.'

'That's ridiculous.'

'Is there someone with a grudge against you? Someone who's out to get you?'

I felt a strange sense of calm, the way I always do when a scientific problem is solved.

'Actually, yes. There is someone.'

We sat in my front room, drinking tea. Croft sat forward on his chair as though afraid of breaking it. He was trying to persuade me to accept twenty-four-hour protection. I refused.

'I spend most of my time at the university where I'm surrounded by students, colleagues, admin staff. If I stay late, there are janitors and nightwatchmen. I'll be perfectly safe.'

'All the same I'd like to put surveillance cameras in your lab and office.'

'Absolutely not. I couldn't bear to be under scrutiny all the time. How would I get my work done? How would I think?'

Croft frowned, looking doubtful.

'I'll be fine. I've done many field trips in inhospitable places. I've learnt to look after myself.'

He ran both hands through his thick fair hair. 'At least let us put a watch on your home at night. I'd say that's when you're most vulnerable.'

'All right, agreed.' I offered the plate of biscuits but he shook his head. 'Any news about Jack?'

'He's not at his flat and no one seems to know where he's got to. A bit of a loner, I take it?'

'I imagine so. He's certainly obsessive and unstable.' I nodded towards the open laptop on the coffee table. 'You can tell that from the emails I showed you.'

Croft stood up and reached for his raincoat. 'Be careful, professor.'

'Don't worry about me. I know what I'm up against now.'

I followed the detective's advice, taking extra care locking doors and windows, not going out alone at night, getting my assistant to vet anyone who came to the office to speak to me.

Jack's emails stopped coming. He wasn't answering his mobile. The police kept an eye on his flat but he didn't re-appear, and there was no sign of him at his parents' house. I didn't like it. Despite what I'd said, it unnerved me. I wanted to flush him out in the open where he could be dealt with. But there was nothing I could do. It was a waiting game.

One night, when I was working late in the lab, I heard noises – a door opening and closing, footsteps. I raised my head slowly from the microscope. The nightwatchman doing his rounds? But his tread was heavy and slow. These footsteps were rapid, and as they came nearer I heard laboured breathing.

I slid silently from my stool. Again I felt that sense of icy calm. I could deal with this. Through the glass panel in the door I saw a shadowy shape, then the door was flung open and Jack Lomax stood there, breathing in shallow gasps. He looked ill. His long hair was scraped back into a ragged ponytail, revealing sunken cheeks. His eyes had lost their wildness. They looked blank, like dead men's eyes.

'Good evening, Jack. Where have you been these past few weeks?'

'On my hols.' He tried to smile. 'Lying low – literally – in a tent by a lake, very remote, very quiet – I didn't see a soul.' His face crumpled like a child's. 'I had to get away – I tried to go home one day and there were policemen outside my flat. I ran.' His expression switched in a moment from bewilderment to anger. 'It was you who put them on to me, wasn't it? What did you accuse me of? Stalking? Harassment?'

'Hardly the worst of your crimes.'

'What?'

'How long have you been back?'

'A few days. I've tried to see you, but there's a policeman outside your house all night. I've tried to get into the department several times but they've changed the security code. Every evening, if your light was on, I've tried the basement service door. No good. Then tonight, for the first time, it was unlocked.'

'That was me. I thought you might come. Tomorrow is your big day after all.'

'My meeting with the dean, yes. I'll tell him how you've treated me.'

'Up to now, Jack, I've treated you very fairly.' My voice was calm but my palms were clammy with sweat. 'But I'm afraid that's about to change.'

'What do you mean?'

'Three murders, Jack. You must be called to account. You must pay for your crimes.'

His eyes narrowed. 'Murders . . .?'

'Your campaign against me has been very useful.' I reached into my pocket for the smooth familiar handle of the bowie knife I used on field trips. 'The police believe the others were a warning, a premonition if you like, that I was your real target, your final victim.'

'You . . . a victim?' He tried to laugh, but only managed a rattling cough.

I closed the short space between us, sliding the blade into his chest. It went in easily, between the ribs and into the heart.

As he staggered and folded to the floor I felt a pang of sorrow for Jack. After all, he had never killed a spider.

I'd seen people destroy spiders before and it had always made me angry. But that was nothing compared to the fury I felt when Demir, shouting absurdly with panic, picked up a huge sauce dispenser and crushed the beautiful Brazilian wandering spider that scuttled across the counter, then flung it out of the back door. Something inside me splintered and a desire for justice overwhelmed me. As a newly-appointed professor I was growing used to making important decisions. Choosing to kill Demir was one of the most crucial. It was like crossing a boundary from one country into another, where the rules were different and I was the one who made them. Jack was right – I was a dictator.

Carolyn had stamped on the spider harmlessly traversing the grey carpet at the dentist's. As for Scott, I'd noticed him acting suspiciously from my window. I fetched my binoculars and saw what he was doing – plucking the legs from a live wolf spider before throwing it on the ground and hitting it with a stone. I knew the research – boys who perpetrate unspeakable acts of cruelty on animals eventually become serial killers. I was doing the world a favour.

Each time, I had rescued the corpse of the spider, planned my revenge and carried it out without a moment's regret. Impaling the dead spiders on their black hearts was a private gesture, of meaning to me alone. Now I saw that it forged a suspicious link between the killings, a link that would now end. In future there would be no connections. The deaths would appear random and inexplicable.

Jack's blood was seeping across the floor. I stepped around him and reached for my phone.

'Detective Inspector Croft,' I said when he answered. 'It's Professor Staples.' I let my voice shake. 'Something terrible has happened.'

MOMENTS MUSICAUX
Judith Cutler

Judith Cutler has produced no fewer than five series of crime novels, and thirty-four books in all. Her first regular detective was Sophie Rivers, and since then she has featured Fran Harman, Josie Welford, Tobias Campion and Lina Townend. She has also published two stand-alone novels.

'Mrs Welford! How lovely to see you!' Sir Charles Orpen greeted me as if I were an honoured guest, not the caterer. Tucking my arm under his, he set off to find his wife. The Orpens of Duncombe Hall were hosting a charity chamber concert. I was providing refreshments for the interval and the post-concert buffet.

'I hear you've brought your own team of waiters,' he observed, sounding doubtful.

'They're all properly trained professionals. I don't want any accidents to spoil the evening. And please call me Josie.'

'I like a spot of professionalism, Josie,' he said, patting my hand. 'Not like this lot playing tonight. They've made a fuss about everything. Couldn't even agree whether to have the piano lid up or down. Madame Thingie wanted it up so that her sound would *prrrrrrroject*. Monsieur Something pointed out that her projection would make his an *impossibilité*. There was a lot of *mon dieuing* all round. At last, I told her straight: that lid will be fixed halfway up, and no more argument. She didn't like that, but the others did – had a good snigger.'

'He's not moaning about the musicians again, is he?' Lady Orpen demanded. 'Hello, Josie, you do look nice. And everything's in place in the kitchen?'

'Absolutely.'

Everyone who was anyone in the district was there in the gold drawing room; being tone deaf, or even stone deaf, was clearly no excuse. DJs and LBJs were *de rigueur*, mothballs vying with Chanel.

'Richard!' He summoned a middle-aged man. 'My good friend Josie Welford.'

'The Mrs Welford of White Hart gastro pub?' Richard smiled.

'There, I can see you're going to get on like a house on fire.' Chuffie patted my hand and left us to it.

'The Mrs Welford who has a nasty habit of telling the police how to do their job? I'm the chief constable,' he said, no longer smiling.

'Chief constable! Does that mean I should curtsy?'

Not a glimmer of a smile. We were both relieved when Dr Kinnersley, the village GP, hove into view, steering me to the long gallery where the concert was being held.

They'd popped the musicians on to a temporary stage in a window embrasure halfway along the room. They couldn't heave the grand piano up onto this, of course, so the string players would have to sit behind it.

The musicians, giving perfunctory bows, might have been about to play at a funeral. Madame looked meaningfully at the half-closed lid – or, of course, if you were a string player, at the half-open lid.

One of the men didn't even nod; he was the double-bass player, needed for the first piece, something short by Bach, but then redundant for the next, a piano quartet by Brahms. The poor man would be kicking his heels for some forty minutes.

The Bach sounded thin to me, like an expensive chocolate with the centre sucked out of it. Only the pianist seemed to enjoy herself; perhaps her choccie had some nougat in it. Wishing I knew more about music, I occupied myself reading their biographies. It seemed that the double-bass player was married to a plastic surgeon, the cellist to a woman who bred poodles. Martine de la Court, the pianist, was a keen photographer. The second violinist played squash. The violist had won some prize at the Paris

Conservatoire. All the string instruments were at least three hundred years old. How about that?

At last the Bach was over.

Leaving his instrument where it was, the double bassist took himself off to the side of the room, where he propped himself up against a door wearing an expression I can only describe as saturnine

During the Brahms, I had time to think about the way the musicians were placed. Surely each should have been able to see what the others were doing? At the orchestral concerts I'd been to, they'd all been in a semi-circle, the conductor at the focal point: just the arrangement I'd have wanted in his place. Now the pianist couldn't see the others at all, and all they could see of her was her head. You could see that the musicians were giving their all. See but not hear: all the string players were completely drowned by Madame.

At long last, after a lot of noise from the piano – quite exciting stuff, I have to admit, some of it – Marion Orpen stood to lead the applause. This was where I stood too, to signal to my team to pop those corks and don their best smiles. For some reason the musicians didn't acknowledge the applause with even a PR smile; if I'd been their manager I'd have given them the bollocking of a lifetime.

Refreshments were served to guests in the gold drawing room, but Madame had demanded a green room. Chuffie was clearly nonplussed. When he saw a tray of champagne and canapés, what did he do but seize it himself and take it off to the room where the players were ensconced.

At length we all trooped back for the second instalment. 'The Trout Quintet'; I knew that – lovely tunes. Someone had closed the piano lid, so we might at least hear some of the string players. Madame, all teeth and poor complexion, opened it fully. Chuffie coughed meaningfully; it returned to halfway.

They all seemed to start together, and probably stayed that way. We couldn't hear them, of course – only Madame and her fortissimo pounding.

At least they all finished together and stood as one to

take their bow. The cellist looked profoundly bored, and the violist's mouth still drooped. But if I'm any judge of people I would say that the double-bass player was looking puzzled.

Puzzled?

And then Chuffie got to his feet. As he opened his mouth, his complexion darkened and he tried to stumble from the gallery. Vomiting, he choked. Hands flailing for his throat, he fell face down, clearly in the most agonising throes, just by the door to the green room.

Shouting through the screams, Richard Pierce cleared the room on the instant.

Dr Kinnersley was already on his knees, trying to see what he could do. Poor Marion mutely did as she was told. I stood where I was and dialled 999: ambulance, and police too.

Since the musicians baulked at stepping over their host to get into the green room, I herded them off to join the guests, disposing of all that valuable wood in a sort of corral of chairs. Madame's valedictory hiss indicated that she would sue if there were the slightest damage.

At last Kinnersley had to admit that despite all his efforts with CPR and injections, he had lost his patient. He moved aside to let the widow say farewell.

We stood together at the door in a spontaneous moment of silence. Then Richard wandered back in, puzzled by the wails of emergency vehicles – clearly more than just one ambulance. He stared at me furiously. 'Why all this for what's obviously a death by obviously natural causes?'

'I was in such a panic,' I said, reluctant, with our courteous host still warm on his own floor, to cross swords, 'that I'm surprised we didn't get a fire engine too. Anyway, they can always guard those instruments . . .'

Kinnersley spoke up. 'I saw poor Chuffie only two days ago and he was in perfect health then.'

'The man was eighty-six, for God's sake! All this must have put his heart under tremendous strain!'

'I've been to even worse concerts than this, and I've never had a corpse on my hands before! Now, if you'll excuse me, I must see to Lady Orpen.' He escorted her gently from the room.

Within seconds, Madame de la Court appeared, arms akimbo, demanding to be allowed to leave. 'We have a ferry reservation from Dover; we must not miss it,' she declared.

I spread my hands in a gesture as Gallic as hers. 'As you can see, Madame, it will be very difficult to gain access to your belongings for just a few more minutes.'

The cellist joined her. And now came Monsieur Viola, too. 'You cannot leave valuable instruments lying around unprotected!'

I pointed silently at the officers. But M. Viola set off for the green room. 'I fear to lose my – my *boutons de manchette*?' he announced.

'And where might your buttons be, sir?' A stolid country constable came to my aid.

'Cufflinks,' I explained in an undervoice.

'On a table.'

'Any particular table?'

'It has the glasses on it. No, not *les lunettes: les verres*.'

You could see that the man was in half a mind to grant permission, but police training asserted itself, almost visibly. He pointed in silence to the corpse.

The musicians withdrew.

Kinnersley reappeared. 'What a woman! They'd been married for fifty-odd years, but Marion still manages to be dignified. And to keep her wits about her. She can't understand why he should die so suddenly. Bless her, she's absolutely demanding a post mortem!'

'Does that make this a crime scene, then, or can I collect up the dirty glasses from the green room?' I asked.

Richard Pierce spread his hands indecisively. Taking that as permission I knew I shouldn't have, I went on through. The empty instrument cases jostled each other on what I strongly suspected was priceless furniture, which shouldn't have had so much as a morning paper laid on it. An assortment of clothes lay on a silk upholstered armchair. And there was my quarry, a tray with seven or eight champagne flutes. There were no cufflinks on it, nor could I see any lying around elsewhere. All the canapés might have gone, but one of the flutes was still half-full. And no wonder. It smelt decidedly unpleasant. Could one of the bottles of fizz have been off? But if it had, why had the others swigged down such vile-smelling stuff? Had they tried it and poured it politely into one of those priceless bowls or vases?

My God: what if my champagne had killed my poor old friend? Without touching the glass itself, I dipped a finger into the remaining liquid and tasted it. No, even the worst wine never had that aftertaste. So it wasn't corked. And if it wasn't corked . . .? More finger-dips established that all the other dregs were fine.

Leaving everything exactly where it was, I returned to the gallery, to locate Richard Pierce, under attack from the pianist. She was waving her hands around as if still at the keyboard, furious that she and her colleagues had to stay. The fact that the room in which she complained of being incarcerated was one of the most elegant in the beautiful building, with exquisite furniture to match, seemed to have escaped her notice. And her more taciturn but equally irate-looking colleagues seemed equally immune to its charms. I searched each face for evidence of guilt, but all remained phlegmatically blank.

I caught Pierce's eye. 'I think you should follow me,' I said quietly, 'to the green room.'

In his place I'd have died with embarrassment, but perhaps the wretched man had had a few too many sips of my champagne to care. Instead, he said, with a sudden inappropriate grin, 'I've always wanted to forbid anyone to leave a country house. Ever since I read those Golden Age detective novels when I was a kid. That was why I joined the police, actually.'

'Are you going to make a great revelation, à la Poirot?' I asked dryly.

'I'm tempted. Let me just pen them in, first. And get a scene of crime team along. Though I've messed it up a good deal,' he added penitently. 'I'd like Kinnersley's opinion of that liquid, too.'

While he did his policeman act, Kinnersley smelt, touched, and tasted. And then frowned. 'No doubt about it! Croton oil!'

'Croton oil!' I scratched my head.

Returning, Richard did likewise.

'Poison,' Kinnersley said flatly. 'One of those things it used to be fashionable to take – oh, a hundred years ago. Fashionable ladies used to take it to keep themselves slim.'

'So why on earth should it surface now?' Richard demanded. 'And why use it to kill poor old Chuffie? I shall leave no stone unturned to get to the bottom of this!'

He sounded as resolute as if he were going to work night and day himself, not get a load of others to do it. Kinnersley and I merely winced at his clichés.

'Far be it for a humble cook to poke her nose in,' I lied, 'but I would swear that the double-bass player looked surprised when they completed "The Trout" without interruption. And we found that glass,' I said, as if it had been all his own work, 'in the musicians' changing room.'

'So we did,' Richard agreed.

'So might not that narrow down the range of suspects a bit?'

'The musicians! And where would they have got this croton oil from?'

'Where would all these elderly ladies and gentlemen have got it from? Or Mrs Welford herself – I take it it's not one of your culinary essentials!' Kinnersley countered. He too could do sarcasm. 'The Internet?'

'What in fact is croton oil used for?' I asked.

'Maybe the pianist is still taking it for her figure's sake. You know these French people – always taking this and that for their liver,' Richard said grandiloquently.

Although I didn't think WeightWatchers would approve I stashed away the notion in case the pounds I'd managed to shed made an unwelcome reappearance. 'Could it be used for oiling fiddles or something?'

Kinnersley shook his head. 'It's commonly used in laboratory conditions to test the efficacy of anti-inflammatory drugs: it provides the inflammation on mice's ears, for instance, and the drugs do their best to cure it. The only time I've come across it in medical practice was when I treated a woman with a terrible skin eruption on her face. She'd been to some quack offering surgery-free wrinkle treatments. Apparently it's a legitimate tool used by a proper dermatologist. It peels the top layer of skin away, and reveals a nice new unwrinkled layer underneath.'

'A sort of extra-strong exfoliation?' I asked.

'Exactly the sort of thing Madame de la Court might use,' Pierce decided.

'It didn't seem to me as if she paid much attention to her complexion,' I said.

'And no amateur would try it, surely!' Kinnersley agreed.

'Just because no one likes her doesn't mean she was trying to kill anyone. Least of all Chuffie,' I pointed out.

'But poison's a woman's weapon,' Pierce insisted. 'And they'd crossed swords. Some business with the piano lid.'

'I doubt if even the French would kill over a piano,' Kinnersley sighed. 'Next you'll be saying Lady Orpen did it because he'd not done his share of the washing up.'

'And we all know that most murders take place within the family,' I added ironically.

Pierce considered this for a moment. 'Not if she's the one wanting a PM. She'd have used something less traceable. No, I'll detain Madame for questioning. Then we can take everyone else's names and addresses so CID can get witness statements tomorrow.'

'Richard,' I ventured, 'I'd love it to be Madame, because she's a loathsome woman and treats her colleagues appallingly. But I don't see a shred of motive. Could she have been aiming at one of the string players and Chuffie drank the brew by mistake?'

'Wouldn't that rather break up the ensemble? And thus cut off their income?' He was engaging with the idea despite himself.

'I think Mrs Welford may be right. The group didn't exactly cohere, did it?' Kinnersley caught my eye and winked.

'It'll all come out when my team interviews everyone

and takes witness statements,' Pierce said with a note of finality. 'We'll get contact details from everyone and – yes?' He broke off irritably as a shirt-sleeved PC appeared.

'Sir, the musicians are absolutely demanding to leave, sir.'

'Bring in CID, fast. Tell everyone in the drawing room that this is a possible crime and they will all have to wait a few more minutes so that we can record their names and addresses to get witness statements from them all later. As for the musicians, tell them that the green room is definitely a crime scene and no one must touch anything.' Richard turned to me, in sudden despair. 'Except you went in there . . .'

'And found the glass contaminated with croton oil,' I observed in my sweetest tones. 'I don't mind giving a DNA sample so I can be eliminated. So long as you promise to destroy it afterwards.'

The constable left, but reappeared a moment later. 'They say you can search the room from top to bottom, but they want their property and they want it fast. Or they'll sue.'

'And was Madame their spokesperson?' I asked.

'Her and some bloke desperate for his buttons. Really worked up, they are.'

Kinnersley raised an eyebrow. 'Why not take them at their word? Find a phial and then you've got some evidence!'

'I suppose . . . OK, constable, contact CID and bring in a team.'

'Tell the waiters there's more fizz in cool boxes in my van,' I said, throwing him the keys. 'That should keep the guests happy,' I added.

'I don't suppose there's enough for us, is there?' Kinnersley asked.

Other people feared Greeks bringing gifts; I feared co-operation from someone who might be a killer. If the phial or bottle or whatever wasn't in a case, where might it be? They turned out their pockets with positively sunny smiles, or what passed for sunny in the violist's case.

The police searched thoroughly, I give them that. Inside the vases, under the cushions, behind the curtains. They found the violist's cufflinks, but no, the cufflinks didn't have an obliging secret compartment containing dregs of oil. His viola case did contain a small cache of cannabis he assured us was for private use only. As was the coke in the cellist's case.

The police didn't even bother confiscating the drugs. Witness statements – the musicians were happy to give those. But really, they had to be on their way or they would miss the next ferry, and thus their next engagement.

'And may we now have your gracious permission to pack our instruments?' the violinist demanded.

Richard shrugged: why not?

I sat down and stared at the bubbles in my champagne glass. More correctly, a flute, of course. Another bloody musical instrument on a night we'd had rather too many. Druggie fiddlers, sardonic and silent double basses, prima donna pianists. And then I thought why not. 'Tell them just ten more minutes,' I said.

The double-bass player. He'd looked on from the back of the room while his colleagues hammered out Brahms. Saturnine, I'd thought him. And then at the end of the Schubert he looked surprised that they'd got through it. And what had I done most of the concert, when I wasn't mentally planning next week's menu, that is? I'd scanned their tedious programme notes.

There were still plenty lying on chairs, as if my fellow listeners never wanted to see them again. So I picked one up, opened it at the relevant page, and passed it quietly to Kinnersley, pointing.

'So we have a source for our croton oil,' he crowed. 'But why the double bass? And where on earth is the receptacle the oil came in?'

Pierce shook his head. 'Why on earth should he want to kill Chuffie, even if he had the means to do so?'

'Perhaps he didn't want to kill Chuffie. Perhaps he put the oil in a glass meant for someone else and the poor man drank it by mistake. He'd be too much of a gentleman to spit it out. How did it keep women's figures slim?' I belatedly asked Kinnersley.

'Some sort of emetic or purge, I should think.'

'That's in small quantities? What about in bigger ones?'

'I should imagine you'd get dreadful stomach cramps. You might vomit. You might get diarrhoea. And at Chuffie's age . . . Well, in sufficient quantities, I suppose it might kill anyone.'

'Suppose,' I thought aloud, 'you didn't like someone. You didn't hate them enough to kill, but you wanted to teach them a lesson. What did you do to teachers you hated?'

Pierce pulled a face. 'Whoopie cushions? Matches in hollowed-out chalk? So you're saying all this might have been a black joke that went wrong?'

'I don't know. But it's a theory.'

'And as good as any. So *cherchez* not *la femme*, but the bottle, whatever that is in French.' Kinnersley stopped abruptly. He looked at me. 'Are you thinking what I'm thinking?'

'Let's just find the bottle,' I said.

Do you remember those children's games, in the days before all those infant hands clutched electronic gizmos? Where you had a small plastic box containing a set of ball-bearings which you had to get into tiny targets, just by jiggling the box? Getting the phial out of the double bass was rather like that. We could hear it rolling around, and sometimes you could see it at right angles to what some musical constable called the F-holes, and others in exasperation called the 'f-ing' holes. At last, however, shaken gently over a pile of towels by two of the strongest officers available, the instrument yielded up our quarry.

The small glass tube had certainly held croton oil: in its concentrated form, the smell was quite distinct.

'So you think the target might have been Madame Thingie!' Pierce said.

'She was a hard-working, capable but ultimately unprofessional woman. And her male colleagues resented her. Didn't you see?'

Kinnersley shook his head. 'We couldn't see anything of them. Didn't hear a lot, either.'

'Exactly so. She was the focus of all our attention: the others never even got a look-in – literally. And if you play in those conditions, day after day, week after week, you must get resentful.'

'Enough to want to kill her?' Richard reflected.

'That,' I smiled sweetly, 'must be for your teams of professional officers to discover.'

The double-bass player tried to brazen it out. Yes, he'd tried to dose Madame de la Tour; all the ensemble had agreed that she must be taken down a peg. During the tour her behaviour had become more and more egotistical. At last, he had resolved to humiliate her. Croton oil was a purgative. He just wanted Madame to have to spend a concert on the lavatory, giving him and his colleagues a chance to shine with a piece they'd privately rehearsed.

'But where did you get it?' Richard asked.

'I told them I needed a replacement bow. It's very easy to get back to France for a day, when you are playing near Canterbury. There was plenty in my wife's clinic. I helped myself to a very little. Alas, when I put it in Martine's glass, the old gentleman – he was very absent-minded, that one – drank it.' He looked relieved to have the matter off his chest. 'But you will not charge me with murder? When all I intended was a simple jest?'

'That, monsieur, will be a matter for the Crown Prosecution Service,' Richard said impassively.

The funny thing was, it was Madame de la Court who protested as he was led away. 'How will we perform without him? Release him this instant. We have important engagements . . .'

'Madame, he killed Sir Charles. And it might have been that he meant to kill you.'

'But he did not succeed. Come, how can we perform without our double bass? Set him free *tout de suite*.'

I listened in amazement; I knew I couldn't understand music. Now I knew I couldn't understand musicians either.

A LIBERATING AFFAIR
Carol Anne Davis

Carol Anne Davis comes from Dundee, and divides her time as a writer between fiction and true crime. Her novels, including *Extinction*, have led to her being described as the 'Queen of Noir', while her non-fiction books include *Women Who Kill* and *Children Who Kill*.

It's always daunting for a man to meet his girlfriend's father for the first time, especially when that meeting takes place on her eighteenth birthday. He'd thrown her a small party, stringing the farmhouse with fairy lights.

'Deborah tells me you're out of work,' he said, minutes after we'd been introduced in the kitchen.

'Yes, sir. I was in sports nutrition, on the sales side, but last year the firm closed down.'

'Less of the *sir*. Everyone calls me Kev around here. And I've got a job going begging,' her father said.

Deborah had alerted me to the fact that he'd probably offer me employment. She'd said that some of the men left after a few hours, that others had nightmares about what they'd seen.

'Well, tonight's Deborah's night,' I murmured, taking her small hand in mine, 'But I'd love to come back for an interview.'

Kev's small eyes narrowed, making his already bloated face look even bigger. 'No time like the present, son.'

'But won't your guests mind?'

'Oh, it's just a few of the locals.'

None of them looked sorry to see him go.

'Do you only keep chickens?' I asked as we traipsed across the grassy fields.

I already knew that he did but was keen to make conversation.

'Only? I feed half the country on them but I'm sure our Deborah's already told you that,' he said.

'She's a lovely girl.'

'Keeps a clean house.'

'Bright, too,' I said, wanting him to see that I appreciated her many qualities.

'Not bright enough to take over the business. Her mum was exactly the same.'

I hesitated, not wanting to speak ill of the dead. I knew that he'd been widowed for three years, that he hadn't bothered with women since.

Fortunately Kev preferred to talk business rather than pleasure.

'How much do you get from the state?' he asked as we reached a huge industrial barn. Looking ahead I could see numerous similar buildings blotting the landscape.

I told him.

'Okay, I'll double that if you start here on the factory floor.'

We entered the building and I found myself in a room stacked with overalls. Kev handed me one and took another for himself.

'Why the masks?' I asked, before slipping the heavy white cotton over my nose and mouth.

'Dust and disease.'

We walked into the factory and I suddenly understood exactly what he meant.

At first I could hardly see the birds themselves, the air was so full of fleas and feathers. Then my eyes adjusted and I saw a vision of hell. It was wall to wall hen, the birds packed like living sardines. Some were pecking at the bird immediately in front of them, causing the blood to flow, whilst others had collapsed and were being trampled and suffocated to death.

Most of the hens were huge, their bodies far too big for their frail legs. They lay there in their own waste, clucking feebly. The floor was so littered with excrement that the lower bodies of the chickens were smeared with it, which probably accounted for the acidic-looking burns on their hocks.

I didn't attempt to speak until I was back in the little room, where I removed my mask and overalls. Kev indicated a wall chute and I dropped them in.

'Why are the chicks so big?'

'We feed them up so they can be slaughtered at six weeks.'

'Do you lose a lot through disease?'

'Not enough to seriously affect my profits, no.' He stared at me challengingly. 'I'm not pretending it's pretty but we're not a zoo – and your Deborah has done very well out of it.'

I took a steadying breath. 'I know she does all your office work.'

'She does but I need someone who can work his way up through the system, keep the supermarkets sweet.'

I'd promised Deborah that I'd keep in with her dad, not be marched off the premises like previous boyfriends, so I started the next day.

My task was to grab as many chickens by the legs as I could and take them outside, forcing them into crates. Needless to say, they tried to escape my clutches. Some of the other chicken harvesters were grabbing up to eight birds at a time, inadvertently breaking their wings.

Kev took me for a drink at the local pub that night.

'How did it go?'

'I felt a bit sick,' I admitted.

'You soon get used to it. You'd have to pay five times more for a free range bird.'

The following week I was shown around the processing plant. It was worse, if anything. Men slotted the overweight chickens into a metal frame by their legs and they were plunged briefly into a bath of water through which an electric charge was passed. The plan was to stun the birds so that they weren't fully conscious when their throats were cut but some hens lifted their heads . . .

I could tell you more, of course, but I trust that I've already persuaded you never to eat factory farmed birds, robbed of their freedom, sunlight and a natural diet.

Speaking of diet, I murdered Kev by putting arsenic in his drink. It seemed fitting. It's regularly used in chicken feed abroad though it's now been banned Europe-wide.

I asked him about the arsenic he was giving his chickens, having heard from Deborah that he was adding it illegally.

'Yeah, it's great stuff. Kills stomach parasites, gives them a better colour and bigger breasts.'

He was a man without a heart . . .

I took a large container of the powdered poison from his safe and added a lethal dose of it to his pint before bringing it to him on the porch. I kept my own unadulterated drink in my right hand, terrified of inadvertently swapping. Within twenty minutes he began to sweat.

'Fuck, it's hot,' he said and I wondered briefly if he'd soon be going someplace even hotter. 'Think I'll have a lie down,' he muttered a minute later and I knew that his bowels were starting to cramp.

He staggered into the bathroom then, a few minutes later, into the master bedroom. I'd unplugged the telephone socket, of course, and had confiscated his mobile and told Deborah to linger at the village hall with her friends after her aerobics class. Now I put my headphones on for an hour so that I wouldn't hear his screams.

The cleaning lady found him dead on his bed the following morning, clutching a photo of his late wife. The arsenic container and pint glass on the bedside cabinet were dutifully taken away by the police.

I'm sure that the coroner's verdict will be that he took his own life: after all, farmers have one of the highest suicide rates in the country. His staffing problems were legendary, with many of his birds dying because he couldn't find men to harvest them, and his near neighbours had seen the lorries of dead and dying birds so chose to keep a wide berth. Deborah will testify that he never got over his wife's death and the cleaner will confirm that he'd spoken of long, lonely days and fractured nights.

So, did I kill a bewildered but essentially hard working man? At the time, I thought not. Deborah had told me that her father had neglected her diabetic mother until her health failed and led to her very premature death. She described him as a control freak who'd disinherit her and leave her penniless if she ever moved away from the family farm.

Fortunately Deborah inherited her mother's compassion for all creatures great and small. That's where she and I met, at a London animal rights meeting. She daren't go on the rallies, or anywhere else where cameras were present, for fear of her dad.

But she listened and learned and, in the six months that I'd been secretly dating her, passed on masses of information about the cruelties that she'd witnessed. These cruelties were an accepted part of the chicken industry, though, so wouldn't be enough to close him down. We needed him to die in order to liberate millions of voiceless victims. We just had to wait until Deborah could legally inherit at eighteen, the day she brought me home for the very first time.

We got married last month. In a way, we had to. After all, she recruited me to be her father's killer so we have too much on each other to ever part. We have to stay here for the fore-seeable future, too, as Deborah is against gassing the existing birds to put them out of their misery so we have to wait for them to resume normal weight and mobility before attempting to find suitable homes.

She wants to sell starter hen kits to organic gardeners. You know the deal – a henhouse, a wire coop, two hens and chicken feed. She also insists on having the henhouses made here in Britain so I'm desperately trying to cut a deal with an ethical firm. I need to run every decision past her as it's her house and her business but she's always gallivanting around town or at her aerobics class.

She decides what we do, who we see, where we go, even how much pocket money I can have on a weekly basis. I was an animal-loving liberal but now I'm ironically caged. I loathe the present, fear the future and cannot escape the macabre memories of the recent past. So I wake up at night, heart almost leaping from my chest and eyes wide open, recalling the groans as I thrust the photograph of Kev's wife into his spasmodically-jerking hands.

'What are you thinking?' Deborah whispers with her usual annoying intensity.

'Nothing for you to worry about,' I quaver and tear my gaze away, with difficulty, from her slender neck.

A GLIMPSE OF HELL
Martin Edwards

Martin Edwards' latest Lake District Mystery is *The Frozen Shroud*. The series includes *The Coffin Trail* (short-listed for the Theakston's prize for best British crime novel), *The Arsenic Labyrinth* and *The Serpent Pool*. He has written eight novels about Liverpool lawyer Harry Devlin, and two stand-alone novels, including *Dancing for the Hangman*. He has won the CWA Short Story Dagger and edited twenty-two anthologies.

A nother day in paradise. Joolz adjusted her sunglasses as she hurried out of the excursion office. Time was tight, but she must text Giddy before she met her group.

Meet me outside Lobster Pot at two. Need to talk. xx

Giddy's face grinned at her from the phone. Dark, tanned, and handsome enough to make your heart stop. His real name was Gideon, but everyone had called him Giddy since he was a kid. He was famously unreliable, but he said he simply liked to dream. She just needed to take care he didn't try to make one particular dream come true.

Waiting for a gap in the traffic, she scrolled through the pictures. Giddy was wary of being photographed with her, said it wasn't safe, but over the past three months, she'd captured a dozen shots of him, starting that very first night they met, at a full moon party on Seven Mile Beach. She'd snapped him through the writhing flames of the huge bonfire. It wasn't just the martinis and the thudding rhythms from the kitchen band that made her knees buckle. He still had that effect on her. But now she had to save him from himself, before it was too late. First, she'd tell Wesley it was all off, whatever he and Giddy had discussed. Then, at the Lobster Pot, she'd insist Giddy make his choice between love and money. He'd surely decide to go with her – wouldn't he?

She crossed the road, and a dozen loping strides took her to the North Terminal. The tourists were chattering outside the souvenir shop. The tender had brought them in from the liner, and they were ready to roll. Most of them looked as though they would roll very easily. Joolz dared not think how much they had eaten since their cruise began at New Orleans. Wait till they discovered the island's cassava cake. Joolz rationed herself to one slice a week. She thought she was too skinny, but Giddy said he loved her this way. He didn't care for fat women.

'Hi there! My name is Joolz, and I'm your tour guide for today.'

Expectant faces beamed back at her. An American woman with dyed red hair as dazzling as the sun said, 'I wanted to go snorkelling, but this guy is all for the easy life.'

The man at her side, rotund and balding, said, 'We're in Grand Cayman for less than six hours, honey. Makes sense to pack in as much as we can. See the sights.'

'Hey, is this our bus?' a small nervous woman asked.

Since this was tour number 7, and the approaching bus had a large placard behind the windscreen bearing that number, the answer seemed obvious, but Joolz beamed and said, 'You're absolutely right.'

Her smile froze as she recognised Seymour's grizzled hair behind the wheel. No dreadlocks, no Wesley. Where was he?

Seymour opened the door. 'Hey, beautiful, ain't you pleased I'm driving y'all today? What's with the frown?'

'What happened to Wesley?'

'Called in sick, I guess.' Seymour grinned. 'Smoked one joint too many last night, huh? Big mistake. Mr Pottinger won't be pleased.'

Joolz caught her breath. What was Wesley up to? She must have been mad to introduce him to Giddy.

'Do we get on now?' The nervous woman had come up behind her, and the rest of the party were only a step or two behind.

'Yes, yes, that's fine.' She hoped she didn't sound as panicky as she felt. 'Please can you show me your tickets as you board?'

They filed past her, and she checked their tickets against the details on her clipboard. All present and correct. Taking a deep breath, she jumped up the steps, and grabbed the microphone.

'Good morning again, ladies and gentlemen, and a very warm welcome to Grand Cayman from me and our driver Seymour. We'll start by heading out of George Town and passing the hotels and condos of Seven Mile Beach. Why it's called that, I'm not quite sure, because it's less than six miles long.'

Everyone tittered, and a wrinkled Englishman in a floppy white hat said in a stage whisper, 'So they have a serious inflation problem here, as well?'

Joolz rewarded the old man with a big smile. Every tour party had one guy who prided himself on his sense of humour. On a really bad day, you were landed with three or four of them.

'After driving by the beach, we have a special treat lined up for you. We'll sail through the amazing mangroves, and you'll get up close and personal with all sorts of wonderful creatures in this very special habitat.'

A woman in an aisle seat put up her hand. Obviously British. 'It *is* a boat trip, isn't it? Not a kayak.'

'Definitely a boat trip,' Joolz promised. 'Anyway, after the boat trip, we rejoin the bus, and then we set off for . . . a glimpse of Hell.'

Cue excited murmuring from a handful of passengers who hadn't bothered to study the itinerary. 'Actually, Hell is a tiny place in the West Bay district. The name comes from a very unusual and distinctive black rock formation. We'll stop there for ten minutes, so you can buy postcards and gifts. Who knows, you may even meet up with the Devil himself!'

The guy from the shop at Hell wore a devil's costume, but Wesley didn't need to dress up for Joolz to suspect he was a devil too. He was always laughing and joking, and the tourists loved his risqué humour. Yet there was a dangerous glint in those dark eyes, and his smile resembled a shark's. What if Giddy had entered into some sort of pact with him?

Enough. No point in dwelling on it. Nothing she could do now until she and Giddy talked. Switching to auto-pilot, she launched into her all-you-need-to-know-about-Grand-Cayman spiel. It only took five minutes.

'So this place is British and you're British?' the red-haired woman deduced. 'Like a home from home, then.'

'You could say so,' Joolz said. She'd been happy here, but she was ready to move on. After all, this was just a small, flat strip of land in the sea, where people only came to chill out or make money.

'Tax haven, eh?' the wrinkly Englishman asked, as they reached the car park at the new marina.

'Off-shore finance makes a valuable contribution to the local economy,' she said sweetly. 'Look, we're here!'

Giddy worked for a financial services firm called McCulloch Stott. Just a small cog in a big wheel. He'd trained as a lawyer in the City, but found it too much like hard work and fled to the Caribbean. He spent a few years as a beach bum before charming the pants off a girl who just happened to be the daughter of McCulloch Stott's senior partner. She'd persuaded her father to find him a job, and six months later they were married. They still were, Giddy confessed to Joolz, just before they slept together for the first time. Joolz didn't mind too much, she'd already figured out he was too good to be true. Easy come, easy go, that was the story of her love life.

Except that Giddy said he would never let her go.

'How's my lovely lady?' Klaus, the skipper, gave her a peck on the cheek. He was sixty, and smelled of raw fish, but she was fond of him. After they had helped the guests on board, he murmured, 'You okay?'

'Never better,' she lied. 'Why do you ask?'

'You look like you didn't sleep too good last night.' Klaus frowned. 'That boyfriend of yours treating you right, I hope?'

'Everything's fine, thanks, sweetie.' Klaus had never met

Giddy, but he knew there was someone. Had Wesley opened his big mouth? He ought to be smart enough to keep quiet, but with Wesley, you never knew. He was a loose cannon. When he was stoned, he might say anything. Or do anything.

'Good.' Out of sight from the guests, Klaus made a swift throat-slitting gesture. 'Any fellow makes trouble for you, he answers to me, okay?'

'It's all good.' Oh, if only . . .

'And where is Wesley?'

She shrugged. 'Off sick, Seymour reckons.'

Klaus gave a sceptical grunt and strode to the wheel. Joolz picked up her microphone, and announced that they were about to sail into the mangroves.

'The nursery of the reef, some people call it. We have everything here, from baby barracuda to green iguanas. Along the way, you'll have the chance to pet a jellyfish.'

Iguanas, yes. It had taken a while for her to spot the similarity between Giddy and an iguana. After all, he was so gorgeous and the iguana – well . . . But there was a sort of sleepy-eyed menace that her lover and the reptile shared in common. Iguanas were harmless, though. As for Giddy, she was no longer sure. He insisted he wanted her, not the spoiled rich neurotic he'd married. The only snag was the money.

'I signed a pre-nup.' He shook his head, as if bewildered by his own naivete. 'Her daddy's one of the smartest businessmen on the island, never believed I was good enough for his darling daughter. He insisted on drawing up a deal. If I divorce Mary-Alice inside five years, I lose pretty much everything. Of course, there's a pay-off, just enough to make sure I keep my mouth shut, but I'd be finished. He pulls the strings of the management board, and they'd have me out on my ear. Word gets around in the business world. I'd be good for nothing.'

She'd never had money, she wasn't like Mary-Alice, with a trust fund to keep her insulated from the real world. But money didn't matter, as long as she and Giddy were together. And hadn't he always dreamed of becoming a beach bum once again, carefree and wild? When she reminded him, he looked at her as though she were mad.

'I bet you were born within five miles of Leeds city centre,' a grey-haired woman in a flowing floral dress said, as the boat drifted over the water. 'Small world, our house is across the road from Oakwood Clock. How long have you lived here?'

'You're quite a detective,' Joolz admitted. 'Harehills, actually. Came over three years ago, to teach Maths. I only meant to stay for twelve months.'

'But you fell in love?'

'With the island,' Joolz said hastily. She waved at the swaying green ferns. 'You can understand, can't you? I decided I'd much rather spend my days outside the classroom.'

'And will you stay here permanently?'

She fobbed the woman off with a smile and a shrug. But her question demanded an answer. It was time to move on. Like Giddy said, you only had one chance in life. *Carpe diem*. He knew more Latin than she did, that was a private education for you.

'You said the island was named after alligators,' the red-haired woman said, giving the water a suspicious stare as the boat puttered to a halt. 'Are there . . .?'

'None whatsoever, you couldn't be safer. Though some of the biggest iguanas look a bit like crocs!' Joolz reassured her so thoroughly that the woman seemed disappointed. She frowned all the way through the homily on the wonders of the mangrove forest's ecosystem.

'There are sharks, though,' the man in the floppy hat said. 'Tells you about them on the internet.'

'Not all of them live in the sea, though,' said Klaus. 'The worst sharks work in those glitzy offices in George Town.'

Too right. Danger on Grand Cayman didn't come from the wildlife. It came from the likes of Wesley, Mister Shark's-Teeth Smile. It had begun as a joke, this idea of Giddy hiring someone to kill Mary-Alice while he established a water-tight alibi, drinking the night away with financier friends at a bar on the other side of the island. He spoke so lightly about it that at first Joolz played along. It was a game, nothing more. He couldn't be serious, and there was no harm in dreaming.

'Those houses must cost a packet,' the floppy hat man said as the boat headed back towards the waiting bus. There was plenty of new building around the marina. 'But why so much concrete?'

'The highest point on Grand Cayman is sixty feet above sea level. When Hurricane Ivan hit us, the island was devastated. Building a house strong enough to survive another hurricane costs a small fortune.'

While the others contemplated the possibility of having everything they'd worked for destroyed in a matter of moments, the woman from Leeds said, 'You need to find a wealthy boyfriend, then.'

'I certainly do!' Joolz said with a laugh.

The woman patted her hand. 'With hair that blonde, and eyes so blue, you won't have any trouble, dear.'

'She's spoken for, lady,' a guttural voice said. Oh God, Klaus had decided to join in the fun. 'Though we have not been allowed to meet him yet. I only hope we are honoured with an invitation to the wedding.'

'See that little lizard on the bank?' Joolz said. 'You can take a photo of him, if you're quick.'

Of course, she had options. She could even break with Giddy if he refused to leave Grand Cayman with her. But she'd hate to leave him alone with Mary-Alice, and a house full of hang-ups. Giddy needed her as much as she needed him.

Joolz wished Mary-Alice no harm, really, but the woman was a flake. No wonder Giddy was sick of her. Even before the wedding, she'd made a half-hearted attempt to slit her wrists. On their first anniversary, after a huge row, she'd taken an overdose, and had to have her stomach pumped. When she wasn't self-harming, she was flying into violent rages and hurling crockery whenever Giddy put a foot wrong. She'd even had a couple of one-night stands with blokes she'd met in clubs and bars. Her father said Giddy was a lousy husband, made him a scapegoat for a money-rich, attention-poor upbringing guaranteed to warp his daughter's personality. Giddy said he felt like a prisoner in a gilded cage.

The tour party climbed back on the bus, and the red-haired woman leaned over to speak to Seymour.

'Say, you come from Jamaica, don't you? Your accent reminds me . . .'

A slow smile spread across his face. 'Ya man. But I live here now. Better way of life. More money, less crime.'

Twelve years ago, Seymour had arrived in Grand Cayman with his wife and two daughters. Lots of people did the same. Wesley had made the journey eighteen months back. Rumour was, he hadn't simply been making a lifestyle choice. Apparently, he'd upset someone important in Kingston, and his survival depended on making a run for it. There were stories that he mixed with drug-dealers and other criminals, that he was a criminal himself. Joolz suspected he encouraged the gossip, thinking it did wonders for his image. What the truth was about his past, she didn't know, and didn't want to know.

'Y'know what we say back in Jamaica?' Seymour asked the woman. 'There are no problems.'

'No?'

'Nah. Only situations.' He gave a wheezy laugh and switched on the ignition.

His homespun philosophy didn't work for Joolz. Wesley could become a very big problem. Why had she been so stupid as to mention him to Giddy? The pair of them had been knocking back mudslides and fantasising about life with enough money to buy a mansion with a private beach and helipad. Joolz had mentioned that she'd never met a hitman, as far as she knew, though she wouldn't be surprised if Wesley . . .

That's all it took for Giddy to talk her into arranging a meeting. He could be so persuasive. Against her better judgment, the three of them had got together at Pedro St James, in a dimly lit bar where they weren't known. Wesley told funny stories about life in Jamaica, they drank too much Tortuga rum punch, and her heart didn't skip a beat. Mary-Alice's name wasn't even mentioned.

'Ladies and gentlemen,' Seymour boomed into the microphone. 'So far you've seen our island paradise. Now you are about to arrive in Hell.'

He turned off the main road, and parked in the open space behind the bright red post office and shop. Everyone trooped off to buy souvenirs and take photos. Joolz sat on the steps of the bus, watching people take it in turns to clamber on to the viewing platform and gaze out at the strange, spiky black limestone behind the barrier.

Yesterday evening, Giddy had let slip that he'd met Wesley at West Beach last week, while she was escorting tourists round a turtle farm, and both men should have been working. When she quizzed him, he passed it off as a casual encounter between two guys who just happened to run into each other, and shot the breeze for half an hour. What could be more innocent?

In the end, she nagged Giddy into admitting that he'd talked to Wesley about Mary-Alice. He said he'd been thinking aloud, just musing about how much simpler and better life would be if he were still a single man. She told him she wasn't stupid, and neither was Wesley. He could read between the lines. For God's sake, they hadn't talked money, had they?

Giddy said he might have mentioned ten thousand dollars.

'I just love the devil!' the red-haired woman said, mopping her brow as she returned to the bus. Her bag was overflowing with gifts from the shop. 'I mean, what a nice guy. He posed for some pictures with us.'

Did Giddy have any idea what he was messing with? During her teens in Harehills, Joolz had come across one or two men capable of anything. Wesley, for all his smiley face and winning ways, was a dead ringer for them. If he thought there was ten thousand dollars to be had from killing Mary-Alice . . .

'You didn't enter into no bargain with that devil, I hope, ma'am?' said Seymour, the life and soul of the tour party.

The red-haired woman barked with laughter. Joolz had stayed awake half last night, trying not to think about Giddy and Wesley thrashing out a deal. That had decided her. When she saw him at the Lobster Pot, she'd say he must leave Mary-Alice and McCullochs, and they'd make do with whatever pay-off he squeezed out of the doting daddy. If he promised to go quickly and quietly, he could negotiate reasonable terms. Okay, they'd need to leave Grand Cayman, but never mind. Plenty of islands in the sea. Countless beaches, innumerable bars. Opportunities would always knock for a hard-working tour guide and a great-looking guy with public school manners and charm.

'So now you can say you've been to Hell and back,' she told her passengers. 'Our next stop is the beach. We'll be there for fifteen minutes before heading back to the terminal.'

While the group wandered out on to the sand, and an adventurous few ventured a quick paddle, she stayed in the bus with Seymour. Having made up her mind what to do, she felt calmer already. This was the only way.

'You going to the full moon party tomorrow night?' Seymour asked.

She shook her head. 'I used to love those parties, but I'm thinking it's time to move on.'

'You don't mean, leave the island?' Seymour put on a sad face. 'We'd miss you, Joolz.'

'Guess I'm stuck in a rut. It's comfortable, but then so is a grave. There's so much else in the world I want to see.'

The passengers straggled back to the bus. Time to head back past Government House. At the terminal, Joolz did better than usual with the tips. A good omen. Every dollar would come in useful in her new life.

'Stay safe,' Seymour murmured as she said goodbye.

The company office was on the other side of the road. She'd tell Mr Pottinger she was resigning, and someone else would have to do this afternoon's Stingray Tour. Then she'd dash to the Lobster Pot. Giddy hadn't texted back, but she'd show up at McCullochs' office if she had to. Threading through the crowd, she saw a *Compass* placard bearing the latest news.

BODY FOUND IN MANGROVE

Oh Jesus, don't say she was too late? Surely Wesley hadn't done something terrible?

Two police officers in crisp white shirts were waiting for her in Mr Pottinger's tiny office. They nodded her into a chair without a word. Mr Pottinger's face was ashen. The older of the two cops, a man whose bulky frame filled half the room, flourished his ID.

'Joolz Ibbotson?'

Her throat felt as if someone were squeezing it hard. 'What is it?'

'I understand you know a man called Gideon Tremlett?'

She nodded, not trusting herself to speak. The expression on the man's craggy face baffled her. It was almost like . . . pity.

'I'm sorry to tell you that we recovered his body from a mangrove near Rum Point earlier today.'

No. She wanted to scream. It was impossible. Wasn't it?

'I'm sorry to tell you that Wesley Stollmeyer has been arrested in connection with his murder, and so has Mr Tremlett's wife. I'm afraid I have to ask you some questions, and it would be easier if you'd come with us to police headquarters.'

The cop might just as well have clubbed her. She felt too dazed to utter a word. Sure, there'd been a Faustian pact. But Giddy, poor Giddy, had not been part of it. Wesley had got into bed with a devil woman.

THE CONFESSIONS OF EDWARD PRIME

Kate Ellis

Kate Ellis was born in Liverpool and studied drama in Manchester. She worked in teaching, marketing and accountancy before finding success as a writer. The latest title in her series featuring Wesley Peterson is *The Shroud Maker*, while she has also written a series about another cop, Joe Plantagenet, and a stand-alone historical crime novel, *The Devil's Priest*.

Edward Prime was a nuisance.

This was the third time that month he'd presented himself at the front desk and asked to see Detective Constable Janet Crowley. And she felt she'd had enough.

'I've got to get it off my chest,' he said, leaning towards her. She could smell something rancid on his warm breath and she edged her chair back a little. 'I've got to make a clean breast of it.' He lowered his eyes to focus on her chest and she raised her hand instinctively to make sure her shirt was properly buttoned.

He began to fidget with the empty plastic cup in front of him. They always gave him a hot drink in the interview room. Maybe that's why he came, she thought. That and a feeling of self-importance.

'What are you talking about, Mr Prime?'

'The woman on Howdale Road. I killed her.'

She took a deep breath and opened the file that lay on the table in front of her. 'That's as well as the post office you robbed in Bucknell Street and the man you stabbed to death outside that nightclub last week, is it?'

'Well, er . . . I've been busy.'

'So I see. In the past six months you've confessed to no less than eighteen crimes.'

'Like I said, I've been busy.'

She looked across the table at him. He was skinny with greasy brown hair and a long face that glowed with perspiration. The cheap yellow T-shirt he wore stretched tightly over his midriff riding up to reveal a not-so-tantalising glimpse of pasty flesh. She could smell his sweat. She wished his mother had taught him to use deodorant.

'Look, Mr Prime. Edward,' she said. 'We know you haven't done anything. We could charge you with wasting police time, you know.'

He lowered his eyes, a small, secretive smile on his thin lips. 'I know about the locket.'

Janet Crowley looked up sharply. Up till now Edward had been so predictable. 'What locket?'

'The one I took from Paula Sloane when I killed her. The one with the picture of the kiddie inside.'

Janet stared at him, lost for words. They knew from Paula Sloane's friends and family that she'd always worn that locket; never took it off. They'd kept the fact that it was missing from the press. There was always something they held back. Just in case.

'Do you know where the locket is?'

Edward shook his head.

'But if you killed her, you must have taken it.'

Edward frowned, as though the logic of the statement was too much for him to take in. If it hadn't been for the mention of the locket, Janet would have sent him on his way by now. But she had to find out more.

'How did you hear about the locket?'

Janet watched as new hope appeared in his eyes. 'Aren't you going to arrest me?'

Janet considered the question for a moment. 'No, Edward. We know where to find you if we need you. You go home to your mum, eh.'

There was no mistaking the disappointment on his face. He was twenty, she knew that from the file, but he looked like a child denied a promised treat. 'But I did it,' he said in a whine.

'You find the locket and we'll have another chat.'

It was the best she could offer. And as she watched him shuffle from the room, she knew it wasn't enough.

As soon as Edward unlocked the front door his mother was there in the hall. He could tell she'd been cooking from the smell of burning that hit him as soon as he'd walked in. She'd never been much of a cook.

'Where have you been?' She stood there, arms folded, a plump vision in velour tracksuit and carpet slippers.

'Nowhere.'

'You've been to that police station again, haven't you?'

Edward could hear the exasperation in her voice. He closed the door behind him and bowed his head. 'No. I never. I've just been out. Walking around.'

His mother turned away and began to shuffle back into the kitchen. 'I'll put the kettle on,' she said.

Edward wasn't listening. Paula Sloane was dead but he knew her secret. He knew who she was.

The DCI stood in front of the whiteboard and gave Janet a disapproving look as she slipped into the room. She was late for the briefing. If the DCI knew why, she knew he'd tell her to charge Edward with wasting police time. But somehow she couldn't bring herself to do that to him. Perhaps she was becoming soft.

'Paula Sloane. Aged forty-five. Divorced. Lived alone. Found stabbed in the kitchen of her house in Allerton the day before yesterday. No weapon found. No enemies that we know of. No suspects. Nothing appeared to be missing apart from a locket she always wore: according to everyone who knew her, she never took it off.'

Janet began to put her hand up, nervous that the DCI would make some cutting comment. She was certain that he thought she wasn't up to the job any more; that she was a middle-aged woman marking time till retirement. She knew she couldn't keep up with the young men and women on the team with their gym-honed bodies and their hungry ambition tinged with a soupcon of callousness. When she spoke they all looked round and she felt her face burning.

'Sir, I've just been talking to Edward Prime. He comes in to confess to any local crime that's been on the news.' She glanced round at the sceptical faces. 'Anyway, he confessed to Paula's murder. Normally, I would have taken it with a pinch of salt but he mentioned the locket. He knew it was missing. Is there any chance the information could have leaked out somehow?'

The DCI was staring straight at her. 'Is he still down in the interview room?'

'I told him to go home. He lives with his mother and we can pick him up any time if necessary.' She held her breath, expecting a public dressing down for letting a potential suspect go.

But the DCI shrugged. 'Any chance he's our man?'

'I wouldn't have thought so, sir. He seems harmless.'

'As long as we know where to find him.'

Janet exhaled. She'd said her bit now and it was up to the senior investigating officer to decide what to do about it.

The DCI continued, 'One thing you should know about our victim is that twenty years ago her baby was abducted. It was a boy called Adam, aged four months. She left him in his pushchair outside the post office on Allerton Road and when she came out the pushchair was still there but there was no sign of the kid. There was a major hunt for him, of course, but he never turned up. According to Paula's family and friends, she never really got over it and her marriage broke up as a result.'

A stick thin young woman with long blonde hair raised her hand. 'Any chance the kid's disappearance is connected to her death, sir?'

'Good question, DC Parker. Truth is we don't know, but it's an avenue worth exploring. She'd recently hired a private detective to try and trace the kid. We've spoken to him and he claims he didn't get very far. However, she rang him on the evening she died and asked to see him the following day. I said I'd send someone round to take a statement.' He looked straight at Janet. 'DC Crowley, can I leave it to you to have a word?'

Janet saw that all eyes were on her again. But this time she felt a small glow of triumph. 'Of course, sir.'

The evening was the only time Bradley Temple, the private detective, was free to see her but at least that gave her a chance to have something to eat at home before she drove to his flat at the Albert Dock for their meeting.

Her son, Russell, greeted her when she arrived home. The house seemed to be in chaos. It always was when he was home from university.

'Hi, Ma. How's crime?' he said as he propelled his lanky body off the sofa. His accent was still decidedly London, but that was hardly surprising as they'd only recently moved up north.

Janet didn't answer. It was a question he always asked, an automatic response to her arrival. After a brief conversation about his day which had been mostly spent in front of his computer screen, she cooked some pasta for them both and Russell wolfed it down as though he'd not seen food for days. Then, when she said she had to go out, he kissed her on the top of her head and told her to take care. She told him not to be daft, she was always careful. But she appreciated his concern.

Throughout her police career down in London and now up in Merseyside, she'd had very little to do with private detectives and most of what she knew about them came from the pages of novels. But she thought Bradley Temple was a good name for someone in that particular profession and her mind conjured a dark, handsome gumshoe in a belted raincoat tramping the mean streets of inner city Liverpool.

She drove into town from the suburbs, through streets of fine Georgian houses, eventually ending up at the waterfront. It was still light when she arrived at the Albert Dock but there was a chill breeze blowing in from the river and it had started to rain. Bradley Temple lived on the second floor of an old warehouse building, now transformed into luxury apartments. And when he greeted her at the door, he proved to be as disappointing as the weather. He was stocky and bald and he wore a shiny suit that had seen better days, but he invited

Janet in with scrupulous politeness and offered her a cup of tea which she accepted gratefully.

'Terrible about Paula,' he began. 'She seemed a nice woman. And she hadn't had it easy. Not since her kid was snatched like that.'

Janet smiled sympathetically. 'I believe she called you shortly before she died. What did she say?'

He paused as though he was about to make a dramatic revelation. 'She said she thought she'd seen Adam; her son who went missing.'

'Where did she see him? And what made her think it was him?'

'She was walking down Allerton Road when she saw a young man going into one of the bars. She said he was the spitting image of her ex-husband so she thought—'

'That's hardly conclusive.'

'That's what I told her. But she was convinced it was him. She asked for a meeting but she died before I could find out what else she knew.'

'She said she had more information?'

'Yes, but she wouldn't tell me what it was over the phone.' He hesitated, as though he was deciding whether to break a confidence. 'But when I'd called on her a couple of days earlier, I'd noticed a young man hanging around. I had the impression he was watching her house.'

Janet leaned forward. 'Can you describe him?'

The man closed his eyes. 'He was around five ten; brown hair that looked as if it needed a good wash; greasy skin; long face; T-shirt that looked a size too small for him. Unattractive character but he didn't look particularly dangerous.'

'Have you seen a picture of her ex-husband? Could there be a resemblance to this young man you saw?'

He shook his head. 'No, I never saw a picture – she said she'd destroyed them all after the divorce. But I don't think that matters too much. I think it was all in her imagination. Clutching at straws – it's what people do when they're desperate. And she was desperate alright. Poor woman.'

Janet took a sip of tea. Surely the man Temple described had to be Edward Prime. Now all she needed to do was to get a confession. Which, given his track record, should be simple.

Edward sat in his bedroom, turning the locket over and over in his hand. He'd taken it from her as a keepsake. After all, it was his by right.

He pushed back the threadbare rug beside his single bed and lifted a loose floorboard before plunging his hand down into the space where he kept his treasures. He could feel the book down there. He'd collected everything together; all the evidence that he wasn't who they said he was. He had kept it hidden from his mother – or the woman who called herself his mother – because he didn't want her to discover that he knew the truth.

He was sorry about Paula. There had been blood all over her nice dress, which had been white with red flowers, and the stain had looked like a massive flower that had spread like some evil weed to engulf the others. He'd wanted to do something to save her but it had been too late. Since then he'd dreamed about it every night. The blood and Paula's dead, staring eyes.

He took out the book and opened it. The whole story was there in yellowing newsprint: 'Child missing'; 'Where is baby Adam?' And then there was the article that appeared in the *Echo* last month saying that Paula had never come to terms with her loss. That was how he'd come to realise that his mum had taken him from outside that post office. That she'd carried him off and left the empty pushchair. When he'd found the cuttings in her dressing table drawer he'd confronted her. And he'd known she was lying when she said she'd only kept them because Paula used to live in the next road and she was interested in the case.

He'd decided to go to Howdale Road to find his real mother. He'd watched her for days and when she'd left the house to go shopping he'd followed her. He felt he must have killed her although he couldn't quite remember doing it. But he felt guilty. He always felt guilty.

He remembered bending over her body and unfastening the locket. And when he'd opened it he'd seen a picture of the baby which must have been himself. He'd taken the locket away with him because it was all he had of hers. He knew that if he took it to the police to prove his story, they'd take it off him. And he didn't want to lose it so he'd lied about knowing where it was. But a lie was a little sin compared to all the others that crowded in his head.

He heard the woman who called herself his mother calling him from downstairs, telling him tea was ready. He'd have to think carefully about his next move.

Janet slept on the problem and, after a sleepless night, she came to a decision.

Russell was still in bed so she grabbed a slice of toast and shut the front door quietly behind her. After what Bradley Temple had told her, she knew she had to bring Edward Prime in for questioning. She had no choice.

As soon as she arrived at work she hurried to the DCI's office. She could see him there behind his glass partition. Busy as usual and half hidden behind heaps of paperwork. She knocked on the door, waited a token second, and then pushed it open. He looked up and, from his expression, she knew her interruption wasn't welcome. But she stepped forward and stood in front of his desk like a schoolgirl reporting to the headmaster.

'Last night I went to take a statement from the private detective Paula Sloane hired. Bradley Temple, he's called.' The DCI put down his pen and appeared to be listening so she carried on with new confidence. 'He thinks he saw a man watching Paula's house. And the man he saw fits Edward Prime's description.'

'Then pick him up.'

'Right, sir. I was going to but I thought I'd better let you know.'

'Take someone with you in case . . .'

'I know Prime, sir. I can manage on my own.'

He returned his attention to his paperwork. It was up to her now. And she knew what she had to do.

Prime lived in one of the streets off Smithdown Road. Most of the terraced houses were occupied by students and the

Primes' stood out from the rest with its hanging basket beside the front door, its fussy lace curtains and its cat ornaments on the windowsill. Most of the students had gone home for the summer so the street seemed deserted as Janet rang the doorbell and waited.

She had been dreading an encounter with Prime's mother. Like all mothers she was bound to be a fearsome defender of her young and she couldn't face the thought of a confrontation. She was relieved when Edward himself answered the door, opening it a crack and peeping out.

'Edward. I need another word. Shall we do it here or shall we go down to the police station?'

Edward's eyes lit up. 'You believe me then? You believe I killed her? I'll come down to the police station.' He suddenly looked disappointed. 'Mum's out at the shops.'

'You can let her know later,' Janet said quickly. 'It won't take long. We just need to talk to you, that's all.'

There was a spring in Edward's step as he walked to the car and Janet tried her best not to feel sorry for him as he sat next to her in the front seat, gazing out of the window like a child on a day trip. He looked proud and excited. He was important now. The police were going to hang on his every word.

'Where are we going?' he asked as she turned onto the road that ran beside the river. 'This isn't the way to the police station.'

'There's no hurry so I thought we'd take the scenic route. It'll give us a chance to have a chat if that's okay.' She had reached Otterspool now and after negotiating the roundabout, she brought the car to a halt on the promenade. She could see the expanse of churning grey water to her right as she opened the window to let the odour of Edward's sweat out of the car.

She turned to him and smiled to put him at his ease. 'Somebody saw you watching Paula Sloane's house shortly before she died.'

'I've told you already. I was there.'

'You admit you killed her.'

He suddenly looked unsure of himself. 'She was lying on the floor and there was blood. I must have killed her, mustn't I?'

'Did you take her locket?'

He nodded. 'It had a picture of me inside.' He said almost in a whisper. 'I wanted to keep it.'

Janet saw the tears in his eyes and she felt an almost maternal urge to comfort him, to tell him that everything was going to be alright. But she knew there'd be no comfort from now on.

'A picture of you?'

'When I was a baby.'

'Think carefully. Did you see anyone coming out of the house before you went in?'

A secretive smile appeared on his lips and his eyes met hers. 'Yeah. I did see someone.'

'Who?'

He looked away. 'I'll put it in my statement.' He said the last word with relish, as though making a statement meant that the police were finally taking him seriously. He was going to be a murderer. A kind of celebrity.

Janet opened the car door. 'Would you like some fresh air, Edward? You're going to need it if you're going to be cooped up in a cell for the next few years.'

'Yeah. But I need to tell Mum where I am.'

'You can phone her when we get to the police station.'

Janet looked round. Because of the bad weather the promenade was empty except for a solitary runner, oblivious to everything except the music from his headphones. She waited till he was out of sight then she walked round the car and opened the passenger door.

The body was washed up at Crosby two weeks later. And because the river had done its worst, it had to be identified by DNA and dental records.

Of course his confession to Janet had no witnesses so it wouldn't stand up in court but the police weren't looking for anyone else in connection with the murder of Paula Sloane. The discovery of the locket in Edward's room had clinched it.

Mrs Prime had sworn her son's belief that he was the missing baby, Adam Sloane, had no basis in fact. Edward got these ideas in his head, she said. He'd always been the same. She had been willing to take any tests they wanted to clear her of Adam's abduction and the DCI had taken her up on her offer.

The results confirmed that she'd been telling the truth. Edward had been her son alright. She had only kept the newspaper cuttings because Paula had lived in the next road: it had been a bit of local excitement, that's all. Maybe if Edward hadn't found them, he would still be alive.

When Janet saw the DCI emerging from his office, she began to study her paperwork, trying to look busy. She was aware of him approaching her desk. Then she heard his voice.

'Have you finished with those witness statements?'

Janet picked up a cardboard file and handed it over.

'I've just had Mrs Prime on the phone . . . Edward's mother. She still can't understand what happened.'

'I've been through it time and time again, sir.' She sniffed. 'Edward wanted some fresh air so I parked at the promenade. We were walking along chatting when he suddenly took it into his head to run off. I did my best to chase after him but . . . He just jumped into the water. I threw a lifebelt but there was no sign of him.'

'There'll be a thorough investigation, you know that.'

She nodded meekly.

'What I can't understand is what you were doing there in the first place.'

'I didn't think it'd do any harm to have a stroll and a chat before we came to the interview room. He was unlikely to see the outside world for years if he was convicted and I felt a bit sorry for him if you must know. I suppose I'll be disciplined.'

'Undoubtedly. You screwed up.' He paused. 'You should know better at your age.'

She looked round and saw the young blonde DC smirking into her coffee.

'I suppose Paula's murder was playing on his conscience and he couldn't face life any more. But if he really believed she was his mum, why kill her?'

'Who knows, Janet? Maybe she laughed at him. He's hardly the son of most women's dreams. I don't suppose we'll ever know for sure.'

The DCI walked away, barking an order at one of the others. Janet returned to her paperwork, trying to ignore the stares and sniggers. As far as they were concerned, she'd miscalculated badly.

That evening she managed to get home at a reasonable time but she found the house empty. Russell was out. He'd left her a note saying he'd gone round to a friend's house and wouldn't be back till later. He couldn't have timed it better because there was something she had to do.

As soon as she'd changed out of her work clothes, she took her collection of old photograph albums from the bottom drawer of the sideboard. It was the early ones she was looking for, the ones containing pictures of Russell when he was very small. She knew she should have destroyed them years ago but she'd been down in London then and it had all seemed so very far away.

It had all been planned down to the last detail. The day after she took him she travelled to London where she stayed with her cousin who'd been completely unaware of her deception. She hadn't told her about her late miscarriage: instead she'd let her believe that she'd had the baby and was struggling as a single mother.

After the miscarriage the need to replace her lost child had become so urgent that she'd searched round for a child to take; a child who would become her own. She'd watched Paula Sloane, sick with envy that she had a beautiful baby when hers had never lived. She'd seen Paula ignoring her baby's cries and leaving him alone in the cold outside the post office. And she'd seized her opportunity.

She began to take the photos of the smiling baby from the album. They were so like the picture in Paula's locket, now in the exhibits store at the police station, that anyone seeing them would guess the truth at once. She carried them over to the grate and lit a match, turning away because she couldn't bear to see the image of the innocent child licked by flames.

Everything had been good down in London: she'd enjoyed her work in the Met and she hadn't even minded when they'd teased her about her Liverpool accent. She'd rented a small apartment that had suited her and Russell just fine. And she'd nursed her secret so closely that she'd almost forgotten its existence.

Then years later she'd had to return to Merseyside to care for her elderly mother because there'd been nobody else to take on the responsibility. By the time her transfer up north came through, Russell had started at university and her mother had died six months later. But all had been well until she'd spotted that piece in the newspaper – the article about Paula Sloane's shattered life – and the reality of what she'd done all those years ago had struck her like a hammer blow.

Everything came to a head when Paula spotted Russell one day and noticed his strong resemblance to her ex-husband. For twenty years Paula had scanned every face in every crowd for that resemblance and all her instincts had told her that she'd finally found the one she'd been looking for. She'd followed Russell home and pushed a note through his door which Janet found. She knew she should have ignored it but she'd needed to know how much Paula suspected. So she'd paid her a visit.

Paula had reacted hysterically, screaming and threatening to report Janet to the police, saying that she'd go to prison for a long time. And, worst of all, she'd threatened to tell Russell – or Adam – what kind of monster had brought him up. Janet had realised that even if she threw herself on Paula's mercy, there'd be no calm reconciliation, no embrace of forgiveness. And, faced with Paula's wild fury, she had been forced to pick up a knife and defend herself.

When she'd realised the full horror of what she'd done, she'd dashed from the house, praying that she hadn't been seen. Being in on the investigation, she knew there'd been no sighting of a fleeing woman so she'd imagined she was safe. Until Edward Prime made his confession. And when he hinted that he'd seen her leaving the crime scene, she knew she had to act.

She was sorry about Edward. She'd always remember the look of terror on his face as she shoved him into those grey inhospitable waters. It would be there with her forever, preying on her conscience.

The last remnants of blackened paper glowed and curled in

the grate. The pictures were burned now. She was safe. As she straightened herself up she saw a car drawing to a halt outside, and when the doorbell rang she brushed the ashes from her fingers and hurried over to the bay window. The DCI was standing at the front door with the smirking blonde. Only this time she looked deadly serious.

When Janet opened the door the visitors said nothing and, as they stepped inside, she knew it was over.

'A witness has come forward,' the DCI began almost apologetically. 'He was running on the promenade and . . .'

Janet bowed her head. Perhaps it was time she unburdened herself. She had so much to confess.

TELL IT TO THE BEES
Jane Finnis

Jane Finnis lives in Yorkshire, near the coast. Her books about innkeeper and reluctant sleuth Aurelia Marcella tells of life and death in first-century Roman Britain, the turbulent province of Britannia, on the very edge of the Roman Empire.

When I was little I told all my news to the bees. Every day after tea I'd run down to the hives at the far end of our garden, and pour out my day's happenings. The bees didn't reply, but their calm buzzing showed they were glad to see me.

Mum and Jeff used to laugh at me, but Grandma didn't. 'It's a good old country custom, Susan. And you're a country girl now. So tell them everything, good and bad, silly and serious.'

I was about six when we moved down to Sussex, Mum and Jeff and me. Dad stayed in London and I never saw him, which was sad, but I had news of him from Grandma. I never saw her either, because Mum and Jeff had fallen out with her over somebody called Will. But she wrote me the loveliest letters every week, funny and wise. I enjoyed reading them to the bees.

Mum and Jeff never came near the hives. Jeff said we should get rid of them, but Mum liked honey, so she paid our next-door neighbour, Mr Crowley, to look after them for us. His garden backed onto ours, and he worked there a lot. He usually gave me a friendly wave over the fence. Sometimes he came through onto our side to tend the hives, and he'd talk to me while he worked. He was a kind old man. I called him Uncle Crow.

When I was nine I overheard Mum and Jeff whispering

together about Grandma. 'Death without pain . . . a blessed
release . . . she's had a good life . . . we must make all the
arrangements . . . not a word to Susan.'

Grandma dead? I was heartbroken. I loved her and I couldn't
imagine my world without her. I was puzzled too. Why 'not
a word to Susan'? But if I wasn't meant to know, I couldn't
ask them about it, much as I wanted to. Jeff had a terrible
temper and Mum always sided with him.

I went straight out to the hives. I didn't even stop to wave
to Uncle Crow. 'It's awful, bees. Grandma's dead, and she's
the only one who really cares about me. I mean cared.' I
wanted to cry, but I made myself go on. 'Even after the falling-
out, she never stopped loving me, and I never stopped loving
her. What will I do without her?'

The bees couldn't answer that, but I was comforted because
I knew they understood.

All next day I waited for Mum or Jeff to tell me about
Grandma, but they never said a word about her, so I couldn't
either. After tea I cried as I walked down and stood by the
hives. 'Bees, I'm so sad. Grandma is dead, but they won't tell
me about it . . .' I stayed there a long time, talking and crying.
Uncle Crow waved to me over the fence, but I was too miser-
able to speak to him.

I didn't mean to get anyone into trouble. Honestly I didn't.

How was I to know that Grandma's death wouldn't be till
next week?

PACIFIED

Christopher Fowler

Christopher Fowler is the author of a series featuring Arthur Bryant and John May, who are members of the fictional Peculiar Crimes Unit. The Bryant and May series is set primarily in London, with stories taking place in various years between the Second World War and the present. Whilst there is a progressive narrative, many of the books focus on flashbacks to a major criminal incident from the detectives' shared past. His other publications include a study of unjustly forgotten authors, *Invisible Ink*.

S uddenly the lights had gone out.

Opening the front door of the apartment and peering into the dimness of the top floor corridor, I became aware of a tall man in a black nylon Nike T-shirt and jogging shorts standing against the distant wall.

'I thought I heard someone outside,' I said nervously. 'Were you banging?'

He lowered his left shoe and came closer. A narrow skull framed by slept-on hair, deep-set eyes that diverged disconcertingly. 'We've got cockroaches. Bloody great brown things like they have in America. I just chased one the size of a small cat out into the hall. They come up from the river at high tide. It's because the lights are out. They come out in the dark. I thought I'd squash it, but if they're strong enough to breed after a nuclear blast I suppose they can survive a rubberised heel.'

He dropped the shoe and wriggled a bony foot back into it. 'So I'm not the only one still here. I haven't seen you before. Hang on a minute.'

He produced a plastic pocket torch and shone it right in

my eyes. When I waved the beam aside he ran it over my body, lingering on my chest, then flicked it to the floor.

'I suppose you know there's no power on for the next twelve hours. I haven't seen him lately. Is he away?'

'Who?'

'The man who lives here.' He gestured to my front door.

'I'm looking after the place for the owner,' I explained.

'Ah. I suppose he's off on business. They always are.'

'I'm sorry?'

'The so-called residents of this block. I'm next door, the corner penthouse of this concrete Shangri-La. North-westerly view. Not exactly Turner's vision of the river, but north-easterly had already gone.' He offered a long hand, with pale fingers that wrapped around mine like crab legs. 'My name's Dr Elliot, by the way.'

'June Cryer,' I said. His palm was unpleasantly moist. I looked down at his running shorts and imagined his testicles sticking to his legs.

'Do you need any light?'

'I found some candles. And a small torch. I didn't know the lights were going to be out when I agreed to—'

'Essential maintenance, apparently. I've got a good alternative. Follow me. It's alright, I don't bite ladies until you know me.'

I realised I was prepared to trust him because his voice was cultured and confident. That's the class system in a nutshell. The BBC might have Indian newsreaders now but they make damned sure they sound like Old Etonians. I knew I must sound horribly suburban to him. 'Estuarine', that's what they call my accent in polite circles. 'Chav', that's what everyone else says. It makes me ashamed, the way I kowtow to people with posh voices. I keep having to remind myself it's not a sign of intelligence. I didn't belong here in this expensive block of flats – sorry, luxury riverside lofts. I was doing a favour for a girlfriend's friend.

Dr Elliot held open the door for me. 'Hurricane lamps,' he suggested. 'I went out and purchased a job lot from some peculiar Turkish shop in Kennington Road. They're only pressed tin but they add a gothic atmosphere.'

'I wouldn't have thought this building needed any more atmosphere.'

'Extraordinary, isn't it? A veritable palace of bad dreams. Makes you wonder what the architect was thinking. A Frenchman, apparently. It's their uncompromising nature that makes them so artistically adroit. And so fucking rude. He must have had a very strange idea of London in his head.'

He led the way into the darkened lounge, stopping to light a pair of the tin lamps on a sideboard. Weak light burnished maroon walls, picking up the glister of expensive gilt frames. He turned and smiled. His eyes were bothersome because I couldn't tell where he was looking. 'At least the water's gas-heated. You should have been given adequate warning about the electricity. *Bad* friend not to tell you. You'll be undressing in the dark.'

'I'm not sure I would have come if I had realised.' I followed Dr Elliot around the room as he lit the lamps. His apartment was squarer and taller than the one I was sitting, with windows on two sides, the walls painted in deep crimsons and browns, lined with medical textbooks. I stopped before the riverside windows to check the view from a different perspective.

From here, London seemed veiled in steel grey mesh. Beside the curtains, what I'd thought was a life-sized statue was revealed to be a full-sized cutaway model of the human body, its skull sectioned to expose a quarter of pink plastic brain, one bulbous eye in its socket, a bright crimson rubber heart, blue-grey lungs, maroon liver and coiled intestines the colour of a flamingo. He had scabby pink rubber arms and legs.

'Oh, that's Maurice. He's a bit startling, isn't he? The idea was to make him look like the sort of chap you'd find in a medical training college in the 1930s. We've grown very attached to each other.'

'You're a doctor?'

'God, no. I'm not interested in the plumbing side of things. Psychiatric research. Motivational stuff for corporate staff training. Physical and psychological effects of sudden life-change. I organise behavioural experiments on patients,

poorly paid volunteers mostly, mess about with their precon-
ditioning, change their diets and stress levels, try to work
out what triggers their responses, generally fuck them about
until they scream like stuck pigs. What do you do?'

'Oh, I'm nobody at all,' I replied without thinking. No
one had ever asked what I did. Dr Elliot frightened me. He
confirmed my assumption that only businesspeople would
live in a building of such peculiarly masculine design. Women
like me would always be invisible here.

'Come now. I rarely find that's true in my line of work.
Everyone's somebody, even if they don't know it.'

'All right. Then I'm a housewife.'

'Is that all? I don't think I know anyone who's just a
housewife. It's such a Fifties word, so redolent of aprons
and baking. Won't you be uncomfortable here? It's very dark.
We might as well be cut off in some ghastly remote part of
the country, instead of being in central London.'

There was something arrogant and suggestive in his manner
that irritated me. 'I've got a friend coming over later,' I lied.
'Anyway, civilisation's just outside.'

'Do you really think so? I look out and see chimps in vans
shouting at cyclists, no one you could actually rely on. The
words "guttural" and "polyglot" spring to mind.' He rolled
the words around in his mouth like brandy, trying them out.
'Guttural. Polyglot.'

'I'll be fine when my friend gets here,' I repeated.

'The outside buzzer's not working and the main entrance
door is open. You'd better tell him to come up the stairs, and
sing so as not to frighten you. It's one of those nights when
you never know who might come wandering in.'

'I won't be frightened, don't worry.'

'That is . . . if your friend is a man.' His distracting eyes
reflected light like some nocturnal animal. He was studying
me too intently, a hazard of his job, perhaps. 'What made
you agree to stay here, I wonder?'

'The money,' I answered honestly, sensing he knew when
I lied. 'My friend's boyfriend is the owner, Malcolm. I have
this friend, Cathy.'

'You mean girlfriend?'

'No, a girl who's a friend. She's seeing Malcolm, and he offered to pay me if I stayed until Monday morning. The security system being out. He has paintings.'

'Yes, the power's off overnight. I don't suppose the insurers would cover that. He didn't tell you the lights would be off as well.'

'No. I've never met him. As I say, it was a favour . . .'

'So you're like one of my paid volunteers. Is this a service you provide regularly?'

'No. I'm just helping my friend out.'

'If you were that much of a friend you wouldn't be taking his money, would you? Or perhaps the exchange of cash eases the social transaction for you both.' He managed to extract a lascivious meaning from every word, using too much tongue. He joined me at the window, standing too close. 'Of course, I knew you weren't like the rest of them as soon as I saw you.'

'In what way?'

'My dear lady, the residents here are the vanished rich. Overseas professionals renting from agents. I've only met three of them, a Swiss banker, a Russian electronic surveillance expert and a plastic surgeon of indeterminate and dubious origin. They're somewhat overcautious about their privacy. Not terribly interested in their neighbours. They like to bring ladies here for a few hours, then let them out to find their way home in tears. You could hammer on their doors screaming blue murder and they wouldn't open.'

'How did you end up here?'

'I see too much of people's emotions at work. We need a place that pacifies us.'

'You could live in the country,' I suggested. As he dropped onto the sofa and folded his legs, I saw that he was wearing see-through socks, pulled up too high.

'In a village with a bad Italian restaurant and a pub with morris dancers? No, my practice is in town, and the building suits my needs.' He stretched out a hairy white wrist and tapped the back of the seat, as though beckoning a cat. Repelled, I remained standing. 'Besides, it's rather interesting as a social experiment. I'm waiting for it all to break down, you see. That's when the real discoveries are made, when organisation collapses into chaos. These lovely properties are built on slum land. The buildings have been pimped into ersatz hotel suites for multicultural money-churners who share no common social skills whatsoever. It's a giant leap back into a dark age, psychologically speaking. Yet there are compensations.'

'It's more cosmopolitan,' I suggested.

'Yes, unsophisticated people always say that. It's a poor substitute for society. In my opinion—'

'My friend,' I interrupted lamely, 'he might be waiting for me.'

He clapped his hands with unnerving suddenness. 'Then I mustn't keep you, must I?' He jumped up and guided me from the room. I felt relieved to be leaving, but he suddenly stopped in the doorway and turned back to me, his face so close that I could taste his breath. 'You know the fun of having a little place in town? This isn't a family building, so there can be . . . experimentation. Only our gallant captains of industry can afford to live here, and it's never a good idea to put them all in a group. Guess what the rates of mental abnormality are in this country. One in five among the general populace, one in three among senior corporate executives. The higher you go, the more fucked-up it gets, psychologically speaking. These people aren't for you. Especially when the lights go out. I think you'd be better off away from here, back in your little terraced house. Here, take one of these with you.'

He handed me one of the hurricane lamps and rested his hand lightly in the small of my back, the supercilious ushering of a doctor seeing off an unrespected patient. 'You'd better go, or I might want to keep you here all night.'

I turned in the doorway and studied him. 'Can I ask you something about Maurice?'

Dr Elliot glanced back at the eviscerated dummy. 'Him?'

'Yes, doesn't he bother you, standing there like that in the dark?'

'Not at all. There's nothing to be afraid of when you've already been as far as you can go. We have no secrets from each other.'

Dr Elliot closed the door before I'd managed to find my way back to the apartment, as though he had quickly decided that I was unattractive and not worth flirting with. Deeply unsettled by the encounter, I returned to Malcolm's flat holding the lantern high so that I could check the stark rooms.

The reflection from the river's palisade of floodlit buildings had robbed the walls of their corrosive colours. I looked in the bedroom cupboards and found plain grey suits and white shirts, as neatly arranged as shop displays. Clearly, Malcolm's wife didn't stay here. A single pair of young women's shoes, gaudy and damaged, lay in the bottom of a cupboard, proof of his unfaithfulness. His wife's home would be more warmly decorated. That was where he lived. This was just for sex, any woman coming here could see that. It was why Malcolm's wife avoided the place; she wouldn't want to be confronted with such obvious evidence. I wondered if Cathy came here in the early evenings after work to strip and pose before him.

I pulled back the glass doors and stepped out onto the balcony. The scene below drew attention in a way that the view from my south London flat never did. In the far corner to the left, I could see into Dr Elliot's penthouse. Even though the rooms were dark it was possible to spot the psychiatrist standing in his window, as motionless as his medical dummy.

I fancied a drink, but the only tonic I could find was flat, so I tipped fruit juice onto what I hoped was decanted gin, and stood proprietorially behind the bar at the rear of the lounge, sipping slowly. The room was stuffy, and the temperature control panel was not apparent in the gloom. I studied the paintings by lamplight. They didn't look especially valuable, but I had only ever seen paintings in books.

I found some fat candles in a sideboard and lit them. Stretched out on an umber couch in the lounge, I watched the creamy flames poised in glowing wax like a line of torch-bearing monks, and tried to summon a sense of independence, but there was nothing. The room grew warmer. No street sounds reached my ears. Up here there was only the soughing of the late summer storm-sky. Cocooned in the huge robe, my eyelids grew heavy.

My dreams were uneasy, dislocated; first I was back at

home in my old sunshine yellow lounge, but stripped bare of furnishings, bright wavering light, and someone was crouching naked in a corner, plangently suffering. Before this hunched child walked a dark creature with blank eyes, rattling something rhythmically in a large steel pot. It held a ladle, clicking against the metal rim, back and forth, back and forth, the sound of a clock, or pipes quickly heating.

When I awoke and looked at my watch it was a quarter to midnight, and I could still hear the clicking. It faded and grew, as if the night air was catching it.

Rising, I took one of the candles and watched its shifting golden sphere raise walls where there had been none. The edges of the light led me to the second bedroom and a floor-length mirror. I studied my spectral reflection, rather pleased with it. Robed in white, candle raised, the heroine of a Victorian novel was distorted in dark machine-rolled glass.

A cool draught stippled my skin. One of the glass doors to the balcony stood ajar. I couldn't remember if I had left it like that. I wanted to close it, but was compelled to step outside and approach the source of the clicking sound.

The breeze from the river was sharper now, cuprous and sour. I looked to my right, across to the corner balcony, scanning the pastel darkness, and flinched when a torch-beam strafed the windows. Placing the candle out of the wind, I looked harder. The third apartment was set at a steeper angle than Dr Elliot's, affording me a dim view of its interior. Its balcony door was open, a thin beam of light bouncing across the walls. I couldn't tell if the girl on the balcony was looking in my direction. Her hands were raised to her throat, long black hair fluttering like flags at her arched back.

A low wave of air attacked my candle and snuffed it out. When I glanced back, the girl was outlined against the pale night like a statue, a memorial to some household divinity, affixed to the building in spiritual appeasement. I could tell she was young by her slender waist, small raised breasts and flat stomach. She could have been a dancer, a model. She lifted her hands high above her tilted head, her fingers spread wide and reaching, as if waiting to be carried up into the night air. High above her, electricity flared within the clouds, like a faulty connection in heaven. For a moment it looked like she had caused it.

The girl was not alone. A tall figure stepped out to join her. Steel sheened her long neck. I heard the passing of a chain, saw the rattle and flash of links. The man was chaining her up.

An urgent whisper escaped her throat and was carried on the thermals trapped between the apartments. I stepped closer to the edge of the balcony and tried to see what was happening. The building's crazed geometry stood against the never-night of the London sky. An unscalable drop fell to the riverside road, seven floors below. When I looked up again the girl had disappeared. Inside the apartment, the torchlight started to recede. I left the balcony, puzzled.

Although my own front door was closed I could hear it shifting slightly back and forth in the jamb. Freed from the grip of electricity, the latch-bolt had slipped from the strike plate. Against the beating of my heart, I peered outside into the hall for the second time in the evening.

Faint light flickered where there had been none before. In the centre of the floor stood a fat black candle, obscenely leaking grease as a question mark formed around its base. Shoe prints, fresh and wet, led across the grey cord carpet tiles into the corridor from the stairs.

Then I saw them.

Beside the door of the next apartment, outlined against a panel of night sky, the man had his captive propped against the wall with her head bowed and a steel shackle attached around her neck. The girl's face was obscured by glossy black hair that fell as straight as pencils.

The man bent awkwardly from the waist, as if he was wearing a back-brace. His legs seemed almost to belong to someone else. The girl was barefoot and bare-breasted, dressed only in pale baggy jeans. She fell forward, to be propped upright by her strange companion. A maze of dark spots glinted around her bare feet on the carpet. She made a vague, hopeless grab at the arms of the broken man and sank drunkenly down the wall, doubling over with a high cry of frustration, or possibly laughter.

I took a pace back in alarm when she suddenly thrust out her arms toward me. The man turned in my direction, his features lost in darkness, but I could see a single lidless eye staring, daring a response.

I didn't wait to find out what he was doing, or what was going on between him and the girl. It was best not to know. In the suburbs you don't talk to your neighbours even if they're being murdered. Be it black mass, buggery or bestiality, the general opinion is that it's best to leave them enjoying themselves so long as everyone's over eighteen.

Slamming the door and running back to the bedroom, I scrabbled for matches and relit the candle, then tore open the zip of my case for jeans, a sweater, a jacket. Unable to lay hands on my trainers, I was forced into heeled shopping shoes, all the while thinking, *Murderers, perverts, I should never have come here.* Why would anyone chain a young girl up like an animal? I wondered if she was an unwilling participant in the kind of sex games you read about every Sunday in the family newspapers.

Remembering my mobile, I ran back to the kitchen, found it, checked the reception meter and saw there were no bars available. End of the ground floor corridor, Malcolm had told Cathy to tell me, that was the only place where you could get reception at the moment.

The front door hadn't been locked or even pushed shut. My feet were numb on the cold floor. Space expanded ahead, folding outward into the rooms as I raised the light. I stopped in the doorway to the guest room and shifted the lantern forward.

She was standing behind the door.

She dropped her arms over my head and I screamed, releasing the lantern. The cheap glass didn't break but oil splashed in a spray of tiny comets, setting the bed quilt alight. I twisted in her tightening embrace, so that her stomach was pushed against my buttocks, and tried to tip her over, but she proved too strong. In my state of panic I couldn't tell if she was trying to get help or hurt me. She suddenly pulled up her hands and I shoved as hard as I could, forcing her against the wall. I had little hope of stopping her, but she fell away.

Grabbing the end of the bedspread I flicked it over on itself, so that the burning patches were smothered. One crackling chunk of material floated and brushed against the wardrobe in a shower of autumn sparks. Acrid smoke hazed the air. The girl had frog-dropped to the floor and closed herself into a foetal position at the base of the wall.

I set the candle on the floor and tried to get a clear look at the collar on her neck, but she twisted from the light. Her lank black hair curtained her eyes. As my fear subsided, I heard her moaning. I waited for her to look up, flinching in anticipation of some terrible sight, but the face that stared back was magazine-beautiful. She was perhaps eighteen, with empty blue eyes and sharp jawline of a photographer's model.

The slim steel noose was fixed tightly at her throat, a metal version of the plastic tags that electronics shops used to bundle cables. She was trying to speak but her voice was undecipherable, a spatula-on-burnt-pan rasp. My instinct was to try and wrench it from her neck, but I was frightened of making matters worse because it was fastened so tightly.

She was clearly in pain. Where the steel edge bit, her skin was ringed with a raw, violet line. Her wrists were connected by a white plastic tag, so that she looked like a product that had been delivered to the wrong address and dumped on the floor in the recipient's absence.

I tried to pull the collar apart, but she flinched and twisted when I touched her, an eel writhing on a hook. I had no idea what to do. The look of fear on her face panicked me even more. Another flinch, more violent this time. Her legs kicked out hard as her muscles bunched. Should I go and fetch the creepy, condescending Dr Elliot, or would that be worse?

I pulled at the steel circle, but I couldn't slip my fingers beneath it. Running to the kitchen I pulled open drawers, searching for a knife. Then I remembered the lethal-looking set of Sabatier knives that lined the wall, and selected one of the smaller blades. By the time I returned to the bedroom she was lying arched on her back, convulsing violently against the collar. I scraped back her hair and held her head steady, trying to slip the knife blade under the band, but it was

impossible to do so without cutting her neck. I needed something else, something that could . . .

In the kitchen I had seen a pair of heavy spatchcock scissors,
designed for chopping chickens apart. Now I ran back and
grabbed them.

She lay still on the beechwood floor of the bedroom, as
pale as bone. The collar was so tight that her face had turned
a mottled indigo, the colour of a bad sprain. Suddenly she
coughed, spattering the walls, the floor and me. Her head
fell back, eyes bulging hard.

I tried to work the tip of the scissors under the band, but
couldn't without slicing her skin. Several times I caused
pinpricks of blood and apologised with a grimace. I could
see I would be forced to dig deeper. I wiggled the blade
under the steel edge and felt her flesh yield.

I was making a mess of her neck. I dug under again. The
metal was thin but incredibly strong. I finally managed to
shift the tip of the scissor blade right beneath it, but it seemed
to take forever to saw all the way through. As it broke she
fell back, sucking in air.

I cut the plastic ties from her wrists and dragged her to
the balcony doors. She had almost no body fat, and weighed
nothing. Her body was cadaver-white and muscular. We left
a skidmark of blood through the flat. She still clutched at
her throat and the side of her head, but was unable to move
her hands properly. Behind me, the light from the tipped-over
lantern fanned and died to a faint blue pulse.

I brought her a beaker of water, blundering and spilling
most of it in the darkened flat. She winced and allowed the
water to overflow her mouth.

'I have to go for help. Who did this to you?'

Moving the lantern closer, I was finally able to see the
side of her head. A sore-looking lump rose at the base of
her right ear, up toward the occipital outcrop of her skull. A
blood vessel had burst in her right eye. She'd been hit pretty
hard. I needed to get her into the light, so I slipped my hands
under her armpits and pulled. The stinging reek of the burned
coverlet made my eyes water.

Her breath had become shallow and fast. I lowered her

against the wall and pulled the scorched eiderdown from the bed, wrapping the unburned part around her shivering body, but when I tried to stand, my legs folded beneath me. The room rotated away as the shock of the last few minutes began to catch up.

I wondered if the psychiatrist next door had any useful medical knowledge. He had warned me about the others in the building, told me to go home, and I had ignored him. I knew I should at least bring him here, but tried to raise myself again and failed.

The girl was laying on her side, breathing more faintly than ever. I gave up trying to stand and lay down beside her for a minute, less a gesture of solidarity than an inability to command my muscles. Shoving the spatchcock shears into the rear pocket of my jeans, I put my head back, listening as our respiration matched and phased.

When I rose and opened the front door again, I made damn sure that her attacker had gone. Only the black candle remained, guttering in the sudden draft. My inability to aid the girl was upsetting, but I was out of my depth and needed help.

I'd left the lantern behind because it seemed wrong to leave her alone in darkness. When I tried to unglue the black candle the wick was extinguished in splashed wax, and as the spirit of the flame departed I found myself stranded with the front door closing behind me, a truly blind panic tamping down my senses.

The bell on the lintel of Dr Elliot's door failed to work without electricity. I slapped my hand against the wood but there was no answer. He's gone out, I thought, he's asleep, he's refusing to help me, just like the others he told me about.

I pressed my ear on the cool maple grain and listened. Nothing. Perhaps I had only seen his dummy at the window. What kind of man would keep a dessicated corpse on display in his lounge? These people weren't my kind, I didn't understand them or want to be like them. The backs of my arms were sweating ice. How much time had passed since I discovered the girl, seconds, minutes, half an hour? The absence of light seemed to rob me of other senses.

Dr Elliot finally answered the door in a creepily short towelling robe. He looked liverish and guilty, his skin as slick and breath as shallow as if he'd been running or having a marathon bout of afternoon sex, and his hair was sticking up on one side like a duck wing. For a moment he didn't seem to remember me.

'Oh, it's you again.'

'I need to talk to you. It's urgent.'

'Then I suppose you'd better come in.'

He seemed reluctant to admit me, not standing quite far enough aside to allow me by. 'You'll have to be quick.' He smoothed his hair into place. 'I'm expecting someone very shortly.'

'Something awful has happened.'

'Really. Do you have to involve me?'

As I passed his bedroom door I caught a glimpse of several leather straps attached with rings and buckles, laid out on the duvet in a fetishistic order that reminded me of the spanners and pairs of pliers my husband kept under our stairs. Dr Elliot led the way into the kitchen, scratching, and poured himself orange juice.

'A girl. I saw her in the third apartment, the empty one. Then she was outside with a man who had . . . there was something wrong with him. Then she came into my apartment. She had a thing around her neck.'

'It sounds as if you were dreaming. I hope so. I have no history of being useful to strangers.' He seemed bored by me and walked away, so that I was forced to follow him into the lounge.

Dr Elliot dropped onto the sofa, his robe falling open at an uncomfortably high level. Either he hadn't noticed or was unalarmed by the notion of displaying his genitals. 'Are you familiar with the legend of Pasiphae?' He glanced over at the bare wall, as if checking to see if it was listening, and I noticed that the eviscerated dummy was missing.

'A Greek myth,' I said, puzzled by the change of subject.

'Oh the Greeks, endless cruel revenges of a sexual nature. The daughter of Helios was cursed by Poseidon so that she lusted after a huge white bull. In order to copulate with it, she had Daedalus build her a portable wooden structure covered with cowhide, which she climbed inside, and the bull raped her. She gave birth to the Minotaur.'

I had no idea why he was telling me this. His robe had opened further, exposing a testicular sac like a fortnight-old peach. I wondered if he did this with all his female guests, in the same way that baboons exposed their backsides to mates. He smiled as he lazily flicked the robe back in place.

'A shocking excess of female sensuality and deceit, don't you think? Painfully penetrated for the pleasure of others, the ruptured Pasiphae was wilfully damaged by her beast. Surely any female who would allow that must be damaged herself.'

There was a noise in the hall. The girl's attacker was standing in the lounge doorway. Maurice's sectioned face, one side skull-bone, the other a Brylcreemed 1930s gent, turned. His single naked eye stared down at me. He seemed to be having trouble staying in one place, and I realised it was because he was balancing on what were presumably prosthetic legs, incongruously clad in grey tracksuit bottoms. A glistening red plastic penis poked up from his waistband below his multi-coloured intestines like some kind of X-rated glove puppet.

Dr Elliot addressed his friend. 'Oh hello, we were just talking about you.'

'The girl didn't want to play,' said Maurice, his sinewy jaw muscles working against bared ceramic teeth. He sounded like a BBC presenter from the distant past, as though a recording was playing inside his chest.

'How is he doing that?' I shouted, standing. 'Is this some kind of trick?'

'God, no, he's like this all the time,' said Dr Elliot, snorting. 'It's just that *you people* never usually see people like Maurice. I'm surprised he managed to keep his mouth shut when you were here.'

Maurice took a step forward, wobbling slightly, like a World War II pilot on calipered stumps. His eyes swivelled over me.

I had to ask. 'How is he moving?'

'Obviously, he's alive, but he's not been well for a long time, ever since he got out of Helmand province. The army surgeons repaired the physical parts but the mind never truly heals. And he's got worse lately. Now he needs a steady supply of girls to keep him calm. They stop him from going strange. You probably get the same effect from – oh, I don't know, shopping.' His crab-fingers traced a pink scar on his inner thigh. 'It's fascinating from a clinical point of view. There are new frontiers opening all the time. Don't get me started, I could bore for Britain on the psychological effects of war. Sometimes the solution is to give the patient exactly what he needs. Maurice, where's our little Pasiphae?' He turned to me. 'Forgive the pun. Pacify, you see?'

Pasiphae. I tried to imagine her hunched on all fours inside the hot darkness of the rough wooden box, her exposed private parts extended back toward the cool opening in the planks, waiting for the burning heat of the bull's great member to tear her apart. One human, one an artificial representation of a human form, reconstructed after God-knows-what kind of horrific accident.

'The lady hurt her, not me. It wasn't Maurice.' Maurice dropped his jaw and laughed in his scratchy recorded BBC manner, staring at me as he wavered in the doorway.

'Don't worry, Mrs Housewife, you're quite safe from Maurice, you're too old for him,' said Dr Elliot.

I still had the spatchcock scissors in my back pocket, and felt like sticking them in his balls.

'Better run away now, though. Maurice doesn't take kindly to people who spoil his nights. Neither do I.'

Maurice wavered on his stumps, guffawing madly, his laughter turning into a string of ragged sobs. I pushed from the room and fled the building, leaving them to their experiments.

You always suspect there's a class that lives so far apart from you that you have no idea what their lives are like. That night, I caught a glimpse inside this other world, and it made no sense to me at all. The curtain briefly parted, then closed again. I know now where these people live, in the darkened luxury apartments that line the Thames, in the backstreets of

Belgravia, in the blind shuttered terraces of Kensington. Their money is accepted with no questions asked, their crimes go unreported, their behaviour remains unchecked.

The next day I asked Cathy to ask Malcolm about the residents of his building, but he never told her anything, or perhaps she never asked, so I never found out.

I walked past the apartment tower in daylight and it appeared normal. But looking up at the sky-reflecting windows, I got the feeling that Dr Elliot and his friends were looking down at me, hoping to find solace in the lower orders again tonight, wishing I would go away and be replaced by someone younger, prettier, poorer, lonelier.

I think – for just an instant – I saw the curtain part again.

THE FRANKLIN'S SECOND TALE
FROM *THE 'LOST' CANTERBURY TALES*

Paul Freeman

Paul Freeman is an English instructor working in Abu Dhabi, where he lives with his wife and three young children. In addition to being a novelist, he has published numerous short stories and is currently working on a series of thirty-three *'Lost' Canterbury Tales*. His contribution to this book is his shortest *Canterbury Tale* to date and offers a foretaste.

Prologue to The Franklin's Second Tale

The hoary-bearded Franklin in our band
Of pilgrims quod: "'Tis time I set my hand
To spinning out a cautionary tale."
He put away his flask of Kentish ale
And added: "Though I generously host
My household guests, not every man can boast
A temp'rament as open-palmed as mine.
In fact I've found that villanelles who dine
On meagre means are likely more to share
What little they possess (with scarce a care)
Than those born high with spoons of solid gold
Betwixt their lips. Ennobled fellows hold
Their riches tight, and always crave more wealth.
So hear you, how a sovereign risked ill-health
To measure those around him. Listen well!
A regicidal yarn I have to tell.

The Franklin's Second Tale

King Egbert, past his prime, felt wont to test
The folk he trusted most ere he divest
His kingship, so he rustled up a plan.
He feigned to be a foolish, deaf old man,
So fragile he was promptly put to bed
To languish in his dotage until dead.

One morning he awoke to find a band
Conspiring to purloin by force his land.

"Usurping father's realm is nothing wrong,"
Prince Fredrick quod. "He's lingering too long.
Perhaps some actions radical and bold
Are needed lest I'm regent when I'm old."

"'Twas mooted that by April he would die,"
Quod Martha, Fredrick's wife. "Yet months go by.
King Egbert's time as potentate has passed,
But still the stubborn ass is holding fast."

The last collaborator of the group
(The King's physician) quod: "Upon thin soup
I've starved him, but his servant girl takes pains
To feed him well, ensuring that he reigns.
Her ministrations need to be curtailed
Lest Egbert's abdication be derailed.
So, if we're in agreement let's dispatch
This millstone through a scheme we'll newly hatch."

The traitors laid their plans and all agreed
On how to carry out the fatal deed.

Prince Fredrick strode towards the bed to place
A pillow over Egbert's pallid face.

The sov'reign thrashed about, then acted dead
Till Fredrick took the pillow from his head.

"Inform the guards of Egbert's sad demise,"
Quod Martha to the doctor. "And advise
The royal court, dear husband, that the crown
Your father donned is due for handing down."

Then once the co-conspirators had left
The chamber, Egbert's servant girl, bereft
And tearful hurried to the regent's side.
She caterwauled, she beat her breast and cried
Until the 'dead man' opened up his eyes
And winked – at which she fainted in surprise.

The moment Fredrick sat upon the throne
To take the right of kingship as his own,
His father yelled across the hall: "This claim
I'm dead is false. My doctor's much to blame.
So sharpen up the executioner's blade,
That with a single swing the bungler's slayed."

The treacherous physician made a plea
For clemency and wept on bended knee;
But nought in mitigation could he say,
So Egbert's guardsmen dragged the man away.

Quod Egbert: "Since the royal court's convened,
I now decree Prince Fredrick must be weaned
Off luxuries, so hereby I promote
My son to head our harshest, most remote
Of garrisons – accomp'nied by his spouse."

Thus Egbert slyly cleansed the royal house
And quietly arranged to see his lands
Would not fall into undeserving hands.

Some twelve months on, a courier arrived
At Fredrick's fort with news he'd be deprived

Of any royal legacy, for writ
Upon a scroll, King Egbert saw it fit
To make, at last, his joyful tidings known –
My servant girl sits by me on the throne,
The message read: *And now a better heir*
Than you my queen's been good enough to bear.

Epilogue to the Franklin's Second Tale

The Franklin, with his yarning done, once more
Uncorked his flask, and passed around its store
Of ale amongst us pilgrims whilst we mulled
The import of his message ere we dulled
Our minds with beer. It seemed his story told
How tenderness affected by the cold
Of calculating greed turns good men bad
And made a son a patricidal lad.
So mark my words, if avarice you choose
To rule your days, the game of Life you'll lose.

SECOND CHANCE
John Harvey

John Harvey has published scores of books under various names, as well as writing poetry, working on scripts for TV and radio, and running a small press. His Nottingham-based series featuring Charlie Resnick began with *Lonely Hearts*, and was adapted for television. His later books include those featuring Frank Elder and Jack Kiley. In 2007, he received the CWA Cartier Diamond Dagger.

He hadn't recognised her. Not right off. A slender woman in blue jeans and a green parka hesitating on the pavement outside the building where he lived. Her hair scraped back into a tight ponytail; make-up an afterthought at best.

'Jack . . .'

'Victoria?'

It had been the voice that had nailed it, Essex laid through with pre-teen years of elocution lessons, a mother with ideas above her station. Basildon, at the time, east from London on the line to Shoeburyness.

'I thought this was the right address, but then, with the shop and everything, I wasn't sure.'

For the past several years, home for Jack Kiley had been a first-floor flat above a charity shop in north London, the stretch of road that led from Tufnell Park down towards Kentish Town. Terry, that morning's volunteer, drape jacket and duck tail, was playing Chuck Berry at near full volume. Midway through the guitar solo on 'Johnny B. Goode', the needle stuck and was lifted delicately clear and set back down a beat before the voice returned.

'You hungry?' Kiley asked.

She shook her head.

'Coffee, then?'

'Okay.'

He threaded her through the lines of buses and private cars to the Vietnamese café across the street. One latte, a flat white, and, for Kiley, a baguette with chillies, coriander and garlic pork.

'Breakfast, Jack, or lunch?'

'Both?'

When she smiled, crow's feet etched deeper around her eyes.

He had first met her when she was just nineteen, a minor sensation at Wimbledon and on her way to being something of a celebrity: Victoria Clarke, the first British woman to reach the semi-finals since Boudica, or so it had seemed. Her world ranking had been twenty-three and rising; in the *Observer* list of *Britain's Top 20 Sportswomen,* she was number seven with a bullet. Canny, her agent had bartered her image between cosmetic companies and fashion houses, settling finally for a figure that tripled whatever she was likely to make out on the WTA tour.

During the Championships, billboards appeared in every major city, showing Victoria in full-colour action: crouching at the base line, racket in hand, lips slightly parted, waiting to receive; watching the high toss of the ball, back arched, white cotton top taut across her breasts. Beneath both, the same strap line: 'A Little Honest Sweat!' The deodorant itself was pictured discretely bottom right, alongside the product's name.

Students tore them down and used them to paper their rooms. Feminists festooned them with paint. Victoria crashed out in the semis, came unstuck in the first round the following year; three years on, advertising contract cancelled, she failed to get through qualifying. Retired at twenty-five.

Since then, she'd done a little coaching, some tennis commentary on local radio, moved for a while to Florida – more coaching – and returned the wiser. The last time Kiley had caught sight of her, aimlessly flicking the remote, she had been modelling heart-shaped pendants on the Jewellery Channel.

'So, how's it going?' he asked.

'You know . . .' Shrug of the shoulders, toss of the hair.

'You're looking good anyway.'

'And you're a lousy liar.'

Kiley bit down into his baguette; a touch of chilli but not too much. 'When you called, you just said you needed to see me. You didn't say why.'

'I was probably too embarrassed.'

'And now?'

She curled the ends of her hair around her finger, sipped her latte.

'I always seem to be coming to you with my problems, Jack.'

'Goes with the job,' Kiley said.

Victoria had fallen pregnant when she was fifteen and persuaded her older sister to bring the child up as her own; an unorthodox way of parenting that had threatened to break into the spotlight just when her big advertising contract was due to be signed. One of Kiley's first jobs as a private detective, having some time previously resigned from the police, had been to trace the root of the problem; help it go away.

'This isn't about Alicia?'

'No. Not at all.'

'So tell me.'

She leaned closer; lowered her voice. 'When I was in the States I met this man, this guy. Adam. He wasn't American, English, he was out there filming. Some, I don't know, documentary. We . . . we had this, this thing. I suppose it was pretty intense for a while.' She lifted her cup; set it back down. 'Anyway, he came back, I stayed. We kept in touch, you know, phone calls, email. It was okay for a while, but then he started getting on at me, trying to get me to change my mind. About living there. Come back to England, he'd say. We had something special, didn't we? It's not as if what you're doing is going anywhere. And he was right, that was the thing, I just didn't like being told. As if I'd made, you know, another mistake. But in the end – he wore me down, I suppose – I packed it all in, what I was doing, the coaching, and came back, and then when I saw him again there was nothing. A big zero. Nothing. It wasn't just I didn't fancy him, Jack, I didn't even like him.'

'And I suppose he didn't feel the same?'

A quick shake of the head. 'When I told him, tried to tell him, he wouldn't listen. Went on and on about how he'd made all these plans, put his life on hold, while all the time I'd been leading him on. I tried to reason with him but he just went – I don't know – crazy. Called me every dirty name under the sun. Punched the wall. The wall, Jack.'

'Not you? He didn't hit you?'

'No, though I think it came close. In the end he calmed down enough to tell me he never wanted to set eyes on me again. If he did, he didn't know what he might do.' She straightened, arching her neck. 'That was a little over a year ago.'

'And now?'

Victoria sighed, twiddled more hair. 'When we were . . . when I was still in Florida, some of the emails we sent, back and forth, they were . . . they were pretty, well . . .'

'Sexy?'

'Yes. Just, you know, what would you do if I were there now? What would you like me to do to you? That sort of thing. Pretty harmless, really. But then, after a while, there was more. More than just, you know, words.'

'Photos? Videos?'

'Yes.' Not looking, looking away, out towards the plate glass of the window, the road. Her voice was dry, small. 'There was a camera on the laptop. He'd make up these little scenes and have me act them out. Download them and then edit them. Send them back. Some of them, they were . . .'

Her voice trailed into silence.

Outside, the driver of a Murphy's construction lorry was embroiled in a noisy argument with a cyclist in full gear, padded shorts, skin-tight top, helmet, the whole bit.

'You want anything else, Jack?' the young Vietnamese woman who ran the café asked.

'No, thanks,' Kiley said, 'I think we're fine.'

Victoria opened her smart phone, went into her emails and passed the phone across the table. Time enough for

Kiley to see the image of a naked shoulder; a woman, clearly Victoria, turning her face towards the camera, the open bed behind. When the image disappeared, a message: 'Listen up, whore. Less you want this all over the internet, do like I say.'

'That's it?' Kiley asked.

'A couple more, the same. Just threats. Nothing spelled out. And then a few days ago another, asking for money. Stupid money.'

'And these emails, they came from the same address?'

'All except the most recent, yes. But any reply bounces back, undeliverable, account closed.'

'And the one asking for money, how're you supposed to pay?'

'It doesn't say.'

Kiley thought he could do with another flat white after all.

'It's someone playing around,' he said. 'Someone's idea of a joke.'

'It's no joke, Jack, especially not now. Not when I'm just starting to turn things around. I've got a shot as a presenter for one thing, only on one of the shopping channels, but it's a start. And I've been talking to BT Sport about maybe doing Wimbledon next year; you know, expert analysis, that sort of thing, other tournaments, too. All it needs is for that stuff to get out onto the internet and for the media to get hold of it, and I wave all of that goodbye. Besides which, there's Alicia. Think what it might do to her.'

Kiley followed her out on to the street.

'She's staying with me now, Jack, term time at least.'

'How come?'

'I arranged with Cathy for her to switch schools last September. Year Eight, Jack, can you imagine that? Alicia, all grown up.'

'And your sister, she's okay with that?'

'She and Trevor, they've been going through a bad patch, and if I'm to be honest, I think Alicia's part of the reason. I think it'll do them good to spend some time without her.'

'Alicia, she's happy about it, too?'

Victoria looked at him in surprise. 'Of course. I am her mother, after all.'

People are rarely, if ever, what you expect. Adam Lucas was shortish – five-five at best – and stockily built; gingerish hair cropped short on top and worn in a trim goatee showing the first signs of grey. Kiley tried to picture him together with Victoria and failed. But then, what did people think when he was out with Kate, when she introduced him to her friends? Her aberration? Her bit of rough? An experiment in social engineering?

Adam's offices were in a basement in Soho, Bateman Street, two rooms liberally festooned with posters: a documentary about illegal migrant workers in East Anglia; a short film about embalming; a recent London Film Festival Poster for *Bad Monkey: Carl Hiaasen's Crazy World*, showing grinning alligators deep amongst the Everglades.

There was a receptionist's desk, but no receptionist. Adam Lucas was editing something on a laptop. He shook Kiley's hand, looked twice at his card.

'This for real?'

'Real as it gets.'

'Never say that to a maker of documentaries.'

There was a low settee along a side wall; all the easier, Kiley thought, for Lucas's feet to touch the floor. Petty, but he enjoyed it nonetheless.

'How about pornography?' Kiley asked.

Lucas looked at him askew. 'Not something we're involved in.'

'Just privately.'

'Sorry?'

'Yesterday, I was talking to Victoria.'

'I don't understand.'

'Little home movies she made in Florida. Your direction. Do this, do that, put that there. Someone's threatening to put them on YouTube, Viddler, Phanfare.'

'And you think that's me?'

'Until you convince me otherwise.'

Lucas shook his head, reached for a cigarette. 'I haven't seen Vicky in twelve months, more. Haven't called, emailed, anything. It's – whatever it was – it's over, finished. Last year's model. She made that clear enough.'

'All accounts, you were pretty angry when she did.'

'She'd fucked me around, of course I was angry.'

'And this is a way of getting your own back.'

Tilting back his head, Lucas let a slow stream of smoke waver up towards the ceiling.

'Tell you something about myself, Jack. It is Jack? I've got a short temper, short fuse. Always have. Got me in trouble at school and just about every day since. But once it's blown it's blown. People I work with, they understand.

'Vicky walked in here now, I'd kiss her on both cheeks, shake her hand. No grudges, Jack. Believe it.'

Kiley thought maybe he did.

'These films, videos, whatever, if they were just private between the two of you—'

'How could someone else have got access?'

'Yes.'

'They're not exactly sitting around on my hard drive, waiting for someone to hit on them by chance. Okay, I could've been hacked into, it happens all the time, but then, so could she.'

Lucas got to his feet.

'I can't help you, Jack. Wish I could. See Vicky, give her my love. And those videos, believe me, compared to what's out there, it's pretty tame stuff. I'd tell her to chill out, whoever it is, call their bluff.'

Since returning from America, Victoria Clarke had been living south of the river, Clapham, a nest of Edwardian terraces between Lavender Hill and the common. Kiley could hear the commotion from the front door. A young voice raised in anger, words scything the air: 'bitch', 'selfish cow', 'bitch' again. Footsteps and the sound of something breaking, smashed against the floor. Helplessness on Victoria's face; helplessness mixed with resignation. Behind her, feet stamping up stairs and then the slamming of a door.

'Hormones,' Victoria said, ruefully. 'Kicking in a little early in Alicia's case.'

Kiley followed her along a narrow hallway and into a living room with French windows out into the garden. Flowers in a glass vase above the fireplace. Tail fuzzed out, a black and white cat scuttled out the moment they walked in.

'Belongs two doors down,' Victoria explained. 'Sneaks in here whenever she gets the chance. Sleeps on Alicia's bed, more often than not.' She smiled. 'Calming influence, cats, or so they say.'

'What was all the shouting about anyway?'

'Oh, she wanted to have some friends round for a sleepover next weekend. From her new school. Three of them. I said I thought three was too many.'

She sat down and gestured for Kiley to do the same.

'She'll stay angry for an hour or so, shut herself in her room. I'll back down a little, compromise on two friends instead of three. It'll be fine.'

Kiley told her about his meeting with Adam Lucas.

Bass prominent, the sound of music from above filtered down.

'Have there been any more emails?' Kiley asked.

Victoria shook her head.

'Maybe it was just someone messing around. Came across one of the videos somehow and decided to chance their arm.'

'I don't see how that could happen.'

'Me neither. But what I don't understand about the internet would fill a large book.'

What Kiley didn't understand, almost certainly Colin Baddeley did. Something of an IT whiz, and briefly attached to the Met, which was where Kiley had first met him, Baddeley now had a very nice and expensive line in electronic surveillance. For friends, he was usually prepared to throw in a little pro bono after hours.

A lover of real ale and British folk music – the two interests irreducibly yoked together – Kiley took him round a generous supply of Baltic Porter from Camden Town Brewery and a copy of Shirley Collins' *The Sweet Primroses* he'd found knocking around at the back of the charity shop.

'These emails she's been getting,' Kiley said, 'is there any way of finding out where they're from?'

It took Baddeley something in the region of ten minutes. From the IP address to the ISP in a matter of moments and from there he was able to access the right geolocation: general area, region, post code. Satellite picture on the screen.

'I owe you,' Kiley said.

Baddeley nodded in the direction of his newly acquired and rare LP. 'I'd say, paid in full.'

He had to ring the bell three times before Alicia came to the door. A One Direction T-shirt over pink pyjama bottoms.

'Mum's out.'

'I know. It's not your mum I've come to see.'

Her room was at the top of the house; a view out through dormer windows towards the common. Kiley lifted a bundle of clothing off the one comfortable-looking chair and set it carefully down; other clothes were scattered haphazardly across the floor. Alicia was sitting cross-legged on her bed, chewing on a length of hair. The computer was on a table against the far wall.

'Why?' Kiley asked.

A small shrug of the shoulders, avoiding his eyes.

'Tell me,' Kiley said.

'So you can tell her.'

'No. So you can tell her yourself.'

'As if.'

He let it pass. Watched. Waited. She hated being stared at, he could see that, hated the silence, the expectation.

It didn't last.

'She was really stupid, right. Thinking just 'cause she'd deleted all that stuff it wouldn't still be there, on the hard drive, somewhere. And, besides, she's got this Time Machine, right, backs up everything. Automatic. I mean, what did she think?'

'She might have thought you'd respect her privacy.'

'Joking, right? Respect. She's spreading her legs for some bloke on camera an' I'm s'posed to show her respect.'

'She is your mum.'

'An' that's s'posed to make it better?'

'No. No, it's not.'

'I hate her.'

'You don't.'

'I do. I fuckin' hate her. Makin' me come an' live down here and go to this crappy school, 'stead of being with my mates. Just 'cause she's decided, after all this time, she wants to play fuckin' mum. Wanted to do that, she should've done it when I was born, instead of givin' me away.'

There were tears in her eyes, the words choking from her throat.

Kiley wanted to go across and give her a hug, but stayed where he was.

Waited.

'You need to talk to her about it,' he said.

'Oh, yeah, right.'

'No, really, you should. Maybe get someone else to help.'

'What, like some counsellor?'

'If that's what it needs.'

Alicia sniffed, wiped a hand across her face. Twelve going on fifteen. Twelve going on seven.

Slowly, Kiley got to his feet. 'No more emails, eh? No more threats.'

Alicia followed him downstairs.

'Your mum would have made me a cup of tea,' he said in the hall.

'Yeah, well, I'm not my mum, am I?'

Not yet, Kiley thought. 'You'll tell her I called,' he said.

'Maybe,' Alicia said. ''Less I forget.'

She was grinning as she closed the door.

ALL YESTERDAY'S PARTIES
Paul Johnston

Paul Johnston, whose father Ronald was a successful thriller writer, was born in Scotland, educated at Oxford and now lives in Greece. He has published three distinct crime series, featuring Quint Dalrymple, Alex Mavros and Matt Wells. At present he is working on the next Mavros novel.

21st

Nick and his college friend Michael took a room above a pub. There had been a rash of twenty-firsts that year and they wanted to do something original. So they hired Napoleonic dragoon costumes with thigh boots and tall hats. People saluted them as they marched in step to the venue. The theme was 'Foot and Mouth' and guests were supposed to come appropriately attired. Which didn't stop one guy showing up with a red plastic fish on his head. There was a prize for the best effort. It was won by Rick, a friend from another college, who managed to keep a candle alight on each of his boots all evening. He was presented with a decrepit copy of *The Veterinarian's Guide to Diseases Afflicting Cloven-Hoofed Animals*, published in 1899. It was fitting. He ended up as a successful writer of Victorian era crime stories. There was further merriment when an unlikely lothario managed to get off with a woman to Led Zeppelin's 'Rock'n'Roll'. At the end of the party Nick and Michael were informed by a knowledgeable gatecrasher that they were actually wearing hussar uniforms. They managed to contain their disappointment.

Things only got out of hand later. Pete, who had a reputation for losing his grip when he'd had more than a few, was in a group heading back to college. He was belting out Derek and Clive's *Cancer*, emphasising every profanity, when a pair of cops walked up. One of them said, 'I don't like your noise.' Pete stopped immediately, his head down. He didn't like authority but, having been at public school, was conditioned to respond to it. They were allowed to proceed after the others said they'd calm him down. But, as soon as they were out of range, Pete started muttering furiously as if he'd been mortally offended. They got past the porter, but then Pete ran ahead and tore into a bed of daffodils in the main quad, ripping them up and shredding the flowers. Nick, who'd seen this kind of behaviour before – and, to be fair, had participated in it – pinned his arms to his sides and hauled him away. Again, that seemed to knock the fight out of Pete, who wandered after the others on the way to the four-storey block where most of them had rooms. He followed them up to the top floor, where Michael, a scholarship-winner, had a flash attic suite. No one had any booze, so cups of coffee were handed out.

'Make his black,' Nick said to Michael, looking around. 'Where is the arsehole?'

One of the windows had been opened and only Pete's bottom half was visible.

'Ha!' he yelled. 'I'll get you next time!'

Nick pulled him away. A post-graduate he didn't know was lying on the grass, staring at the metal object that lay next to him.

'What did you do?'

Pete looked at him and then laughed. 'The Keep off the Grass sign.'

Nick stared at him. 'You dropped it out the window?'

'Hurled it, more like,' said the expert on Napoleonic uniforms.

The only girl in the company was crouching under Michael's desk, quivering like a cornered mouse.

Results: Pete had to pay a large sum for the daffodils. He was also given a serious warning by the dean, following a complaint from the post-grad he'd targeted. He lost the residual interest he had in his classical studies and ended up with a third-class degree.

30th

Nick was the only one of the college friends to have a party: the others were either too horrified by the end of their youth or too skint to bother. Michael was off in the Far East being a ludicrously well paid banker. He sent six bottles of Dom Perignon, which provoked a tirade from Pete, ending, 'I always knew he'd end up a capitalist running dog.'

'Oh yeah?' Nick said. 'And what exactly are you?'

'A free spirit.'

'Yeah, right. Ever since you got fired by the British Library, you've been bumming around like an eighteen-year-old.'

Pete grinned, having already necked three glasses of champagne. 'I have an artistic vision.'

Nick avoided answering by going to greet some new arrivals. He'd fallen in love with Daisy, a colleague from work, and she had introduced him to a different crowd of friends. Predictably, Pete looked down on them because they'd either been to redbrick universities or had gone straight to work after school. They'd met him a few times and nodded at him cautiously as they headed for the drinks table.

'All right?' one of them said.

'On the night,' Pete replied, looking away. He disliked Steve even more than the rest of Nick's new friends. He ran an import-export business and drove a BMW.

'Lovely jubbly,' Steve said, turning away.

Pete shook his head and went over to his two remaining friends.

'Where's your other half?' Al asked.

'Probably asleep under the coats by now. You know how little stamina she has for this kind of thing.'

Al and Luke exchanged glances. Pete's girlfriend, Silke, was German and didn't like them or Nick. She thought they wound Pete up more than was either necessary or sensible. Tonight he had a glint in his eyes that worried them.

They drank, did what they could to control the quality of the music and then got stuck into Nick's present from Daisy's notoriously lively friend, Lindsey: there were pot, pills and a bag of coke. The night got lively. At one point Pete disappeared.

'Where is he?' Nick asked, between host duties.

Al and Luke, their pupils dilated, didn't have a clue. They had just put on 'Kashmir' and were playing air violin-guitar.

With a bad feeling, Nick checked the other rooms. The flat was small, only two bedrooms. Both had piles of coats on the beds. The first, his and Daisy's, was empty. The door to the guestroom was a couple of inches ajar. Nick heard a gasp of pleasure and stayed where he was. The lucky bastard. Then he heard a muffled shriek.

He went in. Silke had risen from beneath the coats, her hair wild. Her eyes were on Pete, who was leaning against the wall. Lindsey was on her knees, blouse open, one hand on Pete's erect member.

'Bloody hell,' Nick said.

Silke looked at him and then turned back to the couple. She started to laugh, at first lightly but soon as if she'd been told the funniest joke in the world.

'I need a drink,' Lindsey said, getting to her feet and doing up her buttons.

'A few more seconds and I'd have given you one,' Pete said, having to shout above his girlfriend's laughter. Then he zipped himself up and ran to the bed. In a second he was sitting on Silke's chest. Then his hands went round her throat. Eyes bulging, she tried to gasp for breath but the grip was too tight.

Nick, a former rugby player, lowered his shoulder and drove into Pete's side, sending him flying off the bed. 'You arsehole, what the fuck are you doing?' he shouted, helping Silke to sit up.

'Murder . . .' Pete said, from the floor. 'It's a fine art, you know.'

Results: Nick called a minicab for Silke and promised he'd make sure Pete didn't come home that night. Pete got thoroughly drunk-stoned with Al and Luke, and they ended the party competing to do the highest Pete Townshend-style leap. Pete and Silke stayed together, leaving the UK a month later to do a modern Grand Tour, ending up in a draughty farmhouse in the Abruzzi. Nick and Daisy got married a year later. Pete and Silke weren't invited to the wedding.

40th

Nick's PR firm was doing well. He and Daisy had two kids, a boy and a girl, and they moved to a detached house in Dulwich. He didn't fancy a party as forty really wasn't an age he'd come to terms with. Instead he hired a private leisure centre and let his male friends loose on the facilities. Several of them were too unfit to do anything other than sit in the sauna or wallow in the pool. Luke and Al flirted unsuccessfully with the lithe waitresses and drank far too many cocktails. After a couple of hours, Nick thought he'd got away with it. Although he'd invited Pete, he doubted he would turn up. Silke and he were living in Antwerp, where he was only just surviving by selling drawings of the city's buildings to tourists. It wasn't clear what Silke did. Nick felt a twinge of guilt about not offering to buy him a ticket. After all, they had been best mates once.

And then Pete appeared, wearing a stained denim jacket and clutching a duty-free bag of Belgian beer. He had lost a lot of hair and was trying to compensate with a Frank Zappa moustache and goatee. They embraced awkwardly.

'Surprised?'

'Well, you didn't RSVP.'

'As if I bother with bollocks like that. I'm a bohemian, me.'

'Is that where Antwerp is?'

Pete laughed, only just on the right side of rationality.

'What have you been taking?'

'Oh, a little cocktail of substances. They're very easy to obtain over there.'

Nick nodded to Al and Luke. 'The boys are back in, er, the pool.'

Pete gave them a glassy look. 'I don't suppose Lindsey's around.'

'No wives or girlfriends. Besides, she's married to Steve now.'

'That prick? What a waste.'

'He's a friend, Pete.'

'Well, choose some better ones.'

Nick walked away. Most of the group were bowling, their shouts echoing around the venue. He joined in, cleaning up several times. He'd always had a good eye for a ball, but not when it was thrown from behind.

'Shit,' he gasped, clutching the back of his head.

He located Pete only after another squash ball came at him. His college friend had climbed on to a joist that ran across the bowling area and was naked apart from a bag tied round his waist. Balls were aimed at the rest of the group, some of whom returned them with interest.

'Wankers!' Pete shouted. 'Lackeys of the Man!' He screamed with laughter as he managed to hit Steve on the nose. Then he threw up over him and several other guests.

Results: Nick and his friends were summarily thrown out of the club. Pete disappeared into the night, while Al and Luke were found passed out in the sauna an hour later. Pete rang Nick a month later, not to apologise but to ask for a loan, which Nick reluctantly provided.

50th

For Daisy, this was the big one. Not only was her husband reaching that significant age – she was a few years younger, so could be objective about it – but their son Ben had turned eighteen. The double celebration was to take place at home, a manor house in a Surrey village with enough lawn for a cricket match to be played. Nick, now boss of the firm, was overworked and ground down, so he concentrated on drawing up the teams for the game. At first he thought he'd have the young play the old, women included if they fancied it. Then he realised that Ben had some seriously handy players among his friends, so he split them up among the old crocks. The wives preferred to have their own tennis competition on the grass court.

'Will Pete come?' Al asked Nick.

'Who knows? He's an art teacher now rather than a bohemian, but he still hasn't bothered with an RSVP.'

'Up north somewhere, isn't he?' Luke put in. Although they'd all been at college together, only Nick kept in touch with Pete irregularly.

'Huddersfield. And they've got a kid – a girl.'

'I'm amazed Silk Cut's still with him.'

'From what he says, she's going through the men of the north hand over fist.'

There was an influx of people, young and old, and Nick went to meet them. Caterers had been hired to provide a long table of food in the garden and there was another table covered in bottles, some in ice-buckets.

'Time to fuel up,' Luke said.

'I think . . .' Al broke off when he saw Pete walk in, Silke behind him carrying a small child. 'Oh-oh.'

'What's happened to his hair?'

'Must be a wig. He hardly had any ten years back.'

'Maybe the witch rubs his head with eye of toad and claw of bat.'

They went to the drinks, laughing.

'Pete,' Nick said. 'And Silke. What a surprise.' He bent over the child. 'And who's this?'

'Christina,' her mother replied. 'How are you, Nick? You're looking well.'

Pete was already on his way to the drinks.

'Am I? I still manage the gym three times a week.' He caught her gaze. 'How is he?'

'He's all right when I'm around,' Silke said. There were strands of white in her hair and she wasn't wearing any make-up, but she still had something. 'And I behave when I'm with Christina.' Her crooked smile confirmed what Pete had told him about her love life.

The noise level rose steadily as the full complement arrived, ate and drank. Nick was apprehensive about the cricket as he knew Pete would want to play.

Fortunately one of Ben's friends had already had too much, so there was a slot for him in the batting order, lower than he would have wanted, but too bad. Then Nick realised that Steve, a fast if wayward bowler, and Pete were on opposite sides. It was too late to do anything about that.

The game passed without incident, the young frequently showing the old up, especially when it came to run-outs. Then Pete came in to bat. Nick couldn't stop Steve taking the ball. Even more bull-chested than he used to be, the bowler ran up faster than he had done previously. Just before he reached the umpire – Nick's father – Pete raised his hand, pointing to the trees beyond the lawn.

'Sorry, mate,' he called. 'Bird flew up.'

Steve glared at him and went back to his mark. Nick shook a finger at Pete to make sure he didn't play any more games. The ball was launched, fast and on a length, and to everyone's astonishment Pete smashed it over the bowler's head and far beyond the deepest fielder. His team mates whooped and clapped. Steve, red-faced and sweating, came again and this time was hit through the covers for four. And so it continued for another two overs, until Nick took him off. Pete was asked to retire on forty to give someone else a chance. He agreed happily enough.

'Shit, man,' Luke said, as Pete passed him in the outfield. 'Have you been practising?'

'It's a question of emotion, my friend. I've always hated that fat tosser.'

Luke watched as Pete went to take off his pads, accepting a beer from an openly admiring woman. Silke and Christina were nowhere to be seen.

The match was declared a draw, Pete having only bowled after Steve was out.

'Right,' said Nick. 'More food and drink *now*.'

The cricketers followed him to the tables.

A DJ had been hired and initially he struggled to cater for the different age groups.

'I suppose a bit of Led Zep's out of the question,' Pete said, after night had fallen. The garden was draped with lights. The DJ feigned deafness. 'Jesus, what a load of shite. Come on, you two, let's go to that statue over there. At least we can smoke.' Daisy had made it clear that she didn't want any ash or butts near the food.

They lit up, then Pete took out a bag of pills.

'Go on, they won't hurt you.'

'What are they?' Al asked.

'Live dangerously. I promise you'll still be here tomorrow.'

The three of them partook and were soon moving to the beat of music they hated.

Then Steve came over. 'Nice batting, mate.' He grinned belligerently. 'What does your old lady get up to when you're on the cricket pitch?'

'Fuck off.'

'Only I saw her round the back of the garages with one of Ben's mates a few minutes ago.'

Pete looked towards the tables and saw Daisy holding Christina.

'Is that kid even yours?' Steve asked.

'Steady—' Luke said.

Pete laughed. 'Course it isn't. You think I fuck my wife when yours is available?'

Steve threw a punch, but Pete swayed backwards, further than he meant to. Then Steve was on him, pummelling his sides after they went into a clinch.

'Nick!' Al shouted. 'Over here, now!'

But it was too late. Pete smashed his forehead against Steve's nose, then slipped free. He grabbed the bigger man by the shoulders and drove his head into the base of the statue five times. It was only when he stepped back that he realised it was a life-size figure of Daisy, standing on one leg like an ancient goddess in flight.

'Nemesis,' he said, as Nick pushed him out of the way and kneeled by Steve's motionless body.

Results: Pete was jailed for Steve's murder, the prosecution successfully proving that he intended to inflict grievous bodily harm. Silke went back to Huddersfield with her daughter and was soon living with another man. Nick never had another birthday party.

PARTY OF TWO
Ragnar Jónasson

Ragnar Jónasson was born in Reykjavik, where he still lives, and is a lawyer. He currently teaches copyright law at Reykjavik University and has previously worked on radio and television, including as a TV news reporter for the Icelandic National Broadcasting Service. His novels include the Dark Iceland series.

'Can I take your plate?' I asked, perhaps too quietly.

I thought I'd cooked the salmon almost to perfection, but he didn't seem to have brought his appetite, which I do think is rather rude. This was a dinner invitation, after all, but in all honesty I think we both knew that it was about more than that. He had a score to settle, of course. The elephant in the room. Neither of us had spoken about it, not yet. Actually, neither of us had ventured into the perilous territory of the past.

'How long has it been?' I finally asked, before removing the plate to take it out into the kitchen. Eventually either one of us would have to open that part of the discussion, and it might as well be me.

How long has it been? Such a silly question, as I knew the answer all too well. Sixty years. We had been friends, best friends, from the age of five. At eleven we went our separate ways and now sixty years had passed.

I probably should have invited him over for dinner a long time ago, but there are things that one tends to keep postponing, knowing they will be difficult.

Did he remember the house, I wondered. My grandmother's old house, a small but cosy cottage perching precariously on the slopes of a mountain on the south-eastern shore of

Iceland, shielded – or perhaps threatened – by the terrifying rocks; overlooking the most magnificent ocean views you would ever see. The sea was sometimes so calm and quiet, like my grandmother, but sometimes more treacherous, perhaps a little bit like me.

My grandmother taught me to make pancakes. The dough was always made from scratch, cooked gently on her old pan, just long enough to make them savory, but not too long, of course. Nobody likes a burnt pancake. And then some sugar sprinkled on top before each pancake is carefully rolled up.

My grandmother tried to teach me a lot after she took me on, but this is really one of the few things that stuck. Probably because I've always had such a weak spot for good pancakes.

She did do her best, I believe. It wasn't easy for her. I never knew my father. My mom, well, she drank too much, as they said. Or as they didn't say, I guess. One didn't really speak of such things at the time, but she did actually drink herself to death. There is no way of sugarcoating that. I was just a baby when she died, so I was sent to live with my grandmother – to live in the middle of nowhere.

The next house to my grandmother's was a couple of miles away, and that's where he grew up. That's how we became best friends.

'I made us some pancakes for dessert,' I said upon returning from the kitchen, holding a plate of some delicious looking specimens. I placed the plate on the table. 'Do you remember the ones that my grandma used to make? It's the same recipe, but only a poor imitation, of course.'

I don't drink alcohol and I never have. To be fair, that is another thing my grandmother taught me – not to drink; although that does not require any great skill, not to do something. 'You don't want to end up like your poor mother, dear thing,' she frequently said. And, no, I didn't want to end up like her; I didn't want to end up dead – so I never started drinking.

I did however buy a bottle of some rather expensive white wine for my guest, as this was quite an occasion. Our first meeting in sixty years. He hadn't started drinking when I last met him, but he was of course only eleven at the time.

I had no idea if he had taken it up since then, but to play it safe I went to the nearest town to get a bottle, about thirty miles of driving for one bottle – and then it turned out that he didn't touch it! Such a waste of time and money.

I didn't have to go into town for the salmon. That I got from an acquaintance of mine close by, freshly caught. And it did taste wonderful, I have to say. I should really cook more often.

Living alone can make you quite lazy. I usually stock up on microwave food on my regular trips into town: pre-cooked chicken in some ill-defined sauce, frozen pizza, etc. This time, however, I took great care in preparing the meal, but still he did not seem to make an effort to try to enjoy it.

Perhaps I should have taken him out to a restaurant instead. We even have a rather nice one just a short distance from here. That's something my grandmother would never have imagined! Thanks to the tourists, who visit the area almost year round to see the glacier nearby, this isn't the middle of nowhere anymore.

Judging by his attitude it was almost as if he knew I had invited him over to ask for a favour. A huge favour, actually . . .

It occurred to me whether reminiscing about the 'good old days' might do the trick. Talk about our summers out by the sea, up in the mountain hills, climbing cliffs so dangerous that venturing up there would only occur to a couple of know-it-all kids like ourselves. But we always made it down safely. Not that anyone cared, in my case. Not really.

One memorable evening, in the mid-summer midnight sun, we had spent walking up the hill behind my grandmother's small cottage, scaring away the sheep, listening to the birds, seeing all sorts of formations on the formidable cliffs above. At the stroke of midnight, or thereabouts, we were sitting on a big rock looking over our kingdom, our land and sea, talking about the future, in the way ten- or eleven-year-old boys do.

I had a pancake, even though he didn't. Perhaps not perfect host etiquette, but it was a bit odd that he wouldn't try my dessert. Finally I brought some coffee. Nothing fancy, not an espresso or latte or whatever they call it nowadays, just old fashioned strong Icelandic coffee. The type my grand-mother used to enjoy.

He hadn't said anything about the . . . the incident. Neither had I, as a matter of fact. I hadn't asked the favour yet, either. And soon he would leave, so time was running out for both of us. It isn't considered polite to stay for long after coffee has been served; although one can of course always ask for a refill. That wasn't about to happen in his case though, as coffee did not seem to be his, well, his cup of tea.

When our friendship came to an end, it was about a girl. Of course, what else? The most beautiful girl I had ever seen. I was only eleven but I knew I was in love. Again, the way an eleven-year-old boy thinks he knows. But at the time I felt it quite strongly, and I thought the feeling was mutual.

We both knew her well, and when I found out the truth it was betrayal on an epic scale. They had been meeting behind my back.

The salmon for dinner was a fitting choice, I think. We do have very tasty salmon in this part of the country, of course, but that isn't the reason. No; the two of us had our own salmon fishing story, and that fact may have contributed to his lack of manners during the meal.

Sixty years ago, a bright summer night, we snuck away to do some salmon fishing in a nearby glacial river, without permission from anyone of course.

This was after I found out about the two of them – although he didn't know that. I'm not sure what my exact plans were, my memory plays tricks on me. Selective memory, one might perhaps say . . .

Neither of us caught anything that night, as far as I can recall. I do however remember him slipping on a rock and falling into the river.

Or did I perhaps push him slightly?

I forget.

Selective memory, again.

But I have to admit that I remember all too well holding his head under the cold water for a little while. Long enough, you know.

And then I went back home to grandmother to tell her the news. Teary-eyed.

He didn't touch his coffee, so after I'd had a few sips of mine, I brought the cups back into the kitchen. It was still bright outside, like that night exactly sixty years ago. When I went back into the living room, the chair was empty.

Gone without a word.

And I didn't get a chance to ask him the favour: 'Please, please forgive me.'

Author's note: This story is a work of fiction. The setting is however based on an area in Iceland called Suðursveit, on the south-eastern shore, which in the past was one of the most isolated places in the country, cut off by glacial sands and rivers (and where the story was in fact written).

READER, I BURIED THEM

Peter Lovesey

Peter Lovesey is the author of four crime series, starting with the Victorian mysteries about Sergeant Cribb, which were adapted for television. In recent years, he has focused mainly on books featuring either the Bath-based detective Peter Diamond, or Hen Mallin. His stand-alone novels include the award-winning *The False Inspector Dew*, and he is a former Chair of the CWA, as well as a recipient of the CWA Cartier Diamond Dagger. His latest book is *The Stone Wife*.

Yes, I was the gravedigger, but my main job was over-seeing the wildflower meadow. I'd better correct that. My main reason for being there was to worship the Lord and most of my hours were spent in prayer and study. However, we monks all had tasks that contributed to the running of the place and I was fortunate enough to have been chosen long ago to be the meadow man. If that sounds a soft number, I must tell you it isn't. Wildflower meadows need as much care as any garden, and this was a famous meadow, being situated at the back of a Georgian crescent in the centre of London. The monastery had once been three private houses. The gardens had been combined to make the two acres people came from far and wide to admire. My meadow had been photographed, filmed and celebrated in magazines. Often they wanted to include me in their reports and I had to be cautious of self-aggrandisement. I had no desire for celebrity. It would have been counter to the vows I took when I joined the brotherhood.

Closest to the monastery I grew rows of vegetables, but nobody except Brother Barry, the cook, was interested in them. My spectacular meadow stretched away beyond, dissected by a winding, mown-grass path. In the month of May we were treated to a medieval jousting tournament, the spring breezes sending the flagged wild irises towards the spikes of purple helmeted monkshood, cheered on by lilies of the valley and banks of primroses. Summer was the season of carnival, poppies in profusion, tufted vetch, ox-eye daisies, field scabious and foxgloves along the borders. Even as we approached September, the white campion, teazle, borage and wild carrot were still dancing for me. At the far end was the shed where my tools were kept and where, occasionally, I allowed myself a break from meadow management and did some contemplation instead. To the left of the shed was the apiary. If you have a wildflower meadow you really ought to keep bees as well. And to the right were the graves where I buried our brothers who had crossed the River Jordan. When their time had come I dug the graves and after our Father Superior had led us in prayer I filled them in and marked each one with a simple wooden cross. You couldn't wish for a more peaceful place to be interred.

And that was my way of glorifying God. The others all had their own tasks. Barry, I have mentioned, was our cook, and had only learned the skill after taking his vows. A straight-speaking man, easy to take offence (and therefore easy to tease), he had done some time in prison before seeing the light. Between ourselves, the meals he served were unadventurous, to put it mildly, heavily based on stew, sardines, baked beans and boiled potatoes, with curry once a week. Although my stomach complained, I got on better with Barry than any of the others.

A far more scholarly and serious man, Brother Alfred was known as the procurer, ordering all our provisions by phone or the internet, including my seed and tools. Being computer-literate, he also communicated with the outside world when it became necessary.

Brother Luke was the physician, having been in practice as a doctor before he took holy orders. A socialist by conviction, he combined this responsibility with humbly washing the dishes and sweeping the floors.

Then there was Brother Vincent, a commercial artist in the

secular life, who was painstakingly restoring a fourteenth-century psalter much damaged by the years. Between sessions with the quills and brushes, he also looked after the library.

Our Father Superior was Ambrose, a remote, dignified man in his seventies who had been a senior civil servant before he received the call.

You may be wondering why I'm using the past tense. I still live the spiritual life and manage a garden, but it is no longer at our beloved monastery in London. One morning after matins, Father Ambrose asked us all to remain in our pews (for your information, the chapel had been created out of two living rooms by knocking down a wall and installing an RSJ. Not everyone knew this was a rolled steel joist and we had fun telling Barry we were expecting a Religious Sister of St Joseph). 'I want to speak to you about our situation,' our Father Superior said. 'It must be obvious to you all that our numbers have been declining in recent years. Three brothers were called to higher service last year and two the year before. I won't say our little cemetery is becoming crowded, but the dead almost outnumber the living now. None of us are in the first flush of youth any more. Tasks that were manageable ten years ago are becoming harder now. I watched Jeffrey cropping the meadow at the end of last summer and it looked extremely demanding work.'

As my name had been singled out, I felt I had a right to reply. 'Father, I'm not complaining,' I said, 'but if I had a ride-on mower instead of the strimmer, it would ease the burden considerably.'

'Jeffrey,' he said, 'I am discussing much more than your situation. I might just as well have used Barry and his catering as an example.'

'What's wrong with my cooking?' Barry asked.

'The curry,' Luke muttered. 'Oh, for an Indian takeout.'

'Did you say something?' Father Ambrose asked.

'Trying to think what could be done, Father,' Luke said.

Ambrose moved on with his announcement. 'In short, the Lord in His infinite wisdom has put the thought into my head that we should move to somewhere more in keeping with our numbers. This beautiful building and grounds can be used for another purpose.'

He couldn't have shocked us more if he had ripped off his habit and revealed he was wearing pink spandex knickers.

'What purpose might that be?' Luke asked eventually.

'I know of a school in Notting Hill in unsuitable accommodation, much smaller than this, and in a poor state of repair.'

'A school?'

'A convent school.'

'You're suggesting they move here?'

'It's not my suggestion, Luke. As I was at pains to explain, it came to me from a Higher Source.'

'Our monastery converted into a school? How is that possible?'

'It's eminently possible. This chapel would double as the assembly hall. The spare dormitories would become classrooms, the refectory the canteen, and so on.'

'What about my meadow?' I asked.

Ambrose spread his hands as if it was obvious. 'The playing field.'

I was too shocked to speak. I had this mental picture of a pack of shrieking schoolgirls with hockey sticks.

'And my studio would become the art room, I suppose?' Vincent said with an impatient sigh.

'I see that you share the vision already,' Ambrose said. 'Isn't it wonderfully in keeping with our vows of sacrifice and self-denial?'

'Where would we go?'

'I'm sure the Lord will provide.'

'Do we have any say?' Barry asked.

'Say whatever you wish, but say it to Our Father in Heaven.'

This is one of the difficulties with the monastic life. There isn't a lot of consultation at shop floor level. Decisions tend to be announced and they have the authority of One who can't be defied.

We filed out of the pew dazed and shaken. If this was, indeed, the Lord's will, we would have to come to terms with it.

I returned to my beautiful meadow and tried to think about self-denial. Difficult. I vented my frustration on a patch of brambles that had begun invading the wild strawberries. After an hour of heavy work, I remembered I had recently put in an order for seed for next year's vegetable crop. If Father Ambrose's proposal became a reality, there wouldn't be any need for vegetables. So I went to see Alfred, the procurer. He has a large storage room with racks to the ceiling for all our provisions. There's a special section for all my gardening needs and beekeeping equipment.

I said what was on my mind.

'Good thinking,' he said, looking up from his computer screen. Eye contact with Alfred was always disconcerting because he had one blue eye and one brown. 'I'll see if it isn't too late to cancel the order.'

'Did you know what Father Ambrose was going to say this morning?'

'Not at all,' he said. 'Has it upset you?'

I knew better than to admit to personal discontent. 'I don't like to think about our departed brothers lying under a hockey pitch.'

He shook his head. 'Those are only mortal remains. Their souls have already gone to a Better Place.'

He was right. I wished I hadn't spoken. 'Are you in favour of this?'

'It's ordained,' he said. As the second most senior monk, he probably felt compelled to show support.

I heard the slap of sandals on the floorboards behind me. We had been joined by Vincent, the scribe. He was a more worldly character than Alfred, always ready with a quip. 'What's this – a union meeting?' he asked. 'Are we going on strike, or what?'

'Brother Jeffrey is here to cancel his order for next year's seeds,' Alfred said. 'We have to look to the future.'

'A future without a meadow? That's going to leave Jeffrey without a garden shed for his afternoon nap.'

'We don't know where we'll be,' I said, ignoring the slur about my contemplation sessions. 'Wherever it is, I expect we'll have a garden.'

'No problem for me,' Vincent said. 'All I need is a small room, a desk and a chair. And my art materials, of course. Do we have some more orpiment in stock?'

'Plenty,' Alfred said.

'What's orpiment?' I asked.

'A gorgeous yellow,' Vincent said. 'The old scribes used it and so do I, but modern artists prefer gamboge.'

'If it's so gorgeous, why isn't it used more?'

'Because it's the devil – if you'll pardon the expression – to grind the natural rock into a pigment. In fact, the variety I use is man-made, but based on the same constituents. I'll take some with me, Alfred. Chin up, Jeffrey. I'm sure there'll be a little patch of ground for you at the new place. If we leave London altogether, you could find yourself with acres more to grow things on.'

But you never know what the Lord has in store. The concerns we had over moving from the monastery were overtaken by a shocking development. Our Father Superior reported to the infirmary with stomach pains, vomiting and diarrhoea. Some of us suspected Brother Barry's cooking was responsible, but Brother Luke diagnosed an attack of gastro-enteritis brought on by a virus infection. All that could be done at this stage was to make sure the patient drank plenty of fluids. Normally the infection will subside. But poor Father Ambrose didn't rally. His condition worsened so quickly that we barely had time to administer the last rites.

Was it a virus, we asked each other, or food poisoning? The latter seemed unlikely considering all of us had eaten the same food and no one else had been ill. A post mortem would have settled the matter, but, as Luke remarked, it wouldn't have altered anything. Being a qualified doctor, he issued the death certificate and nothing was said to the local coroner. I dug a grave and we buried Father Ambrose the following Monday.

After a period of mourning, we resumed our worship and work. Life has to go on for the survivors. Vincent returned to his restoration work. Barry got on with the cooking, and assured us all that he was using fresh ingredients and regularly washing his hands. Luke, with no patients to tend, scrubbed the infirmary. And I made a wooden cross for Ambrose, carved his initials on it, placed it in position and then went back to caring for my wildflowers. The ever changing, ever beautiful, meadow was a source of solace. Already the bee orchids were appearing.

There was no debate about installing our next Father Superior. Alfred, through seniority, was the obvious choice. And he had gravitas. We held a token election and he was the only candidate. A well-organised monk I haven't mentioned, called Brother Michael, took on the mantle of procurer and computer operator.

One afternoon I was in my shed having a few minutes' contemplation when I was startled by someone tapping on the window. It was Michael.

'Did I wake you?' he asked when I invited him in.

'I was fully awake,' I said. 'Meditating.'

'I've been doing some thinking myself,' he said.

'What about?'

'Father Ambrose's sad death.'

'He was getting on in years,' I said. 'It comes to us all eventually.'

'But not so suddenly. He was gone in a matter of hours. I was wondering whether he was poisoned.'

I was aghast. 'Food poisoning was mentioned, but we all eat the same and no one else was ill, so the virus seems more likely.'

'I don't mean food poisoning. I'm speaking of murder by poison – as in arsenic.'

'Oh, my word! You can't mean that.'

'I'm sorry,' Michael said, 'but I have some information that I feel bound to share with somebody. When I took over the store I decided to do an inventory and there was one item that was new in my experience, called orpiment.'

'It's paint,' I told him. 'Brother Vincent needs it in his work. It's a shade of yellow the medieval scribes used.'

'So I understand. But have you seen the packet it comes in? There's a warning on the side that it contains poison. I checked on the internet and it's produced by fusing one part of sulphur with two parts of arsenic.'

Shocked by this revelation, I tried to answer in a level voice, not wishing to turn our peaceful monastery into a hornets' nest. 'I didn't know that,' I said. 'Presumably Brother Vincent is aware of it.'

'I also looked up the symptoms of arsenic poisoning,' Michael said. 'Nausea, vomiting, abdominal pain, diarrhoea – easily confused with acute gastro-enteritis.'

'What exactly are you suggesting, Michael?' I said, still trying to stay calm. 'None of us had any reason to poison Father Ambrose.'

'The motive may not have been there, but the means was.'

'Let's not get carried away,' I said.

'It's tasteless,' he said.

'You took the words out of my mouth.'

'No. I'm saying that arsenic has no taste. And if you remember, it was a Friday – curry night – when Father Ambrose died. The orpiment wouldn't show up in curry.'

'But no one else was ill. We all had the curry.'

'If someone meant to poison Father Ambrose, they could have added some of the stuff to his bowl.'

'But when?'

'As you know, Barry spoons the curry into the bowls with some rice and then one of us carries the tray to the table. Then we bow our heads and close our eyes for the grace. The opportunity was there.'

Clearly, he'd thought this through in detail and believed it.

'Are you accusing Brother Barry of murder?' I asked.

'Or whoever carried the tray. Or whoever was seated beside Father Ambrose, or whoever was opposite him.'

'Any of us, in fact?'

'Well, yes.' His eyes widened. 'And when I said just now that there was no motive, I was trying to be charitable. If one thinks the worst, there *is* a motive – Father Ambrose's master plan to remove us all to another monastery. No one likes change. Let's face it, we were all shocked and distressed when he announced it. By getting rid of Ambrose, we would save the monastery.'

I shook my head sadly. 'Michael, if this were not so silly, it would be a wicked slander. Do I need to remind you of the vow of obedience we all took? It's unthinkable for any of us to question our Father Superior, let alone cause him harm.'

He appeared to see sense. 'I hadn't thought of it like that.'

'Then I suggest you put it out of your head and don't mention it to anyone else. I'm going to forget you ever spoke of it.'

Months passed. I cropped my meadow late in August after the seeds had spread and Michael's alarming theory was as weathered as the bronzed hay. I'm bound to admit I had been unsettled by it. Despite my promise to forget about the conversation, I couldn't stop myself casting my brother monks in the role of poisoner. Once the seeds of suspicion are sown and growing, they are as difficult to root out as ground elder. Take Alfred, for example. He had attained the highest position in our community through Ambrose's death and as the procurer he had easy access to the orpiment. Equally, Vincent was in possession of the deadly stuff and although he professed to be indifferent to a move, he'd reacted strongly when it was first mentioned. Luke, with his doctor's training, probably knew more about the dangers of poisoning than any of us. Barry, as the cook, was best placed to administer the poison, and had been deeply upset by the criticism of his culinary skills. And Michael had benefited from Ambrose's death and risen to the position of procurer. What was his reason for spreading suspicion of everyone else? Uncharitable thoughts come all too readily when you're gardening and most of them are best ignored.

Late in October, when the last butterflies had gone and autumn mists were appearing over the meadow, the harmony of our community received another jolt. Alfred, our new Father Superior, had made almost no significant changes to our routine since being called to lead us. Then he announced he would be leaving the monastery for a week on a small mission. From time to time, the calls of family disturb the even tenor of our existence, so we thought nothing of it. In Alfred's absence, our services were led by Brother Luke. But when Father Alfred returned, he addressed us in chapel and my heart sank, for he stood to one side of the altar, just where Father Ambrose had been when he announced his ill-omened plan.

Alfred cleared his throat before saying anything. 'You may not all appreciate what I have to say, but hear me out and when you have had time to absorb it, you will be better able to consider the matter without personal feelings intruding. Six months have gone by since our dear departed Father Ambrose raised the question of vacating this building so that the school could move in. As his successor, I feel bound to give consideration to his last great idea. It had been revealed to him, as he made clear, in the nature of a divine vision. After much prayer, I was moved this week to take the process a step further and I am pleased to tell you I have been to see a building that with the Lord's help we can transform into a monastery better suited to our numbers.'

After a moment's uneasy silence, Luke asked, 'What is it, a private house?'

'No, a lighthouse.'

'God save us,' Barry said in a stage whisper.

'These days, the warning lamps are automatic, using solar powered batteries, so there's no need for a keeper, but the living space is still there,' Alfred said. 'The rooms are wedge-shaped, most of them, smaller than the dormitory you're used to, but they will actually provide more privacy.'

'I don't think I'm hearing this,' Vincent said in a low voice.

'There are kitchen facilities,' Alfred went on, warming to his theme and sounding awfully like an estate agent, 'and a telegraph room that we can convert to the chapel. The building isn't just a glorified cylinder, you see. There's a keeper's house attached and most of our communal activities would take place in there.'

'Where exactly is it?' I asked.

'Off the north-west coast of Scotland.'

'*Off* the coast?'

'It's a lighthouse, Jeffrey.'

'Some lighthouses are on land.'

'This is an island a mile out to sea, a crop of rocks known as the devil's teeth.'

He wasn't doing much of a selling job to a bunch of London monks. 'So it's built on solid rock?' I said. 'Isn't there a garden?'

'That's one thing it does lack,' Alfred admitted.

I was speechless.

'When you say "kitchen facilities",' Barry said, 'can I run a double oven and two hobs, as I have at present?'

'I believe there's a Primus stove.'

'I don't believe this.'

'Where will I do my restoration work?' Vincent asked. 'I need a north-facing light.'

'Top floor, in the lamp room,' Barry unkindly said.

But there was no question that Father Alfred was serious. 'Brothers, we must be flexible in our thinking. It can only do us good to adjust to a new environment. Try to come to terms with the concept before we discuss your individual needs.'

We had curry as usual on Friday. Brother Barry's curries were notable more for their intensity than their flavour, so nothing was unusual when Father Alfred gasped and reached for the water jug. We always drank more on curry night. We smiled and nodded fraternally when he complained of a severe burning sensation in the mouth and throat, extending to his stomach. There was more concern when he retched and ran from the table.

Four hours later our Father Superior was dead.

Brother Luke, who was with him to the end, could do nothing to reverse his rapid decline. The patient vomited repeatedly, but brought up little. Severe stomach cramps, diarrhoea and convulsions set in. He complained of prickling of the skin and visual impairment. Before the end he became intensely cold and was talking of his veins turning to ice. A sort of paralysis took over. His facial muscles tightened and his pulse weakened, but his brain remained active until the moment of death.

You will have gathered from my description that Luke gave us a full account next morning of Alfred's last hours. A chastened group of us discussed the tragedy after morning prayers.

Barry insisted it couldn't have been the curry. 'It must have been the same virus that killed poor Father Ambrose.'

'Again?' Michael said. 'I don't think so.'

'Why not?' I said. 'The symptoms were similar.'

Michael gave me the sort of look you get from a dentist when you insist you brush after every meal.

Then Luke said, 'I must admit, my confidence is shaken. I've never come across a viral condition quite like this. In fact, I'm thinking I should report it to the Department of Health in case it's a new strain.'

'Before you do,' Michael said, 'let's consider the other option – that he was poisoned.'

I raised my hand to dissuade him. 'Michael, you and I went over this before. Speculation such as that will damage our community.'

'It's damaged already,' he said. 'Aren't two violent deaths in six months serious damage? I was silent before, at your suggestion, but this has altered everything. We know for a fact that a poisonous substance is stored here.'

'What's that?' Barry said.

'Orpiment. The pigment Vincent uses is two-thirds pure arsenic.'

'*Vincent?*'

All eyes turned to our scribe.

Michael added, 'It doesn't mean Vincent administered the stuff. Any one of us could have collected some from his studio or my shelves. I don't keep the store locked.'

'And used it to murder Ambrose and Alfred? That's unthinkable,' Barry said.

'Well, maybe you can think of some other way it got added to the curry you serve,' Michael said, well aware how the words would wound Barry. He wasn't blessed with much tact.

While Barry struggled with that, Luke asked, 'What possible reason could anyone have for murdering Father Alfred?'

'Come on,' Michael said. 'Just like Ambrose, he was about to uproot us. None of us wants to see out his days on a lump of rock in the Atlantic Ocean.'

'So there was motive, means and opportunity, the three preconditions for murder.' A look of profound relief dawned on Luke's features. As our physician, he was no longer personally responsible for failing to contain a deadly virus. 'You must be right. I'm beginning to think we can deal with this among ourselves.'

'What – a double murder?' Michael piped up in disbelief.

'We don't want a police investigation and the press all over us.'

I added in support, 'They'll want to dig up Father Ambrose for sure. Let him rest in peace.'

Barry agreed. 'No one wants that.'

Michael, in a minority of one, was horrified. 'We'd be shielding a killer. We're men of God.'

'And He is our judge,' Luke said. 'If we are making a mistake, He will tell us. Shall we say a prayer?'

This was the moment when we all became aware that Luke, as the senior monk, was the obvious choice to be elected our new Father Superior. Even Michael bit his lip and bowed his head.

I dug another grave and we buried poor Father Alfred with the others at the edge of the meadow next morning. None of us asked what Luke had written on the death certificate. He was now our spiritual leader and it wasn't appropriate to enquire. I constructed the cross and positioned it at the head of the grave.

The lighthouse wasn't mentioned again. Father Luke had more sense. He wasn't quite as paternalistic as some of his predecessors. He believed in consulting us as well as the Lord and we left him in no doubt that we wanted to remain where we were, in our beloved monastery in the heart of London. Life returned to normal. I managed my meadow and kept the graves tidy. Vincent worked on his psalter. Barry kept us fed. Michael ran the store with efficiency and ordered our supplies online.

It came as a surprise to me one afternoon in January when I was in my shed wrapped in a quilt, indulging in my post-prandial contemplation, to be disturbed by a rapping at the door. Michael was there, hood up, arms folded, looking anything but fraternal.

'Is something up?' I asked, rubbing my eyes.

'You could put it that way,' he said. 'The Father Superior wants to see you in his office.'

'Now?'

'He's waiting.'

The office was in the attic at the top of our building. Michael escorted me and said not another word as we went up the three flights of stairs.

Father Luke's door stood open. He really was waiting, seated behind his desk, hands clasped, but more in an attitude of power than prayer. 'Come in, both of you,' he said.

There wasn't room for chairs, so we stood like schoolboys up before the head.

'This won't be easy,' Father Luke said. 'It's about the deaths of Father Ambrose and Father Alfred. Michael has informed me, Jeffrey, that he spoke to you after Ambrose died, about the possibility that he was poisoned with arsenic.'

I said, 'I think we all agree that he was.'

Michael said, 'But at the time you told me to keep my suspicions to myself.'

Now I understood what this was about: a blame session. I'd never felt comfortable with Michael, but I hadn't taken him for a sneak. 'That's true,' I said. 'It was the first time anyone had suggested such a thing and it was certain to cause friction and alarm in our community.'

'Go on,' Father Luke said to Michael. 'Tell Jeffrey what you told me.'

Michael seemed to be driving this and enjoying it, too. 'When I took over as procurer, I gained access to the computer and this enabled me to confirm my theory about the orpiment. It is, indeed, a pigment made of sulphide of arsenic that was used by monks in medieval and Renaissance times to illuminate manuscripts.'

I couldn't resist saying, 'Clever old you!'

Father Luke raised his hand. 'Listen to this, Jeffrey.'

Michael went on, 'However, when I searched the internet for information about the effects of acute arsenic poisoning, some of the symptoms Father Luke reported didn't seem to fit. Typically, there's burning in the mouth and severe gastro-enteritis, vomiting and diarrhoea – all of which were present – but the second phase of symptoms, the prickling of the skin and visual impairment, the signs of paralysis in the face and body, aren't associated with arsenic.'

Father Luke said, 'Symptoms very evident in Ambrose and Alfred.'

Michael said, 'It made me ask myself if some other poison had been used, something that induces paralysis. I made another search and was directed away from mineral poisons to poisonous plants.'

I was silent. Already I could see where this was going.

'And eventually,' Michael continued in his self-congratulatory way, 'I settled on a tall, elegant, purple plant known, rather unkindly, as monkshood, the source of the poison aconite. Every part from leaf to root is deadly. After the first violent effects of gastroenteritis, a numbing effect spreads through the body producing a feeling of extreme cold and paralysis sets in. The breathing quickens and then slows dramatically and all the time the victim is in severe pain, but conscious to the end.'

'Precisely what I observed,' Luke said, 'and twice over.'

'This proved nothing without the presence of aconite in the monastery,' Michael said. 'There are photos and diagrams of the monkshood plant on the internet, so I knew what to look for and where best to search. It prefers shady, moist places. I spent several afternoons while you were taking your nap and checked along the edges of the meadow where the water drains, close to the wall. Of course you hacked the tall stems down, so the plants weren't easy to locate, but eventually I found your little crop. The spiky, hand-shaped leaves are very distinctive. Some of the ripe follicles still contained seeds. Are you going to admit to using it, adding it to the curry?'

Father Luke said, 'The Lord is listening, Jeffrey.'

I didn't hesitate long. I'm not a good liar. I hope I'm not a liar at all. If you read this account of what happened, you'll see that I always spoke the truth, even if I didn't always volunteer it. 'Yes,' I said. 'I used some root, chopped small. I made sure I was sitting beside our Father Superior when he spoke the grace. Then I sprinkled the bits over the curry. I couldn't face life without my beautiful meadow.'

'So you took the lives of two good men,' Michael said to shame me.

Our Father Superior shook his head sadly. 'Now I'll have
to notify the police.'

I said, 'I'll save you the trouble.' I walked to the window,
unfastened it and started to climb out.

'No, Jeffrey!' Father Luke shouted to me. 'That's a mortal
sin.'

But he was too slow to stop me.

I was indifferent to his plea. I'd already committed one of
the mortal sins twice over. Here on the roof I was at least fifty
feet above ground. Below me was a paved area. When I jumped,
I was unlikely to survive. If I had the courage to dive, I would
surely succeed in killing myself.

With my feet on the steep-pitched tiles, I edged around the
dormer to a place where no one could lean out and grab me.
Then I climbed higher, intending to launch myself off the
gable end.

Father Luke was at the open window, shouting that this
wasn't the way, but I begged to differ.

Up there under an azure sky, on the highest point of the
roof, I was treated to a bird's-eye view of my meadow and if
it was the last thing I ever saw I would be content. Glittering
from the overnight frost, the patterns of my August cut were
clearly visible like fish scales, revealing a beauty I hadn't ever
observed from ground level. This, I thought, is worth dying
for.

I reached the gable end and sat astride the ridge without
much dignity, collecting my breath and getting up courage. A
controlled dive would definitely be best. I needed to stand
with my arms above my head and pitch forward.

I grasped the lightning conductor at the end and raised
myself to a standing position.

And then I heard a voice saying, 'Jeffrey, don't do it.'

For a moment, teetering there on the rooftop, I thought the
Lord had spoken to me. Then I realised the voice had not come
from above. It was from way below, on the ground. Brother
Barry was standing in the vegetable patch with his hands cupped
to his mouth.

I called back to him. 'I'm a wicked sinner, a double
murderer.'

'That's not good,' he called back, 'but killing yourself will only make things worse.'

I told Barry, 'I don't want to live. The police are coming and I can't bear to be parted from my meadow.'

He shouted, 'You'll get a life sentence. It's not as bad as you think, believe me. You'll share a cell with someone, but what's different about that? The food is better, even if I say it myself. And with good behaviour you'll be sent to a Category C prison where they'll be really glad of your gardening experience.'

I was wavering. 'Do you think so?'

'I know it.'

What a brother he was to me. I'd never considered the prison option, but Barry had personal experience of it. And he was right. I could pay my debt to society and make myself useful as well. Persuaded, I bent my knees, felt for the lightning conductor and began to climb down.

In the prison where I have been writing this account of my experiences, I am proud of my 'trusty' status. Barry was right. I can still lead the spiritual life and I always remember him in my prayers. The governor has put me in charge of the vegetable garden and I have persuaded him to allow me a wildflower section. No monkshood or other poisonous plants, of course. But by May we'll have an explosion of colour. And I built my own tool-shed. Every afternoon I go in for an hour or so. Even the governor knows better than to disturb me when I'm contemplating.

THE LAST GUILTY PARTY
Phil Lovesey

Phil Lovesey was born in 1963, and is the son of Peter Lovesey. He studied art and took a degree in film and television studies, later working as a freelance advertising copywriter. He is the author of four crime novels and is a past winner of the CWA Short Story Dagger.

L ooking back, Eric Trimble couldn't remember exactly when, or how, the first Guilty Party ever happened. Save to say, it was probably sometime during their second year at university, far too many years ago. And, of course, it was also certain to have been Geoff's idea. What idea wasn't, in those days . . .?

Eric looked in the mirror, pulling gently on his Windsor knot, noticing how his neck seemed to sag ever more grotesquely on to the top of his stiff shirt collar these days. Age the great leveller; mortality the inescapable sentence.

'Guilty,' he muttered, trying not to take in the lines in his face too much. Instead, he distracted himself picking idle threads from his tweed jacket, and inspecting his shoes – both having seen better days, too.

He wondered how many of the others would be there. How many were still alive, even. Each year, the annual meeting of the Guilty Party played wearisome host to fewer and fewer members. Last year, it had been just five of them, and he knew for sure that Bob had passed on in October, and he hadn't had a Christmas card from Stan either – Death's dark warning for folk his age.

Which would leave just himself, Tim and, of course, Geoff. The three of them, the last three, all of them guilty . . .

Not that all had died, of course. Some members had drifted

in and out over the years, or simply quit what they considered to be little more than an annual university reunion that merely offered the chance to impress the others with exaggerated tales of their successful lives, careers and families whilst drinking far too heavily in a cheap seaside hotel.

All activities which Eric knew far too well he was guilty of himself. But wasn't it precisely what folk did at these reunion dos? Sugar the old pill a bit, tell a few whiskied whoppers to anyone still sober enough to listen? It was form, Eric suspected, and certainly almost *de rigeur* in the Guilty Party.

As he drove to the Welsh coast, he was glad of the finality of this last occasion. Geoff had written to him in the spring as always, informing him that, due to dwindling membership and increasing infirmity, this September's meeting would be 'the last Guilty Party'. Something Eric was secretly (guiltily?) more than pleased about. For it wasn't simply the driving, the cost of all the drink and staying in the hotel . . .

It was Geoff.

And how had it started, all those many years ago? Quite simply, with the words, 'Ah, here comes the guilty party,' muttered by an irate lecturer as a bunch of them had stumbled late into a morning seminar nursing obvious hangovers from a heavy night on the sauce the previous evening. The phrase had stuck, taken instantly by Geoff as some sort of badge of boozy student courage.

That night, they'd all gone out again, celebrating the first-ever official meeting of the Guilty Party, an elite group of heavy-drinking boisterous students, whose sole intention was to say (or scream, depending on the time of night) the word 'Guilty!' as often as possible during the evening's raucous pub crawl.

For some, of course, the 'fun' lasted only the one night, finding it too exuberant, too high-spirited, too damned expensive. Stalwart members (of whom Eric and Geoff were legend in the university campus) were frequently warned about their 'high jinks' by the exasperated dean in his office. At which time, the only approach was to hang heads, snigger and then yell 'Guilty!' right in his face.

They weren't ever sent down, because Geoff's family had

'connections'. He'd been to the right school, had bundles of loot, and his father (glad to be rid of his tearaway son for a few precious years) paid for the upkeep of the university library. All of which, it has to be said, suited Eric handsomely. For as long as he was in tow with Geoff, he was just as impervious to any disciplinary issues.

'Bloody good times!' Geoff would always say at annual Guilty Party reunions. 'Best goddamned years of my life!' And then he'd elbow Eric in the ribs. 'We did some things, eh, didn't we?'

And Eric would have to force some sort of laugh, and return with the club call of 'Guilty!' while others managed to force a few laughs, too; perhaps making a mental note that this was to be the last time they'd attend a Guilty Party reunion. Eric knew for sure that one member had got his wife to write back to Geoff explaining that her husband wouldn't be attending that year, as he'd unfortunately passed away. A fact that Geoff was able to dispute, after he'd driven three hundred miles overnight to the member's house, then waited outside most of the morning, eventually to catch him about to go shopping with his wife.

Geoff was like that . . . unshakeable.

Eric checked into the flaking sea-front hotel with an hour to spare before lunch. Guilty Party tradition dictated that all members meet in the lounge bar at midday, wearing suits, shirts and their club ties – Windsor-knotted, green silk with judge's gavel and pint-glass emblem embroidered onto the front – and ready to indulge in the afternoon and evening of alcoholic debauchery.

Mindful of this, and far too old now for this caper, Eric had taken to spending an hour in his room, eating corned beef sandwiches and trying to ready himself for the forthcoming 'celebrations'. It had become a dispiriting hour of almost morbid examination, as he followed the fortunes of his life that had ended in that precise moment – alone, eating corned beef sandwiches in a shabby hotel room he couldn't afford, wondering at the inanity of it all.

But, of course, this would thankfully be the last Guilty Party.

Taking a deep breath, and one last look at the rumbling grey sea from his window, he made his way slowly downstairs.

'You must be Eric Trimble!' boomed a familiar voice in the far corner of the deserted lounge bar.

'Guilty as charged!' Eric replied, trying to muster some enthusiasm as he made his way over to the table. 'And you're Geoff St John!'

'Indeed, Mr Trimble!' the large, balding figure replied. 'Guilty, and awaiting sentencing!'

Eric went through the rest of the required motions. 'Then I sentence you to attempted death by alcohol, Mr St John! Whisky, your weapon of choice?'

'Guilty!' Geoff drained his glass and offered it to Eric. 'Double's fine, Mr Trimble. Your round, I believe?'

'Guilty,' Eric replied, a little less enthusiastically now, wondering just how much of his widower's pension would be left by the evening. He ordered drinks from a colossally bored foreign barman, before returning to the table. 'No Tim then, this year?' he asked.

Geoff shook his large head. 'Chap couldn't make it. Passed away to the great bar in the sky five weeks ago. I know, I checked. Went to the ruddy funeral, didn't I? Wasn't invited, so caused a tad of a stink.' He winked and raised his glass. 'Guilty again, eh, Eric? Always bloody guilty, aren't we?'

'I'm sad about Tim,' Eric said, simply because he felt he ought to.

'Don't be. Funeral was all right. Lousy do afterwards, though. Don't know why I bothered, really. I tell you, when my turn comes, I'm having a proper send-off. Got myself booked into the cathedral, haven't I? Bishop, choirboys, bell, all the trimmings.'

'Gosh.'

'What's the point of strings, if you can't pull them?'

'Indeed.'

'You sorted your bash, then?'

Eric nodded. 'Co-op's doing it for me.'

Geoff frowned. 'Oh dear. Oh dearie, dearie me. Dreadful.'

Eric took a careful sip of his whisky. 'It's budgeting, really.'

Geoff muttered something, then said, 'Another drink, old man?'

'Guilty,' Eric managed, noticing how it ached to hold his cheeks in a false smile as he tried to resign himself to the rest of the day in just Geoff's company.

'Course,' Geoff said when he returned with more drinks and eased himself back behind the table, 'there are one or two guilty pleasures to be gained from the aftermath of funerals.' He was looking at Eric in a way that demanded further questioning.

'Such as?' Eric obliged.

Geoff lowered his voice, which Eric felt was almost absurd in such an empty room. 'Comforting the grieving widow,' he whispered salaciously. 'And if that makes me one of these so-called sexual opportunists, then guilty as charged, Your Honour.'

Eric took a moment to take it in. He hadn't known Tim that well, but he'd seen pictures of his wife that the most recently deceased member of the Guilty Party had once proudly displayed many years previously. 'You're . . . with . . .?' He couldn't even begin to place the name.

'Helen,' Geoff replied. 'Indeed, yes. Well, not exactly "with" . . . just sort of . . . you know . . . from time to time.'

Eric pressed back in his chair and found himself grinding his remaining few teeth. 'When it suits you, presumably?'

'Guilty!' Geoff guffawed in that overtly loud way that always signalled the double whiskies had found their mark.

'And Cecily?' Eric asked. 'Doesn't she suspect anything?'

'Oh, I hardly think so,' Geoff replied. 'My dear battle-axe wife finally saw fit to shuffle off the old mortal coil a few weeks ago.'

Which came as a bombshell to Eric. Cecily – dead? He'd last seen her only four months ago when Geoff was away on another of his golfing trips to Florida.

'Stroke,' Geoff confirmed. 'Initially.' The booming voice dropped back down. 'Whole left side paralysed, completely wonky. Had to push the bloody woman around in a damn chair.'

Eric was still reeling. Cecily *couldn't* be dead. She'd seemed so full of life, so full of love . . .

Geoff was watching him carefully. 'You always had a thing for her, didn't you?'

Eric was stung by the words. *'Thing?'*

'Oh, come on, Eric!' Geoff insisted, slurring slightly, and wafting his tie towards him. 'This is the last ever meeting of this bloody-shambles Guilty Party. The last time that thankfully we'll ever have to see each other's faces again. At least be *honest* and plead guilty, man!'

'To what?' Eric was beginning to panic.

'Good God!' Geoff sighed. 'To fancying my Cecily, of course!'

Confused, ambushed, Eric sought temporary solace behind a whisky glass before draining it in one go.

'Right back at university, you always had a thing for her. You couldn't stand the fact that I got her, could you? Could you?'

'You're talking horseshit, Geoff.'

'Just say you're guilty.'

'No!'

'Can't?' Geoff sneered. 'Or won't?'

Eric was silent.

Geoff reached into his pocket, pulled out a sheet of paper, unfolded it and pushed it across the table between them. 'When she was in hospital,' he said, his eyes fixed on Eric, 'she thought she was going to die. So she dictated this letter to one of the nurses to give to me.'

Eric picked up the letter and began reading the unfamiliar handwriting, yet hearing his dear Cecily's voice in the way it was expressed.

'The words of a guilty woman on her deathbed,' Geoff continued, watching as Eric read. 'Dates, times, sordid little hotels, it's all there. Addressed to me, in order to clear her wretched guilty conscience. And before you try to deny it, Eric, let me remind you, Cecily thought she was going to die. Why the hell would anyone make this kind of thing up, eh? And in such detail, too?'

Eric rubbed the corner of one eye, took a deep breath and passed the letter back. 'Guilty,' he whispered.

Geoff waited a moment, then suddenly switched to a

full-beamed smile. 'Indeed, Mr Trimble! Guilty as charged of having a long-standing affair with my wife! And I sentence you to . . . go get the next round in at the bar! Off you go, Trimble. Methinks there are lifelong reparations to be made up!'

Eric took a breath. 'If it's all the same to you . . .'

'You'd rather be going, wouldn't you?' Geoff sneered. 'Rather be toddling off in your cheap little car to mourn your "dearest Cecily"?'

'I'm going to leave, yes.'

'Except, if you do,' Geoff explained, folding his arms, 'then you'll never discover those precious final few words that dropped from her disloyal lips, will you?' He waited a moment, then said with sarcasm, 'I assume they were meant for you.'

'What were they?'

Geoff gestured to his empty glass.

'What were the damn words?' Eric begged.

Again, Geoff simply gestured to the glass. 'And I'll also tell you how she died, too. Quite pleasantly, really. They'd probably have hanged her in the Middle Ages.'

'Well, we're not in the Middle Ages, now, Geoff.'

The large man laughed. 'Indeed not! Definitely not middle-aged, either of us. Old, sagging. Look at us both. But here's the difference, Eric. I'm happy. Led a happy life. Pulled strings, enjoyed the party. Still do.' He grinned, pointed at Eric. 'Have you enjoyed your time on the planet? Made the most of every-thing, did you? Or did you simply live for those times you could spend with my wife?'

'You hated her.'

'True. But you were just as disloyal as she was. Now get some drinks, for Christ's sake. A man's dying of thirst here.'

Eric did as asked, his mind almost in the same state of utter turmoil as when he'd finally plucked up the courage to tell Cecily of his love for her, and – joy of joys – she'd returned it. He paid for the drinks, hands shaking, and returned to the table.

'Tell me what she said and I'll leave.'

Geoff took a moment, looking around the bar, then drained his drink in one go, wincing slightly. He eventually whispered,

'You've got to understand it was difficult to hear precisely, as I was smothering her with a pillow at the time.'

Eric stuttered, 'You were . . . what?'

'I believe the correct medical term is "assisting". Bit frowned upon these days, apparently. Controversial, you know, *Daily Mail* outrage sort of stuff.'

'You *killed* her?'

'Not according to the coroner,' Geoff replied. 'Had to pull a few strings, mind. Leaves me conveniently old, free and single like you, eh Eric? Except, of course, I'm the lucky one. The luckiest guilty party of the lot.'

Most murder pre-trial hearings warrant precious few lines of press coverage. Reporters tend to wait for the actual trial before devoting valuable column inches to whatever events led to the calamitous act. But the pre-trial hearing for Eric Trimble, 72, a widower from Dorking, Surrey, accused of strangling one of his oldest friends to death in the lounge-bar of a seafront hotel using the victim's own silk tie – was quite different.

Police and sources acting for the defendant had leaked enough details to the press prior to the hearing regarding the full confession, the bizarre Guilty Party reunions and the various entanglements of these two unassuming pensioners, that the gallery was full.

True to expectations, their hopes weren't diminished, as the neatly dressed defendant stood in the dock, listening as the charge against him was read out. For a moment he said nothing, then slowly he turned to all in the gallery and bowed slightly, before turning back to the presiding judge and announcing, in a clear voice that all could hear, and would always remember:

'Never, in all my years, your honour, have I had as much pleasure in saying this one, most despicable word that has dogged me for almost an entire lifetime. Guilty.'

WHAT'S THE TIME, MR WOLF?

Christine Poulson

Christine Poulson has a PhD in History of Art, and has written widely on nineteenth-century art and literature. She worked as a curator of ceramics at Birmingham Museum and Art Gallery, has taught for the Open University and was a lecturer in Art History at Cambridge. Her latest novel is *Invisible*.

'Soon be over,' Frank said.

'Thank God.' Sheila exchanged a wry glance with her husband.

Before the party he hadn't seen the need to hire an entertainer. 'How hard can it be to keep a few kids occupied for a couple of hours,' he'd said. Sheila knew better. It had to be planned like a military campaign, every minute accounted for.

The woman had those kids in the palm of her hand. She was a passable ventriloquist and the fluffy white toy rabbit under her arm was singing, 'Happy Birthday to you, Squashed tomatoes and stew.'

Shrieks of mirth went up from the four-year-olds sitting cross-legged on the floor.

'Whatever we're paying her it's not enough,' Frank conceded.

Sheila taught Year 6 at primary school, a job-share since she'd had Harry, but controlling a bunch of four-year-olds was a very different matter. And perhaps because she was an older parent – she and Frank had been over forty when Harry was born – she did find it a strain being responsible for so many little ones. Once again she counted heads. Yes, all present and correct. She could relax. Everything was under control. The birthday tea was over. Frank's mum was in the kitchen, putting slices of birthday cake in the party bags. No one had been sick, no one had hurt themselves, hardly anyone had cried. And looking at Harry, who was actually holding his sides laughing, she knew it had all been worthwhile. But thank God she wouldn't have to organise another children's party for a whole year.

After the entertainer there was time for two more games, pass the parcel with Frank carefully manipulating the breaks in the music so that everyone would get a little gift, and then 'What's the Time, Mr Wolf?' That was Harry's favourite. He adored being the wolf and shouting 'Dinner-time'. There was lots of shrieking and everyone got thoroughly over-excited, but it didn't matter, because by then the parents were beginning to arrive. One by one, prompted by mums and dads, the children said, 'Thank you for having me,' and off they went. The party dwindled until there was only Harry left and one other child.

'Where's Evan's mummy?' Harry asked.

'Oh, she'll be here in a minute,' Sheila said.

It was odd all the same. It was half an hour past pick-up time and it was parental etiquette to be prompt on these occasions. She settled the children down in front of a DVD of *Shaun the Sheep*. Evan wasn't making a fuss. He was a serious little boy, rather pale, with shadows under his eyes as if he didn't get enough sleep.

'Shall I ring her mobile?' Frank asked.

She nodded. Thank goodness he had thought to take contact numbers.

She watched him tap in Jennifer's mobile number. He listened and shook his head. No one was answering.

'Do you know where she lives?' he said.

'Somewhere out towards Ely?' she hazarded. Jennifer and her husband had only recently moved into the area and she didn't know her that well. 'She's probably got muddled up about the time, that's all. There's sure to be a simple explanation.'

'Of course. Wires crossed somewhere. Bound to be.'

But half an hour later Jennifer still hadn't arrived and she still wasn't answering her mobile. She hadn't left a landline number. Sheila rang round the other mothers and managed to find out where she lived.

'We'd better drive over,' Frank decided.

'Shall we take Evan?' Sheila asked.

'Better leave him here with Mum. Jennifer or her husband might arrive while we're gone. If they do, Mum can ring us.'

They looked up Jennifer's address on Googlemaps. Sheila printed out the map on the other side of the sheet of paper with the phone numbers.

Frank got the car out and they set off.

They drove in silence on long straight roads that cut across ploughed fields, ready for their winter crops. Pigeons pecked the dark, chocolately earth.

Sheila pieced together what she knew about Jennifer. Not much; they'd only exchanged the odd 'hello' at the nursery gate. Jennifer was always dauntingly well turned out, always carefully made-up in contrast to Sheila's old jeans and barely brushed hair. And though Sheila knew she shouldn't judge, she felt a bit sorry for Evan who seemed to be at the nursery all day every day.

'Maybe Jennifer thought her husband was collecting Evan,' Sheila said.

'And he thought she was. Very likely,' Frank agreed.

It wasn't only dusk that was darkening the vast Fenland sky. Grey cumulus clouds were advancing, dragging curtains of rain.

Sheila shivered and leaned forward to switch on the car heater. She looked at her watch. Six o'clock and the party had finished at four.

'Or maybe she's had an accident. She could be lying injured somewhere. Maybe we should ring the police.'

'We'll try the house first.'

It was a nineteenth-century farmhouse, some way from the nearest village, and set back from the road behind a windbreak of trees. As Sheila got out of the car a gust of wind lifted her hair. Dry leaves rattled on the trees and it was suddenly colder. Even before they reached the door, big drops of rain began to fall and they ran to shelter in the porch. Sheila was looking round for a bell, when she noticed that the door was ajar. Frank saw it at the same time and they exchanged glances.

Frank ran the bell and they waited in silence. When no one came, he pushed open the door and called out, 'Hello?'

There was still no answer.

'Should we go in?' Sheila asked.

Frank nodded.

Inside it was very quiet and darkness was gathering in the corners of the hall. When Sheila saw the bloodstains on the wall she gasped and grabbed Frank's arm. He reached for the light and switched it on. The stain wasn't red, but brown, and there was a sweet, pungent smell. It triggered off a memory, something elusive that slipped away before she could grasp it. It was something unpleasant that she'd rather not remember, she knew that.

Frank said, 'That's cough medicine. Look, there are bits of glass, too, on the floor.'

They moved on further into the house, glancing in at rooms as they passed. The place was immaculate, all chintz and pale, thick carpets. It was exactly the kind of place where Sheila would have expected Jennifer to live. But how did she manage to keep it like this with a four-year-old? At the end of the hall they found themselves in a kitchen that was all of a piece with the rest of the house: exposed beams and gleaming copper pans. Frank went across and pushed open a door that led into the conservatory. Sheila looked around. There wasn't a thing out of place except . . . on the scrubbed oak table lay the body of little tabby cat. Sheila exclaimed and moved towards it, placed a hand on the furry flank. It was cold. A dent on the side of the head suggested a fractured skull.

Sheila was startled when Jennifer appeared from the hall, pushing back wet hair with one hand. The rain drumming on the glass roof of the conservatory must have masked the sound of a car driving up.

Jennifer looked amazed to see Sheila.

'What are you doing here?' she asked.

'You didn't come to collect Evan, so—'

'Didn't I say? Barry was coming for him.' Realisation was dawning and with it, alarm. 'You mean – he didn't?'

Sheila hastened to reassure her. 'Evan's fine. Frank's mum—'

'Sheila.' Frank's voice was hoarse.

She turned to see him standing in the doorway of the conservatory. His face was white.

'Better call the police. And an ambulance.'

It's a strange experience, reading about yourself in the news, actually more like reading about someone else, Sheila thought, as she scanned the headlines on the BBC website.

'Yesterday the body of banker Barry Brunswick' – no wonder they could afford that house – 'was discovered by Sheila Cumming, 45' – how on earth had they managed to get hold of her age? – 'and her husband Frank after Mr Brunswick failed to collect his four-year-old son from a birthday party at their home.' There was a photo of Jennifer, looking haggard under her make-up, carrying Evan who had his arms around her neck. The article reported that she had been out walking with a friend and had returned home to find her husband dead from a single stab wound to the heart.

Sheila was supposed to be teaching today, but Frank had persuaded her to call in sick. She had scarcely slept the previous night. She couldn't stop thinking of Cluedo: Colonel Mustard and a dagger in the conservatory. It was one of those awful inappropriate mental tics. She must be suffering from shock.

The phone rang yet again, another journalist probably. Sheila waited for Frank to pick up the phone on the extension. He was screening their calls.

A few moments later he put his head round the door. 'Elaine.'

Sheila picked up the phone. Elaine was one of her oldest and best friends. They'd been at school together. It was one of those friendships that survives against the odds. Sheila was quiet and reflective. Elaine, who had become a leading theatrical designer, was not. But that was what Sheila liked about her. There was no pussy-footing around. With Elaine what you saw was what you got.

'Sweetie! I've just seen the news, you poor darling. How *are* you? Tell me all about it.'

Sheila told her.

'Now, you won't believe this,' Elaine said, 'but I know Jennifer too. They used to live a few doors down.'

'No, really?'

'Well, that might be pitching it a bit high. They kept themselves to themselves. I didn't like her at first, thought she was a stuck-up bitch, then I realised that she was just terribly shy.'

Sheila couldn't help smiling. She could just imagine. Conversations with Elaine tended to be overwhelming until you learned just to sit back and let it wash over you.

Elaine went on: 'She was such a mouse of a woman. You know, brown hair, brown clothes . . . But judging from this photo that I'm looking at on the screen, she must have bucked up her ideas a bit. I wonder . . .'

'Yes?'

'He was so good-looking. You know, one of those men who's almost too good-looking? I took against him after I saw him in a restaurant looking into another woman's eyes. I'm sure he was having an affair. I wondered, when they moved to the country – maybe a new start and all that? Oh Lord, is that the time? I've got to be at the theatre. See you very soon, my sweet. Kiss kiss. Big hug.'

And she was gone. Sheila always felt better for a phone call from Elaine: perhaps it was the sheer energy she exuded. But she was perceptive too. She might be right and Jennifer's aloofness was really shyness, her reliance on make-up and smart clothes, a sign of insecurity.

'Are you alright, love?' She looked up to see Frank hovering over her anxiously.

'I just can't help thinking about that poor woman. And they'd just moved in, too, she hardly knows anybody.'

The doorbell rang.

'That's them, now, the police,' Frank said.

The police inspector was overweight, his belly straining the buttons on his shirt and his tie was slightly crooked. For all that Sheila got a sense of a keen intelligence as he took them through the events that had led up to the discovery of the body. Just when she thought he'd finished and was about to leave, he flipped back through the pages of his notebook.

'If we could just go back to when Mrs Brunswick arrived to

drop off her little boy. Three o'clock, you said? Pretty hard to be certain about the exact time when you were busy getting ready for a party. Could it have been somewhat after three? Or even before?'

'Do you have children, inspector?'

'A boy and a girl.'

'Then you'll know that a children's party isn't like a cocktail party. People don't arrive fashionably late. They arrive on the dot. I looked at my watch at ten to three, wondering when the first one was going to arrive. And by five past they were all there, including Evan. I remember thinking we'd better get going on the first game. I'd got it all organised more or less down to the minute.'

'So how did that go, exactly? Mrs Brunswick drove up . . .'

'A whole load of them arrived at once, and she was one of them. The kids ran in together, and Frank's mother took them off to join the others. The parents handed over birthday presents, we took their mobile numbers, including hers, and off they went.'

'So she definitely dropped her son between ten to three and five minutes past?'

'That's right.'

'How did she seem? Did she say or do anything out of the ordinary?'

Sheila tried to picture the scene. 'I'm not sure that she said anything at all. I wasn't really noticing.' All the same something was tugging at her memory. She appealed to Frank. 'Can you remember, love?'

He shook his head. 'It's all a bit of a blur to be honest.'

The inspector nodded and shut up his notebook.

After he'd gone, Frank said, 'I suppose he was eliminating her from their enquiries. The husband or wife's always the first to be suspected.'

'As if it wasn't bad enough for her to have lost her husband!'

Frank put his arm around her shoulders and squeezed. She leaned into him. Darling Frank. With the almost-telepathy of a happy marriage, she knew that he was thinking about her first husband and his death in a climbing accident.

'Well,' Frank went on, 'let's hope we've supplied her with an alibi.'

'That poor, poor woman. I'll give her a ring. At the very least I can offer to take Evan off her hands for a few hours.'

'I still can't believe it,' Jennifer said. 'It just seems . . . unreal.'

It was two days later and Sheila had finally managed to get through to her.

Sheila had stopped thinking about Cluedo, but now her thoughts were returning obsessively to the broken bottle of cough mixture and the dead cat. There was something so strange – almost surreal – about finding them in that house where nothing else was out of place. Of course she couldn't ask.

Instead she said, 'Have the police let you go back to the house?'

'Just to collect clothes and things. My friend, Annie, the one I was out walking with, we're staying with her. I can't ever live there again. And we'd been looking forward so much to moving to the country, thought it would be safer than the city, a good place for Evan to grow up.'

Perhaps Sheila had misjudged Jennifer. After all, she was just another mother, wanting to do the best for her child. The old freemasonry of motherhood was kicking in.

'How is Evan?' Sheila asked.

'He thinks Barry's away for work and keeps asking when he's coming back. I know I'll have to tell him soon. But he's already so upset about Tabitha.'

'Tabitha?'

'Our poor little cat. She got hit by a car. We were going to bury her that afternoon. We got her for Evan when we moved in.'

So that explained that, now there was only the cough medicine. Sheila reproved herself for her flippancy.

Jennifer was saying, 'I can't help thinking . . . a friend rang the house around three o'clock and spoke to Barry so he was still alive then. If I'd gone straight home instead of going walking with Annie, then everything might have been different.'

Yes, Sheila thought, you might be dead too, but she didn't say that, just murmured a sympathetic response.

Jennifer said, 'The police think it was someone wanting money for drugs. That's all they took. Just money and some of my jewellery. Our bedroom had been ransacked.' Sheila could tell she was on the verge of tears.

'Anything I can do to help,' Sheila said. 'If you'd like me to have Evan . . .?'

'You're so kind. Oh, I almost forgot to ask. I can't find Evan's coat anywhere. I know he had it when I dropped him off for the party. I was wondering . . .'

'I don't think it's here, but let me just check.'

Sheila put down the phone and went to look in the hall, but the coat wasn't there.

She returned to the phone. 'I'm sorry, no.'

Jennifer said, 'The worst of it is, it had a little teddy bear in the pocket. Evan won't go to bed without it. I'll just have to try to get a new one from somewhere.'

Sheila was at a party and it was for grown-ups, but they were playing 'What's the time, Mr Wolf?' She didn't know who was playing Mr Wolf, and she was afraid to find out. Yet she was compelled to move stealthily forward. She was only two steps away, when someone called out 'What's the time, Mr Wolf?' and the figure began to turn. She knew that what she would see was a real wolf's head. She wrenched herself out of the dream, and woke up, shuddering.

She lay quietly in the dark, letting her breathing settle. Two weeks had passed since they had discovered Barry's body, but she hadn't recovered from the shock of it. It had shaken things loose, had brought to the surface memories that she usually managed to suppress. Was the figure Kevin? Her first marriage hadn't been happy, and no one knew – not even Frank – quite how bad it had been.

But that was all over. She was safe now. And how lucky she was, how amazingly lucky, to have gentle Frank asleep beside her and dear little Harry in the next room.

She wondered how Jennifer and Evan were getting on. Jennifer had taken Evan out of the nursery and she hadn't been in touch. Perhaps Sheila should ring her again.

It was later that morning as she was getting ready to go out with Harry that she discovered Evan's coat in the hall closet. Frank must have thought it was Harry's, and put it away. The little teddy was still in the pocket. She was intending to go to Ely anyway. It wouldn't be much of a detour to go past Jennifer's house.

As she drove up, she saw that a 'for sale' sign was already up. A car was parked outside. She tucked her own car in behind it.

'Mummy,' Harry said. 'I want a wee.'

She reached over and undid his seatbelt. 'Come on then. We'll see if anyone's there.'

She stepped into the porch and rang the doorbell. She was beginning to think the house was empty, when she heard footsteps, the door opened and there was Jennifer. Sheila held up Evan's coat. 'I found this just today, I'm so sorry—'

Harry interrupted her. 'Mummy, mummy.' He was clutching his crotch and squirming.

'Harry's desperate for the loo,' Sheila explained.

'Oh, come in, come in,' Jennifer said, ushering them through the door. 'There's one just here.'

Harry darted in.

Sheila's eyes strayed to the brown stain on the wall. It looked almost as though the bottle had been thrown against the wall. Washing wouldn't be enough. That would have to be painted over. Jennifer caught her looking and Sheila looked away, embarrassed. There was an awkward silence. It was broken by Evan appearing at the sitting-room door.

'Is Harry here?' he asked. 'Can we play?'

He looked different, more animated, and there was some colour in his cheeks. Jennifer put a hand on his shoulder and drew him close. 'Have you got time, Sheila? Can you stay for a cup of tea?'

Harry emerged from the loo. Without a word, the two little boys disappeared into the sitting room.

The two women smiled at each other.

'Thanks, I'd love one,' Sheila said.

The kitchen seemed different, not untidy exactly, but more things left out on the counter, more homely. Sheila watched

Jennifer fill the kettle. She was as immaculate as ever. Her honey-coloured hair was cut in a long smooth bob and not a hair was out of place. The eyeliner had surely been copied from the Duchess of Cambridge and she must have used a lip-brush to get that outline. Was that what had delayed her coming to the door?

Jennifer said, 'It was lucky you caught me. I've just come to start packing things up.'

As she talked, she was getting out mugs, looking for milk in the fridge.

Sheila felt uneasy. Of course it wasn't surprising, given what had happened the last time she was here, but it was more than that. Something wasn't right . . .

There were footsteps in the hall and a woman's voice called, 'Jenny!'

Jennifer said, 'In here! I've got a visitor.' It sounded almost like a warning.

A woman appeared in the doorway. She was slim, dressed in jeans and a sweater, with smooth hair tied back in a short pony-tail.

'I wasn't expecting you so soon,' Jennifer said. 'This is Sheila. Sheila, this is my friend, Annie.'

Sheila stood up and offered her hand. Annie shook it. Her grip was firm and she had a pleasant smile. Yet Sheila's sense of discomfort was increasing. She wondered if she could make an excuse and leave.

On the kitchen table Jennifer's mobile began to buzz and vibrate.

'That'll be the estate agent,' she said. 'Can you pour the tea, Annie, when it's brewed?'

'I'll just check on Harry,' Sheila murmured.

She went into the hall and put her head round the sitting-room door. When she said, 'Five minutes, Harry,' he didn't even look up. He and Evan had their heads together and Lego was scattered all over the floor.

Back in the kitchen, Jennifer was sitting at the table with her organiser open. 'So tomorrow at three o'clock then,' she was saying.

She wrote down the appointment.

That was when Sheila knew what was wrong. Jennifer had her pen in her right hand. But when she'd dropped Evan off at the party, she'd written down her phone number with her left hand. Sheila was left-handed herself and she'd been trained to notice it in the children she taught. In her mind's eye she could see Jennifer curling her hand round in that awkward way that some left-handers have.

She looked at Annie, who was pouring out the tea. With her left hand. And she was wearing her watch on her right hand, just like Sheila did. That must have been what had bothered Sheila earlier. Annie glanced round and saw Sheila standing transfixed. Sheila saw her look back at the hand on the teapot and realise her mistake.

Sheila felt giddy. She reached for a chair and lowered herself into it. She closed her eyes. Absurdly, she found herself thinking, what's the time, Mr Wolf? Three o'clock! But it wasn't so absurd after all, because timing was the key to it all.

When she opened her eyes, Annie had moved to stand between her and the door. Both women were staring at her. Her thoughts flew to Harry. No one knew they were here. She got to her feet. Her mouth was dry.

The silence was electric. It was broken by brmm-brmm noises. Out in the hall Harry and Evan were playing with cars on the tiled floor.

Jennifer got up and closed the door. She came back and sat down at the table. 'It's alright,' she said. 'You're quite safe, you and Harry.'

'Why did you . . . ?' Sheila asked.

Annie took a seat next to Jennifer. 'Barry was a monster,' she said. 'A sadistic brute and a bully. Show her, Jenny.'

Jennifer grimaced, but she pulled up her jumper to show a midriff dotted with small, round scars.

'Cigarette burns,' Annie said. 'I'd been working abroad, wondered why I hadn't heard from Jenny, and when I got back, I understood why. Jenny didn't have friends any more. Barry didn't like it. He didn't want people getting too close in case they guessed what was going on. I told her that she had to get out. I could see what it was doing to Evan.'

Jennifer said, 'Barry told me he'd kill me if I tried to leave. And Evan, too.'

Sheila didn't say, why didn't you go to the police? She had tried that with Kevin and it hadn't worked. The police couldn't lock someone away forever or protect you for the rest of your life. She remembered the relief that had flooded through her when the police broke the news that Kevin – ever the risk-taker – had died on a climbing holiday in the French Alps. It had been all she could do not to dance round the room.

'But then Barry decided that we were going to move to the country, and that was when . . .' Jennifer hesitated, glanced sideways at Annie.

'Yes,' Annie said. She put her hand over Jennifer's. 'It was my idea to pass myself off as Jenny. We used to swap clothes all the time when we were students. People thought we were sisters. But it had to happen before people got to know her, when all they really saw was the distinctive make-up and the expensive clothes and the haircut.'

Sheila thought of what Elaine had said about Jennifer's mousy appearance: so that had been the reason for the make-over.

'I didn't think it would work and I really didn't think I'd be able to, well, you know, I didn't think I could do it,' Jennifer said. 'The day of the party – that was supposed to be an experiment. I pretended that Harry's party was an hour earlier than it really was. I dropped Evan off at Annie's and came home. And when I got back—' She put her head in her hands.

'Tell her what that bastard did to the cat,' Annie said grimly.

'So she wasn't run over,' Sheila said.

Jennifer shook her head. 'He lost his temper when she got under his feet and tripped him up. He picked her up by the back legs and swung her against the wall. That was what did it, I didn't see red or anything like that, it was more as if I was somehow standing outside myself. I saw myself going into the kitchen and getting the knife . . .' Her voice trailed off.

Annie squeezed her arm.

Jennifer cleared her voice and went on, her voice stronger.

'By the time Annie rang after she'd dropped Evan off, Barry was dead. Annie told me she thought she'd pulled it off and that you hadn't realised.'

'I wasn't really looking for Jennifer as a separate person, I just saw Evan's mum,' Sheila admitted.

'I don't suppose we could leave it like that?' Annie said. 'That it was Evan's mum you saw?'

Sheila said slowly, 'I suppose there isn't any real evidence. At least nothing a halfway decent barrister couldn't demolish. I was so distracted by the children and the party and everyone arriving at once. And eyewitness testimony's notoriously unreliable. Although . . .' she was struck by a thought. Was this the coat she had been wearing? Yes . . . She fumbled in the pocket and brought out a folded sheet of paper with the contact numbers from the party on one side and the directions to Jennifer's house on the other. Would a handwriting expert be able to tell that it was Annie who had written the phone number? Better not risk it.

She handed the piece of paper to Jennifer.

'Here, have this,' she said. 'I should burn it if I were you.'

They lingered in the garden, reluctant to say goodbye.

'Where will you go?' Sheila asked.

'The States, I think,' Jennifer said. 'Annie's been offered a job in Denver. We'll go with her at least for a while.'

'That'll be best,' Sheila agreed. 'Send me a postcard. Let me know how Evan's getting on.'

'I will.'

Sheila strapped Harry into his child seat and got behind the wheel.

She had pulled away and waved goodbye when she remembered something. She braked, told Harry she'd only be a moment, and got out of the car.

Jennifer came part of the way to meet her.

'There's just one thing I have to know,' Sheila said.

'Yes?'

'The cough medicine. How did it get on the wall?'

'I found it like that when I got home. Barry had smashed it on purpose so that he could order me to clear it up.'

Sheila nodded, satisfied. 'I thought that was it.'

With Kevin it had been a bottle of maple syrup.

Even after all these years the smell of it still made her gag.

THE WIDE OPEN SKY
Kate Rhodes

Kate Rhodes went to the University of Essex and completed a doctorate on the playwright Tennessee Williams. She has taught at universities in Britain and the United States, and now writes full-time. Her first books were two collections of poetry, and her novels *Crossbones Yard* and *A Killing of Angels* are both set in London, her birthplace.

Nan's breathing sounds like a full force gale. When I get back from school at lunchtime the mask is pressed over her face, pale blue lips gasping for air. I twist the dial on her oxygen tank to maximum, and soon she's well enough to tell me off.

'Why are you home early, Shane? What have you done this time?'

'Nothing.'

Her eyes pinpoint me. 'They'll separate us if you get in trouble. You know that, don't you?'

'I didn't do anything, Nan.'

'How long have they excluded you for?'

I study the scuff marks on my trainers. 'Just till Monday.'

The look Nan gives me would kill anything within twenty miles, but she's the reason I've been fighting again. Jamie Wilcox made jokes about her being a cripple, so I went at him with both fists. There's no point in trying to explain, because she'd never believe me, so I leave her gasping into her mask and go back downstairs.

Nan always sleeps in the afternoon, which suits me fine. From the back step I can see the fen rolling away into the sunshine, flat as a bowling green. Sometimes it feels like I could run through the parched fields, and keep going till I touch the sky. I try not to make a sound as I lift the rifle from the cupboard. Nan keeps it for shooting rabbits, and I'm not meant to touch it, but I can't resist the smooth wooden carriage, the trigger's cold metal. Sometimes I take it into the woods and shoot pine cones from the trees. I slip a cartridge into the carousel, stow a couple more in my pocket then head outside, with the rifle slung over my arm.

Our neighbour, Barry, is working at the bottom of his garden. I always know what he's doing, because our cottages are connected, and there are no other houses until Rawlings' Farm, half a mile away. Nan doesn't like Barry, but that's not unusual. She's not keen on the health visitor either, or any of my teachers. She says that people have lost their manners, more's the pity. The hole he's digging is waist deep, circles of sweat darkening his T-shirt. A smell of rain, fresh turned grass, and decay rises from the ground.

'What's that for, Barry?' I ask.

'None of your business. Why've you got that gun anyway?'

I shrug at him. 'Target practice.'

'Watch your feet, kiddo. Don't lose any toes.'

Barry always calls me kiddo, but I'm as tall as him, even though I'm only twelve. He's an odd looking bloke; thin arms held together by strings of muscle, always struggling to stand still, dancing from foot to foot. One of his eyes stares straight ahead while the other spins in circles, like it's stuck in a whirlpool. Maybe that's why he lives alone. If he had a girl-friend she wouldn't know which eye was watching her.

'That must have taken ages to dig,' I say.

'I'm planting an apple tree here.' He rests his spade on the dry soil. 'Listen, I'm going to town later, want to come along?'

'Can't, the health visitor's coming.' I've been out with Barry a few times, but he just drives around in his van for no reason. He stares at girls walking by, muttering things under his breath, and never talks to anyone.

'See you later then, kiddo.'

Barry scowls at me, so I leave him to his digging and run down to the canal. It's so hot that I feel like diving in, but I haven't brought a towel, so I throw stones instead, counting the ripples that reach the bank. I lift the gun and take a pot shot at a rat, but miss by yards. When I get tired of the water I lie on the bank and watch a blur of swallows changing shape overhead. Every way I turn, the sky goes on for miles, no buildings or tall trees to interrupt it. The last time mum visited I spotted her car, miles away – a red mark between the fields, slowly growing bigger, until she pulled up outside. She doesn't come often anymore, just birthdays and Christmases. The last time her hair was black instead of blonde and she cried when she said goodbye. She told me to learn from her mistakes so I wouldn't have to make any of my own.

When I get back, Nan's staggering around in the kitchen in her dressing gown, so I hide the gun in the log pile. She's insisting on tidying up, each breath rattling as she wipes the surfaces. She likes the place to be spick and span when the health visitor comes. The woman's name is Denise and she's always on time. When I open the door at three o'clock her hair is a frizz of orange curls, and her expression is so bitter, it looks like she's sucked a lemon.

'Off school again, Shane?'

There's no point in replying because she writes everything down in her black book. I take her into the sitting room then make some tea. After I've delivered the tray, I wait outside, earwigging. Denise's voice is as sour as her face, and I can hear every word.

'It's better to forward plan, Mrs Wilcox, that way you're in control. There are plenty of foster parents who would take Shane if you go into a care home.'

Nan's reply is too quiet to hear, but it must have been sharp, because Denise opens the door so fast it almost smacks me in the face. Her Nissan Micra disappears in a cloud of dust. Soon it's a speck of metal vanishing into the potato fields, and Nan's eyes are so black it's like staring down a well.

'That woman's not coming here again, Shane. There's no way on God's earth she's splitting us up.'

I can't help smiling. This is the Nan I remember, the one who could chop wood all afternoon, and never sit down, before the emphysema began. But the fight soon fades out of her. She lies on the sofa with the fan at full blast, panting for air.

It's five o'clock when Barry's van pulls up. He opens the

doors and lifts out a big cardboard box, and whatever's inside must be heavy, because he staggers under its weight. I want to find out what he's bought, but I'm making our dinner: beef burgers and oven chips, a tin of baked beans. It's so hot it feels like the air has stopped circulating, but at least Nan's peaceful. She eats a few mouthfuls then drifts back into sleep.

After I've washed up I go outside to listen to the crickets. There's plenty to watch at the edge of the field – dormice and ladybirds. I catch a Red Admiral and feel its wings brush my cupped hands before letting it go. The air smells of dust and a hundred different types of pollen. By the time I get back, Nan's awake again.

'Put the news channels on, can you, Shane?'

She always makes me watch the headlines, even though they've got nothing whatsoever to do with me. A blonde woman talks about another war starting, then men in suits argue about why London's run out of money. It's only when the local stories come on that something catches my interest. I recognise the girl's face straight away. She's called Eva, and she's in year seven. I've seen her loads of times in the playground with her mates. She's smiling in the picture, wavy brown hair flying in the wind. The newsreader explains that she's gone missing on her way home from school.

'There are some sick creatures in the world,' Nan mutters. 'It's time you went to bed.'

I help her upstairs then go to my room, but I can't stop thinking about Eva. She's been stuck in my head for weeks, because she's so pretty, and she never calls me names. Sometimes she even smiles at me in the corridor.

It's so hot that I lie on the bed with the window open, longing for a breeze. Something brings me round hours later. My alarm clock says that it's three fifteen and moonlight's flooding through the window. At first nothing seems to be moving, but when I look outside, Barry's in his garden, digging with all his might. The hole is deeper now, almost up to his shoulder.

Barry's so hard at work, he doesn't notice me slipping outside and climbing over the fence. The cardboard box I saw him lift from his van is beside the compost heap, the lid half-open. I have to rub my eyes to believe what's inside. Eva is lying on her back, naked skin pale as a ghost, and fear hits me out of nowhere. I'm still frozen when Barry grabs my arm. There's a froth of spit on his lip when he speaks, and a stink of fresh sweat.

'Listen to me, kiddo,' he hisses. 'Your gran'll get hurt if you tell anyone. Do you understand?'

I blurt out the question before I can stop myself. 'What happened to Eva?'

'She wouldn't shut up.' Barry's lazy eye crawls across my face. 'Some girls are like that, you'll understand one day.'

I look at Eva's bruised face and reach out to touch her hair, but the punch knocks me to the ground. Barry's hands close around my throat.

'I could put a pillow over your gran's face, right now. Remember that, kiddo.'

I manage to break away, and after that everything spins into fast forward. I run back to collect the gun, and my thoughts stop as I edge along the fence. My mind's empty when I point the barrel between his shoulder blades, and he collapses forwards into the dirt. A puddle of red gushes from his chest, staining the clean moonlight. Then I sit still, too shocked to cry, but the light in Nan's room never comes on. She takes sleeping tablets, so there's a chance she never heard anything.

Eva's skin is cold when I lift her into the hole. It feels wrong to make her lie beside someone who hurt her so badly, but there's no other way. It takes a long time to pile the earth back with Barry's spade, and by the time I've finished, the sun's rising above the lip of the fen. There's no way I can stay here, because Nan would get into trouble, and she's too sick to go to prison, so I pick up the gun and set off down the path. I sprint until my lungs empty, and the cottage is a brown thumbprint in the distance. Then I turn away and start running again, even faster now, aiming for the wide open sky.

SKELETON CREW
Chris Simms

Chris Simms graduated from Newcastle University then travelled round the world before moving to Manchester in 1994. Since then he has worked as a freelance copywriter for advertising agencies throughout the city. The idea for his first novel, *Outside the White Lines*, came to him one night when broken down on the hard shoulder of a motorway. His latest series features DC Iona Khan and is set in Manchester.

T he place is quiet. Always is last thing on a Friday. Guy in a Volvo estate dragging sheets of cardboard out of the boot. An old lady – sixty-five, seventy? – she's at the railings, dropping all of three jars down into the recycling container for glass. Why drive all the way out to the edge of town for that? Daft old bat, should have used the collection-point at the local supermarket.

I look around the little cabin. These bloody things shouldn't be here. Mutilated teddies. Heads of decapitated dolls. Action figures with missing limbs. I recognise that one – it was on the telly the other day. Stupid advert: garish and shouty and too fast. Military drums, camera swooping jerkily down from the sky to a close-up of the manikin. Transfigurer, was it? Something like that.

Next to it on the windowsill is a grotesquely-muscled wrestler, face contorted in a snarl. He only has one arm – and that's been placed round the slender shoulders of a naked female figurine. Her legs make up two thirds of her height, pinched waist and high, jutting breasts. But she has no hair and her eyes are missing. Is it any wonder the country's going down the pan? Kids playing with this kind of rubbish.

Need to put a message out to the site staff: no collecting

items deposited in the containers. This is a council tip, not an opportunity to amass unwanted toys.

The Volvo bloke's carrying the cardboard towards the wrong container. Imbecile. I fold the copy of the local newspaper on the article about another young adult going missing. 'Excuse me, sir. That's for non-recyclable waste.'

He turns to the half-open door of the cabin with a lost look. I step fully out, and zip up my fluorescent tabard. 'Cardboard goes in number four. The one to your left.'

He's staring at me like I'm speaking a foreign language.

'Number four,' I repeat. 'To your left – that's the one for cardboard, sir.'

In the restricted-access area below us, the JCB revs its engine. The vehicle's cabin has been raised up to its maximum height. The front of it is fitted with a long pair of hydraulic arms that clutch a cast-iron scoop. This allows the driver to reach over into the various containers and rake smooth the piles of debris within. But more often, he simply uses the heavy bucket like a pile-driver, smashing it down to compress everything inside.

The member of the public nods at number four. 'This one, you say?'

A safe guess, I want to reply, judging by the three-foot-high sign marked with the word 'cardboard' attached to the front of it. I incline my head in agreement and he slings his armful of squashed boxes over the railing. They drop down into the container where, in due course, they'll be battered lower by Rick, the JCB driver.

The vehicle approaches the waste-to-energy container and the scoop hits the mound of bin-liners that have built up in one corner. Plastic bursts and the shrivelled remains of carrots and potatoes tumble out. The bucket lifts and drops again, sending a chicken carcass scurrying down the slope. It comes to rest behind a fading bunch of carnations, as if it's hiding there. The cloying smell of rotting fruit wafts up. Lorry will be here soon to ferry that lot to the incinerator at the borough's main site.

I watch as Rick backs the JCB away. There shouldn't be that silly registration plate propped up behind the vehicle's windscreen. CD R1C. Not CD now, though. Not since I banned him from listening to music while working. Ear protectors? A valid item, perfectly permissible for a site such as this. Not earphones, though. That's a safety hazard, plain and simple.

The JCB's engine growls as he heads off to the container reserved for timber. The one for small household appliances looks a bit full, too. Get that collected first thing tomorrow morning.

The old Cortina passing under the height barrier at the entrance catches my eye. Hey up, it's them again. Tweedle-dum and Tweedle-dee. A right pair, these two. Quick glance at my watch: six fifty-five. Always the same. Seconds ahead of when the lorry arrives to take the waste-to-energy container away.

As I walk down the ramp to unlock the main gates in readiness for the lorry turning up, their battered old Cortina stops alongside the container for unwanted clothing. One bag goes in, but the flap isn't able to close completely. Thing must need emptying, too.

Here comes the lorry, as I knew it would. 'Evening, Harry,' I say to the driver as he slows to a halt. 'How's things back at base?'

He gives me an awkward glance as I swing the gates open. 'Same old, same old.'

As he steers the lorry towards the waste-to-energy container, I can see Tweedle-dum and Tweedle-dee standing at the railings above it. Even though one's lost most of his black curls, they must be twins. The same jowelly-cheeks and squashed-out bottom lip. Sad, droopy eyes that are devoid of life. Open-mouth-breathers – that's what Trevor, my ex-policeman friend, calls their type. Both are wearing hideous, cheap-looking leather jackets that end in thick elasticated waistbands. Shapeless jeans tucked into black wellington boots that are caked in manure, or something similar.

Every time they reach over to drop a shoebox-sized package into the container, the waistbands of their leather jackets ride up over their fat stomachs. Tugging them back down in unison, they turn to the boot of their car and repeat the process, avoiding eye-contact with me all the while. Something's not right about them, I just know it.

The fruit machine lets out a burst of flashing light. Coins chunter into the tray. I look at the young man playing it and sigh. 'Bloody thing. Why did Dave let them put it in?'

'Brewery said so,' Trevor replied. 'Dave's hands were tied.'

'Well, even so. He could have insisted.' I turn to my friend of over fifty years. Trevor and I schooled together. Two young lads in baggy shorts, our barm-cakes in snap-boxes over our shoulders.

I got a job with the council – or Corporation, as it was once known. Trevor went into the police. Rose to sergeant before retiring last year. Every Friday we meet for a pint, come rain or shine. You need routine in life. Everyone does.

I take a sip of Mild and adjust a beer mat before setting my glass down. 'Another went missing this week, I see from the local paper.'

'Another what?' He sits back, a hand resting on each knee.

'A lad. Or vulnerable young adult, as they like to call them. Which means one from that council care home in the town. It's up near the old mill, apparently.'

Trevor is watching my hands. He has an uncomfortable expression on his face. I turn a beer mat over and study its underside. 'That's the second one in three months that's vanished. Gone.'

'Teenagers like that are always going missing. Dozens disappeared during my time in the job. They run away. We catch them and take them back. They run away again. It's all a big game.'

'I haven't heard of these two being caught.'

Trevor sips on his beer and then passes a knuckle across his moustache, smearing a trace of foam into the bristles. 'And your thoughts on this are?'

I stare down at my drink then reach across to the neighbouring table for a fresh beer mat. 'There are these two men who turn up at the tip . . .'

'The Glen Hill site?'

There's an edge in his voice. I don't need to glance up to know his right eye will have narrowed. 'That's correct. This pair, they always show last thing on a Friday. It's like they wait out on the main road for the lorry that comes from the main processing site.'

'From Shawcross?'

I nod. 'Comes to pick up the waste-to-energy container. For the big incinerator they put in there last year.'

'You told me all about it. Enormous thing.'

I lift my gaze. His arms are crossed and he's examining the wall above me. 'Well, anyway. They were there again today. Same routine. Just before the container's winched onto the back of the lorry, they drop these packages in and are on their way.'

Trevor's now staring directly at me. The corner of his eye twitches. 'And?'

'Last thing on a Friday, Trevor. That's when staffing levels are at their lowest. Just me and the JCB driver by then – and as soon as the clock hits seven you can't see him for dust. The main processing site will be the same.'

'I'm struggling to see why you're so concerned.'

'They're up to something. It's not normal to have a regular routine for dropping off rubbish. Not domestic, anyway. The contents of that container will go direct into the incinerator – within hours, it's ash. Nothing survives the temperature in that thing. Not even bones.' I give him a meaningful look. 'I know the lazy bunch at the main site won't be inspecting it. Not last thing on a Friday. They'll all be clock-watching.'

'Peter, are you forgetting why you're now supervising the Glen Hill site and not the main one at Shawcross?'

I feel my teeth clench. I knew he'd bring this up. 'They were guilty. Just because I didn't catch them red-handed—'

'You accused your co-workers of taking backhanders. Formally accused them.'

'And they were.'

'But you weren't able to produce any evidence. You hid yourself on that site for how many nights?'

I say nothing.

'Not once did you witness them allowing commercial vehicles through. But you ignored me and went ahead with the accusation. Peter, if it wasn't for your circumstances, you wouldn't have got away with a formal—'

'They were doing it!'

The young man at the fruit machine glances over, eyebrows raised. Behind the bar, Dave pauses in the act of hanging up a wine glass. I see a reflection of myself in the mirror on the opposite wall. My temples and cheekbones seem to stand out more sharply than I remember them. There's a gap between the collar of my shirt and my neck. The knot of my tie looks too big. 'They were doing it,' I repeat more quietly, reaching to the next table for another beer mat.

'Peter, are you . . . have you been . . .?'

'Taking my blood pressure pills? Yes, thank you for asking. I have.'

'You seem agitated. Was Dr Phillips happy with this latest lot when you last saw him?'

'He was.'

'It's just that when you change medications, there can be side effects. I know with my brother's blood pressure – when they tried him on a different one it triggered off all kinds of things. Itching, insomnia, all sorts . . .'

'I'm fine, Trevor. I lost my wife, that's all. She had the medical condition, not me.' The pain of Linda suddenly going is back. 'Would that it was me,' I whisper, adjusting the mat's position on the table.

Trevor places a hand across my forearm. 'Peter?'

'I'm fine.'

He doesn't answer and I look up to see him regarding the table between us. At its centre are eight beer mats. I've arranged them in as near to a diamond-shape as possible. But I need a ninth to complete the pattern. There are no more on the next table. It frustrates me, the fact my arrangement is flawed.

Resignedly, Trevor lifts his drink and slides his mat over.

'Thanks.' I fit it into place and some of the tightness in my chest recedes.

Trevor clears his throat. 'These two men who keep showing up. They're concerning you because . . .?'

'You could check with your old colleagues, couldn't you? I noted down the registration of their vehicle.'

Trevor's shoulders sag.

'And there's this,' I continue, reaching under the bench to retrieve the plastic bag.

He sends an uneasy glance toward the bar. Dave is nowhere to be seen. 'What's in there?'

'They dropped it off this afternoon – in Oxfam's clothing container. I managed to pull it back out once I'd closed up.' Using the tips of my fingers, I open out the crumpled plastic so Trevor can see in. The muscle in the corner of his right eye is going off as he leans forward slightly, arms tightly crossed. 'What is it?'

'A men's top. Not men's – more a teenager's. The label says Super Dry. You can tell it's for a youngster.' I start to take it out.

'Leave it be,' Trevor hisses. His hands are still tucked firmly under his armpits. 'Put it back on the floor, for Christ's sake.'

'What would two men like that have a teenager's item of clothing for?' I can see he won't say another word until it is safely out of sight. I slide it beneath where I'm sitting. 'Do you want their vehicle's registration?'

The fingers of his left hand emerge from beneath his right arm. A forefinger taps against his jumper. 'I'm worried you're getting fixated again, Peter. Like with your colleagues at the Shawcross site.'

I immediately shake my head. 'They're up to something. It's bloody obvious.'

'Do you feel unsettled? How often have you been washing your hands lately?'

'The hand-washing is under control. This isn't about me.'

He drops a heavy glance at the beer mats. The slight crumpling in the corner of the third one on the right mars the diamond's appearance. Knowing he's now scrutinising me, I fight the temptation to turn the mat over. But I know the underside will be nice and smooth. I know it.

'What's this registration, then?' he sighs, reaching for his jacket on the next seat.

But I produce my piece of paper quicker. 'Here, I wrote it down earlier.'

*   *   *

Five-to-seven. Intently, I watch the approach to the main
entrance. They're normally here by now. Rick is reversing the
JCB into its corner and, as the diesel engine chokes to a halt,
I hear the puffing hiss of a lorry applying its brakes. Harry,
turning into the side road that leads to the site. No Cortina is
ahead of him as the lorry comes into view and pulls up beyond
the main gate. Where's the Cortina? Where is it?

'Boss!'

I blink and look to my right. Rick is leaning out of the
JCB's cab, gesturing to the main gates.

I raise a hand in acknowledgement and extract my set of
keys from the jacket behind the cabin's door. Why didn't they
show? The local paper is open on page five. An update on the
missing teenager. A possible sighting over in Liverpool, where
his family was originally from. I can't help feeling irritated.
By breaking their routine, the two brothers have disturbed mine.

As I stride down the ramp, I hear Rick's car starting up
over in the spaces reserved for staff vehicles. With him setting
off home, my Honda is the last car left.

Once Harry's driven the lorry through, I walk round to the
public entry point. Even as I swing the barriers shut, I'm
listening for the sound of their Cortina behind me. But it
doesn't come.

Within minutes, Harry has winched the waste-to-energy
container up onto the rear of the lorry. As he drives back out
I give him a farewell nod. He doesn't turn his head. His name
was on the list I submitted to the Regional Manager.

After padlocking the main gates, I make my way back up
the ramp to the cabin at the far end of the railings. The route
takes me past the row of cages for car batteries, oil containers
and hazardous chemicals. But it's the cages that draw my eye.
The thick wire mesh and solid hinges of the doors it is now
my duty to secure. A person could never break free once shut
inside. Especially a young one. I wonder where the twins live:
how private their home might be. Did they live alone, the two
of them? At the end of an isolated lane like this one? Did it
have outbuildings or cellars where a cage like one of these
could be concealed?

I continue back to the cabin to get my jacket. The site is

now quiet, everything packed away in its place. A group of crows have alighted in the tallest tree in the copse behind the rear fence. The containers have eliminated the problem of vermin, but there's nothing that can be done about the crows that swoop down the moment the place is free of people. Every dusk they appear, creatures of habit as much as any other. As much as me.

The interior of the cabin is nice and tidy. No plastic flowers in salvaged vases. No silly toys lining the windowsill. No decorations nailed to the walls. Just my notice saying such items are not permitted. Looking over the restricted-access area one last time, I realise I've forgotten to tell Rick that his personalised number-plate cannot remain in the JCB's cab.

'So.' I place my pint in the centre of a beer mat and sit back. It's obvious Trevor has news. There's a tenseness about him. Stored information that has to come out.

The young man at the fruit machine taps futilely at the plastic buttons before turning round. 'Dave, this bloody thing's just swallowed my money.'

The landlord frowns. 'What did you put in?'

'Two quid.'

He comes out from behind the bar and also presses a couple of buttons. 'Strange, thing's completely dead.'

I make sure no amusement shows on my face.

The young customer nods. 'Refund button, included.'

Dave's crouched down and is peering round the back. 'Bloody plug's come out. Cleaners, I should think.'

Trevor narrows his eyes at me and I sip innocently at my drink.

'I had a quiet word,' he murmurs.

'And?'

He crosses his arms and raises both shoulders in a slow shrug. It's his way of saying, I'm not sure. What's the best choice of saloon car? The slow shrug. Would he recommend the hotel he and Margaret booked in Tenerife? The slow shrug. Pros and cons. Advantages and disadvantages. Good news and bad news.

'What did you find out?' I ask.

Trevor gives me an unhappy look. 'Neither of the missing two lads were wearing a maroon top from Super Dry when they disappeared. Where is the thing, anyway?'

'In my garage. Safe and sound.' The news about the top isn't causing Trevor's glum expression. 'What about where they live? Did you get an address?'

He nods.

'Well?'

'I'll tell you on one condition, OK?'

'I don't know. You'll need to tell me, first.'

Suddenly, he looks irritated. And tired. 'This isn't you playing bloody Miss Marple. If I tell you this, you agree to leave those two brothers alone . . .'

'So they are brothers?' My mind is like the fruit machine: connections lighting up. The police know about them. Why?

'Twins. Non-identical. Walter and Stanley Eggerton.'

'What have they done?'

He leans forward and lowers his voice. 'They've not done anything – which is why you must drop your . . . suspicions.'

I wait for more.

Trevor takes a good sip of his beer before continuing. 'They had an older brother called Cedric. Twenty-three years ago, he killed their parents at the farmhouse where they all lived. Up in Northumberland, it was. Walter and Stanley were eleven. Older brother was seventeen. The dad's Land Rover was found abandoned at the ferry port in Hull. A blood-stained axe was lying across the backseat. The older brother was sentenced in absentia.'

'My God.'

'Exactly. The twins moved to the place out near Glen Hill almost nine years ago. Only a few know about the family history – social services and the local police. You're not either of those.' He stares at me without blinking. 'Point taken?'

I fumble for a spare beer mat, pick it up and put it down. I want to ask where Walter and Stanley were when it happened. Did they witness the murders? How come the older brother spared them? But I know Trevor won't tell me any more, even if he knew. 'Where is this place they live?'

'It's a big cottage. Out past that mill. Very isolated.'

I look up, keeping my thoughts from my face. But Trevor

is studying his drink as he adds, 'They don't lead the kind of life you or I would class as normal.'

From the battered old Cortina and their Seventies clothes, I could tell that.

'It's just the two of them out there, for a start. And loads of dogs, apparently. They breed them in the out buildings. They also take in waifs and strays. The RSPCA have visited a few times following complaints from walkers passing near the property.'

'Cruelty?'

He gives his slow shrug. 'Not malicious. More born of ignorance. They're just not very bright, according to the person I spoke to. The place is a tip. Very badly maintained. But they do their best by the animals; they certainly don't keep them in any worse conditions than they live in themselves.'

I think about how their wellington boots are always encased in a crust of dried-out muck. Disgusting.

'Now you know. And last thing, Peter – they buy bones, offal and the like from the two butchers out in Glen Hill. For their kennels. So, the packages they drop off could well contain bones and similar. I don't know. I just didn't want you retrieving one like you did that maroon top and jumping to the wrong conclusion.'

'Bones and similar? Are the kennels out at this farm commercial?'

He cocks his head. 'I don't know. Why?'

'Because if they are, they shouldn't be dumping refuse at a facility for domestic waste. That's illegal.'

Trevor's eyes close for a long second. 'Peter, you said it's just a few shoebox-size packages. Be reasonable.'

I wanted to say that was a fine attitude to take for an ex-police officer. Instead I adjusted the positioning of the three beer mats before me. The triangle of space between them wasn't quite a perfect equilateral.

'So you'll let this go now,' Trevor states. It wasn't a question: it was an order.

I sit back. 'I have my responsibilities, Trevor. And ensuring the facility is used correctly is one of them.'

'You only know what you do because I told you. And I told

you on the condition you let it go.' Two red dots had formed
high on his cheeks. 'That information was passed to me by
an old colleague doing me a favour. You cannot act on it.'

I say nothing.

'White vans pull up outside the entrances to tips all the
time. I've seen them on a Sunday. People unloading all sorts
and carrying it up to the containers. Old sinks, broken tiles,
all sorts. You know as well as I do that's commercial waste.'

'We're in the process of clamping down on that type of
activity.'

'For Christ's sake, Peter. Leave the pair of them alone.
Promise me you will.'

'I can't do that, Trevor.'

'You'd bloody better.' He seizes his coat and stands.

Over half his drink is still on the table. 'You've not finished,'
I say, peering up at him.

He glowers down. 'Forget it. And forget next Friday, I'll
make other plans.'

'But how will you get home?' I ask as he walks away. 'I
drove you out here, remember?'

He waves goodbye to Dave and steps out of the door. I
can't understand. That's a ten-pound taxi fare, right there. And
no meeting up next Friday? That's over thirty years of tradition, that. Surely he didn't mean it.

A watched pot never boils, as they say – and Friday seemed
to take an age to arrive. When it did, the day started with
something that stopped me in my tracks. One of the lads had
left a copy of the local paper in the cabin and there it was on
page two: another young person had vanished from the council
home up near the mill. They'd included a photo of him –
fourteen years old, black hair and pimples on his forehead.
His eyes were older though. Like they'd watched things
happen. Bad things.

The rest of the day crawled by, the arrival of each car a
welcome distraction. Old mattresses, their secret stains exposed
to the day. Rolled-up carpets, broken cabinets, warped buggies
– over the railings they all went. Flocks of magazines, pages
flapping as they fell. An aquarium with a tidemark where the

level of water once stood. What had lived and died in there? It shattered outwards on hitting the bottom of the container.

The levels of rubbish would gradually rise up and every so often Rick squashed down each container's contents, the vehicle's arms whining with the effort of supporting the sheer weight of the great bucket.

Finally, five o'clock arrived and the bulk of the day shift made swiftly for their cars. Six o'clock and just the skeleton crew remained. Six thirty and they started looking hopefully to me for permission to leave a bit early. Only three cars had dropped off in the last twenty minutes. I surveyed the site. The restricted-access area had been swept. Everything was in order. The waste-to-energy container was three-quarters full, the exposed metal of its inner sides moist from where lobbed bags had burst.

All that refuse would be going nowhere tonight. Not if Tweedle-dum and Tweedle-dee arrived with their usual deposit. 'Have a good weekend, lads.'

They grunted their thanks and started filing across to their cars.

I settled onto my stool in the cabin.

Five-to-seven and the Cortina appeared. My heart gave a little jump. The lorry was twenty metres behind. The Cortina made its way up the ramp and backed in towards the railings. I watched from the corner of my eye as they climbed out. The one with the full head of hair opened the boot of the car and I could see a layer of boxes inside sitting on a sheet of plastic. Do they think I'm stupid? I make my way down to the main gates as they start dropping packages down.

'Evening, Harry,' I say through the chain-link fence. 'Pick up for the energy-to-waste container is rescheduled. Tomorrow morning, now.'

His eyebrows lift. 'Since when?'

'About one minute ago.'

His jaw was set tight as he rammed the gear into reverse. 'Could have let me know before I set off all the way out here,' he mutters, eyes fixed on the rear-view mirror as he backs away.

After closing the barriers for the car entrance, I turn on my heel and march up the ramp. Rick had just parked the JCB in its corner. He poked his head out of the cab. 'Boss?'

'You can go,' I say.

The twins were standing at the railings, looking down at me with mouths half-open. The lorry's engine roared as Harry trundled back toward the main road. 'Site's now closed,' I call out to them. 'Can you please leave the premises.'

They hesitate and I see the balder one's eyes shift to the boxes that now lay on top of the bin bags some twelve feet below. Too far for you to reach, I thought triumphantly. But not too far for me and my ladder. 'Please move your car, we're closed.'

The curly-haired one looks at his brother, then at the JCB, then at me. He was close to tears. They both were.

'On your way now,' I say, copying the tone Dave uses in the Rising Sun at closing time. The interior of the pub flashes up in my mind. Trevor has made no attempt to call me all week. And it's his turn to drive. Maybe there'd be a message waiting for me at home. Perhaps he'd just show up at the normal time like nothing had happened.

The boot of the Cortina bangs shut and, moments later, they drive slowly past, faces pale behind the windscreen. I watch the vehicle start down the exit ramp then unhitch the cat-ladder from the side of the cabin.

The crows are back, their hunched forms shifting impatiently on their perches. Rick's car starts up as I lay the aluminium ladder across the railings above the waste-to-energy container. I slide it outwards, letting the feet gradually drop closer to the bumpy surface of bags. I'd judged it just right: the ladder's hooked ends fitted over the uppermost railing, allowing me to climb across the narrow gap then down the sloping succession of rungs and into the container itself.

The smell seemed to have pooled within the sheer metal walls – a heavy cabbage-like aroma laced every now and again with the sharper notes of rotting meat. By the time I step off the final rung, the sky has been reduced to a rectangle of darkening blue above me. The boxes are to my right. Unsteadily, I make my way across the marshy surface. My foot sinks into a crevice and I have to place a hand onto a bin bag to keep my balance. On the other side of the thin plastic, something cold and lumpy shifts.

The uppermost box is now in reach and I remove the Stanley knife from my tabard. The blade slices through the wrapping of gaffer tape securing its end. I shake it gently and bones cascade out. Not chicken ones; too big. And with ragged fragments of red meat clinging to them. The ends are bloody stumps, sinew and tendons poking out like bad wiring. Cow bones? Sheep? As I open a second box and shake it, the sound of the JCB starts up. Rick. I thought he'd set off home.

A clump of debris drops out. Clots of hair. Black hair. And an ear. A human ear. Oh God. Oh dear God. I twist my torso round, flailing desperately with my arms as I begin to fall. My right hand makes contact with the edge of the ladder and I'm able to drag myself across the slippery surface, kicking and scrabbling with my feet all the while. By the time I make it onto the lowermost rungs, my front is dripping with slime and fragments of food.

Gagging, I climb up a few more rungs and the main part of the site comes into view. Oh, thank God: Rick is still here – back in the JCB. I'm about to shout when I realise he's talking to a pair of people at the locked main gate. The twins. Their Cortina is parked just outside. Their fingers are hooked in the fencing and they're nodding eagerly as Rick continues to speak down at them from the vehicle's cab. Then the curly-haired one sees me and points. Rick looks over and immediately grabs the wheel. The metal bucket raises up, several hundred kilos of cast iron. As the vehicle rapidly approaches the container I'm inside, the twins watch in dead-eyed silence.

I would shout to Rick. Call the police! Those two are murderers! Ring for help! But I know it's futile. My eyes are glued to the registration plate propped behind the windscreen. I realise the letters spell a name. CD R1C. The family resemblance is suddenly clear. The same pouting bottom lip, the over-hanging cheeks. And I cannot move. Even as he manoeuvres the bucket directly above me and reaches for the lever, I cannot move.

FLATMATE WANTED:
SMOKERS WELCOME
C.L. Taylor

C.L. Taylor lives in Bristol with her partner and young son. Born in Worcester, she studied Psychology at the University of Northumbria and works for a London university. *The Accident* (*Before I Wake* in the US) is her debut psychological thriller. She is currently writing her second novel – about friendship, mind control and murder.

I sense the atmosphere the second I walk through the front door. When you know someone as well as I know Gavin – and I know my big brother pretty damned well – you don't need to hear, or even see them to know how they're feeling. It's in the air, the electrons are whizzing around the nucleus faster than normal, or something. The house *feels* different, that's what I'm saying.

'Mark?' Rob, the newest member of the household, calls out my name. 'Come into the living room, Gavin's called a *house meeting.*'

He says the last two words like he's trying to suppress a laugh.

The electrons whizz faster. Gav's seriously pissed off.

'Alright guys?' I poke my head around the living-room door and place my tool belt on top of the sideboard. Rob's sitting in my armchair so I sit on the sofa next to Gavin instead. He stiffens as I sit down but otherwise doesn't acknowledge me. He's too busy glaring at Rob who's just swung his legs over the arm of the chair. It creaks ominously under his weight. At 6'3" tall and about eighteen stone he's the biggest flatmate we've ever had but Gavin's not intimidated by a man twice his size.

'Right,' he says, 'now Mark's back from work you can admit it.'

'Admit what?' Rob gives an exaggerated shrug, a smile playing on the corners of his lips. 'I don't even fucking *like* milk. I drink black tea, you've seen me.'

'Only because you're too tight to buy your own milk.'

'Why don't you look a bit closer to home for the milk thief.' Rob glances at me. 'Or Mr Cereal as I like to call him.'

I stifle a laugh. Mr Cereal? Rob's a dick but he's funny. I'll give him that.

'Mark?' There's no hint of amusement on Gavin's face. 'Did you finish my milk this morning and then put it back in the fridge?'

'No.' I meet his gaze. Neither of us blinks. His pupils are tiny pinpricks, barely visible in the murky brown of his irises. 'I've got my own milk.'

Gav looks back towards Rob. 'I know it was you. Admit it and this won't go any further.'

Silence descends as Gavin stares at Rob and Rob stares right back at him. No one's laughing now.

'I don't like thieves,' Gavin says evenly. 'And I won't have them in my house.'

'Ooh.' Rob purses his lips and fakes a shiver. 'I'm so scared.'

I say nothing, although I probably should.

'What's his fucking problem anyway?'

It's the next evening. Gav's out at pool and Rob and I are in the living room watching *All Star Mr and Mrs* because there's fuck-all else on TV. I just caught him watering down Gav's milk from the kitchen tap but I didn't give him shit. Instead I laughed when he said, 'Two can play at this game' and pointed to the biro scribble where Gav had marked the level of the milk on the side of the carton.

'He was starved as a kid,' I say. 'There was never any food in our house.'

'Seriously?'

'No.' I lie. I'm not about to tell him that Gav and I grew up in a grotty sink estate and that Mum didn't have two quid to rub together. It didn't help that she'd introduce us to a new 'uncle' every couple of weeks, some itinerant alcoholic drifter who'd throw her a few compliments, shag her, nick what little money she had and then disappear as quickly as he'd appeared. We were always glad to see them go, particularly the one that paid a late-night visit to our room when Mum was out shelf-stacking at Tesco.

There's always a tale to tell with the guys who rent our third bedroom – families they fell out with, girlfriend's kicking them out, flatmates who hated them (never their fault, of course). And, funnily enough, they never get any visitors. It's almost as if they don't want anyone to know where they are. None of them stick around for long but that's not a problem. As long as they stump up the £150 deposit and a week's rent, they're in.

Rob lights up a cigarette and I reach into my back pocket for my own fags. I don't know what it is about the kind of guys that respond to our 'flatmate wanted' ads but we haven't had one yet that didn't smoke.

'Can I borrow your lighter?'

He throws me his lighter and I close my fingers around it. It's a Harley Davidson one, chrome and gold-effect, with 'Born for Style, Born to Ride' etched onto the side and a big pair of wings wrapped around the side. Looks like a limited edition. Expensive too. I wonder who he nicked that off.

Gav unscrews the lid of his whiskey, pours a tiny measure into his glass and then sits back in his armchair and closes his eyes. He breathes in – deeply – then out again, then opens his eyes and raises the glass to his lips. He takes a sip, audibly sighs, then swallows.

It's Sunday night, the end of another week and he's celebrating, as he always does, with a single shot of his favourite single malt. Just one shot, never more. I swig at my bottle of Bud. Gav's never offered me a shot of his whiskey and I've never asked.

'Alright boys?' Rob swaggers into the living room, a towel around his waist, his broad chest glistening with water after his shower. He really is a huge bastard. 'Hard day mowing lawns?'

Gav raises an eyebrow at him. He takes his job as a landscape gardener seriously. He takes most things seriously, my brother.

'What're you drinking?' Rob spots the golden bottle at Gav's feet. He takes a step towards it and reaches down.

Gav grabs his wrist. 'Don't touch what you can't afford.'

Rob tenses and, for a second, I think he's going to swing at him. Instead he twists his arm out of Gav's grip and laughs. 'Depends how much it costs.'

'£200. You can't buy twenty-five-year-old Glenmorangie for a penny less.'

Rob whistles. 'Expensive taste for a man who mows lawns for a living.'

'Says the man who's never done a hard day's work.'

The room falls silent as Gav looks at Rob and Rob looks at the bottle. I break the silence by sparking up a fag.

'New lighter?' Rob clocks the white object in my hand.

'Nah, I've got a few.' I hold it up so he can read the black print on the side – *buy your own fucking lighter* – and he laughs.

'I'm getting a sandwich then I'm going out,' he says as he crosses the living room towards the kitchen.'

'Not using my cheese you're not.'

Rob turns back. 'What was that, Gav?'

'You heard.'

'I haven't touched your cheese.'

'Then why is it half the size it was on Friday?'

'Mice?' Rob laughs, but he's the only one smiling.

'I told you not to touch my stuff,' Gav says.

'I haven't touched your fucking stuff.'

'Maybe it was the cleaner,' I say, more to lighten the atmosphere than anything else.

Gav looks at me like I'm deranged.

'What?' I say. 'She's got a key. She can let herself in whenever she likes.'

'For a slice of cheese?' Gav narrows his eyes. He doesn't always appreciate my sense of humour.

I glance at Rob who's standing by the kitchen door, but he's looking at Gav's whiskey again.

*   *   *

When I get back from work at midnight on Monday, after another late night re-fitting a shop, the house is in darkness. Gav's at pool and Rob's god knows where so I unbuckle my carpenter's tool belt and reach for the light switch at the bottom of the stairs. Nothing happens. The light bulb must have blown while I was out.

I make my way up the stairs in darkness, feeling my way along the bannister, when a loud thud – swiftly followed by a low moan – makes me freeze. The noise came from further along the landing, just outside Gavin's room. I slip a chisel out of the tool belt and creep up the last few stairs. Whoever it is has chosen the wrong house to burgle.

I round the top of the stairs, keeping low. My eyes adjust to the gloom as I pass Rob's closed bedroom door and I recognise the shape of the man curled up on the floor outside Gav's room.

'Rob?'

He doesn't look up. Instead he groans and grips the end of one of his knackered trainers. 'Fucker broke my toe.'

'Who . . .?' I start to say but then I notice the hammer and dessert spoon lying on the ground beside him. The padlock on Gav's door is still intact.

'Fancy a wee dram, did you?' I say, though from the cloud of beer fumes I'm inhaling, Rob doesn't need any help getting pissed.

'Your fucking brother put a mousetrap in with his bread.' He holds up the fingers of his right hand. 'I could have lost a finger!'

You'll lose a lot more than that if you go after his whiskey, I think but don't say.

'He thinks he's clever, but he's got no idea who he's messing with. My bitch of an ex thought she had one over on me –' he reaches into his pocket and pulls out his Zippo. He flips it over then squeezes it open and lights it with a flick of his fingers – 'but she was wrong. Wish I could have seen her face when she came home to an empty flat. That grubby little brat of hers is in for a shock if he thinks Father Christmas is going to bring him anything next month.'

I force a grin but my mouth is so dry my lips are stuck to my teeth. Sometimes it's hard being the good guy.

Rob keeps his head down for the next few days. We don't get so much of a glimpse of him during the day and the only sign he comes back to sleep is the stinky pair of Nike trainers that appear outside his bedroom door. Then, when I come home from work on Wednesday I find him smashing his hand into the fridge door.

'Fucking arsehole. Mother fucking twat!'

His eyes are watering, his cheeks puce. I assume he's drunk again but then I spot the upturned Tupperware lid on the draining board and the piece of paper sellotaped to the lid – 'Gav's chilli. Touch at your peril'.

'He booby-trapped it! Flicked red hot chilli into my face. Fucking psycho!'

He yanks open the fridge door and reaches for the milk – Gav's milk – and unscrews the lid. He tips his head back and pours the cold, white liquid over his eyes and face. A split second later a piercing scream fills the kitchen and he throws himself at the sink and grabs the cold tap. He turns it on full blast then puts his head under the faucet.

'Bleach,' he gasps between breaths. 'He watered it down with bleach!'

I take a step back out of the kitchen and into the living room. I'm not retreating because I'm scared, I'm retreating because I know exactly what he'll do next.

'You don't have to do this,' I say evenly as Rob grabs my tool belt from the sideboard in the living room and speeds up the stairs, taking them two at a time. 'You've got a choice. You could still be the bigger man.'

Rob spins round and I brace myself for a smack in the face. Instead he grabs me by the T-shirt, thrusts a hand into my jeans pocket and pulls out my phone. He pockets it, smiling, 'Just to make sure you don't warn him.'

I hang back as he inserts my chisel behind the lock plate on the door frame then hits it with the hammer. He pulls at the chisel, changing the angle as he rains down blow after

blow and I wince as the wood splinters from the wall. He's
making a total pig's ear of a relatively simple job.

'I'm going to drink his fucking whiskey and then I'm
going to put the empty bottle in his bed. No,' he laughs to
himself as the padlock, hasp and staple fall to the floor and
he yanks the door open, 'I'm going to drink half then piss
in the bottle and put it back. We'll see how much he likes
surprises . . . What the fuck?'

His eyes flick from the black vinyl flooring to the grey
glossed walls to the bars on the windows to the large oak
wooden cabinet in the centre of the room. In it, glowing like
golden treasure behind a strong metal mesh, is Gavin's
whiskey.

The chisel hangs loosely in one hand, the hammer in the
other. I could overpower him now if I wanted to. He's left
my tool belt on the floor and there's a Stanley knife still in
its strap. I could drive it between his shoulder blades if I
wanted to.

Choices, choices, choices. Rob has a choice. I do too.

'Your brother's one screwed up tight-arse, neat freak,'
Rob breathes as he walks towards the cabinet, 'or maybe
he needs all these wipe clean surfaces because he's such a
massive wanker.'

He laughs at his own joke and crouches down in front of
the cabinet. He reaches out a hand to touch the mesh.

'Careful!' I say and he jumps.

'What's it going to do?' Rob says, looking over his
shoulder at me. He lifts the hammer over his head, then
looks back at the box. 'Explode?'

'Yes,' I say. 'You saw what happened with the chilli.
That's got nothing on this.'

Rob sneers but he lowers the hammer anyway. He peers
around the box and shakes his head. He's confused but he's
bought the lie. The oak chest is strong enough to withstand
a hammer but he could still put some ugly nicks in it and
I'm proud of my work.

'What kind of psycho makes an exploding box and keeps
his whiskey in it?'

'Have you got fast reactions?' I ask, crouching beside him.

He frowns. 'What's that supposed to mean?'

'See this . . .' I point at a small, letter box-shaped hollow in the wood, just below the shelf the bottle is sitting on. 'In there, and just around to the right, is a button. Press it and remove your hand in under two seconds and the mesh will open and you can take the bottle.'

'And if I take longer than two seconds?'

'A blade will slice your hand off at the wrist.'

Rob laughs, then twists to look at me. His expression changes from mirth to confusion. 'Bullshit.'

'Try it then.'

He looks back at the whiskey, then at the hollow, then back at the whiskey. The fingers of his right hand twitch.

'You do it.' He grabs my hand by the wrist. His fingers dig so deeply into my flesh that I feel sick. 'You press the button.'

'No.' I try to pull away but he's got me fast.

Rob presses his face close to mine, his breath hot and sour. 'You think you're so clever, don't you? Pretending to be all chummy chummy when really you're laughing at me behind my back with that scrote of a brother of yours.' He leans even closer. 'You made this, didn't you? And those other traps? I should just chop off your hand right now!' He shoves my hand towards the letter box and I shout out.

'Not so clever now are you, Mark?'

'My brother's the clever one. I'm just good with my hands.'

'Is that so?' He holds the chisel to my neck, digging the sharp metal edge into a tendon. 'Then press the button, Mr Good With My Hands.'

'Okay, okay.' My heart races and my stomach twists with anticipation. 'Let go of my wrist or I won't be able to fit my hand in there.'

Rob deliberates, then in one swift move, lets go of my wrist and twists round me so he's grabbing me round the neck instead. I'm forced forward onto my hands and knees, my head in the crook of his elbow.

'I can't do it like this,' I say. 'If I lift up my right hand I'll have to balance on my left.'

'Oh boo fucking hoo. DO IT!'

Rob breathes more heavily as I lift my right hand up from the floor and move my fingers towards the letter box. He inhales through his nose – short, sharp excited sniffs that remind me of another dirty, sweating bastard that put his hands on me without asking. There are some things no one should steal.

'Okay . . . okay . . .' I slip my hand into the letter box, keeping my fingers pressed tightly together, my palm sliding along the grain until the tip of my middle finger reaches the end of the alcove and stops. Now I twist my hand round and extend my middle finger towards the right. The button is indented in the wood, five millimetres further into the cabinet.

'Three . . .' I say, then take a breath. I'm nearly there, I've nearly done it. But things could still go wrong. 'Two . . .' If Rob is the man I think he is he'll do exactly what I predict. 'One!'

I press the button and wrench my hand out of the box. At exactly the same time the metal mesh drops away, freeing the twenty-five-year-old bottle of Glenmorangie from its wooden prison.

'Yes!' I'm yanked upwards by the neck as Rob punches the air then dropped to the vinyl as he reaches across me with his right hand. His fingers graze the neck of the bottle. 'Yes you beaut—'

His horrified roar fills the room.

'My hand!' he screams, holding his stump aloft as it pumps blood all over the wipe clean walls, the floor and himself.

His hand is motionless, still wrapped around the bottle of whiskey on the shelf of the oak cabinet.

'So sorry,' I say as I back towards the door. 'I forgot to tell you the second part of the instructions. You're supposed to press the button a second time before you take the whiskey or you risk being chopped by another blade. See, I'm really not very clever at all. I did warn you.'

I snatch up the chisel and hammer, dart out of the bedroom and slam the door shut behind me, then reach into my pocket for Gavin's spare key and deadlock it. The padlock is just for show, to get our 'guests' to think there's something worth stealing inside. We leave the door itself unlocked – until they're inside.

I wait outside the door until Rob stops screaming and falls silent and then set to work repairing the damage to the door frame and fit a new hasp, staple and padlock. I take my time, savouring the sound of rasping saw and the gentle chk chk of the chisel on the virgin piece of wood.

The first time I saw a man bleed to death I was ten years old. Me and Gav were in the kitchen and Mum was preparing dinner. Spag bol it was, my favourite. Mum had her back to us and I was pretty sure she was crying, and not just because she'd been chopping onions. We'd just told her about what Simon had done to us the night before, while she was shelf stacking at Tescos – me and Gav taking it in turns to speak, secretly holding hands under the table – and she hadn't said a word. She just kept chopping onions with the great big cleaver her dad, a former butcher, had given her for Christmas.

Chop-chop-chop-chop.

I nearly peed my pants when I heard the key go in the front door. A second later Simon was in the kitchen, all leery drunken smile and great broad shoulders filling the door frame.

'Alright darlin'.' He breathed, then nodded at us. 'Boys.'

Mum didn't turn round and she didn't say anything. She just carried on cutting up onions.

Chop-chop-chop-chop.

'What's that, then?' Si crossed the room in one great stride and gestured towards the chopping board. 'Give us some, I'm starving.'

One second his hand was outstretched, the next it was on the floor.

Mum got eight years inside for manslaughter and we spent the rest of our childhood in a children's home. We

had a lot of time to talk about what we'd do when we got
out. A *lot* of time.

'I got your text.' Gavin strolls into the living room, two
white 2.5 litre plastic cans of muriatic acid in each hand.
He looks at me and grins. 'Good day at work?'

'Yeah.' I lean back in my armchair and put a cigarette
between my lips. 'Most satisfying.'

He sets the cans down in the middle of the living room then
sits down on the sofa. 'There's some more in the van.'

'Burn out a few tree stumps today, did you?'

'Not as many as I thought. Hence the surplus.' He raises
an eyebrow. 'We couldn't have it going to waste could we?
Not when it's so good at dissolving troublesome crap.'

'Nope.' I flip open my lighter and click it alight. 'Want
me to take it up to the bathroom ready for the cleaner?'

'In a bit, I think she's—'

Gav's interrupted by the living-room door swinging open.
A small, blonde-haired woman steps into the room carrying
two buckets loaded with cleaning equipment. She places
them on the floor in the centre of the room, next to the cans
of acid and surveys the two of us, shaking her head.

'The cleaner, indeed,' she tuts. 'Have some respect. I
thought I brought you two up better than that!'

Gav and I share a look. 'Sorry, Mum,' we chorus.

'Well?' She holds out a hand. 'Money first, cleaning
afterwards.'

Gav reaches into his back pocket and pulls out a roll of
notes. 'A hundred and fifty quid,' he says as he hands it to
her, 'same as normal.'

Mum pockets the cash and shakes her head. 'We need to
put the deposit up. You've had some right dirty bastards to stay
recently. In the bath, is he?'

I nod. 'Want me to help you carry the stuff upstairs?'

'Nah,' she flops onto the sofa next to Gavin and reaches
for his cigarettes, 'finish your fag first. Lighter?'

I throw my lighter over. My brother snatches it from the
air and turns it over in his hands. 'New?'

'Nah,' I watch as he runs his thumb over the chrome

and gold-effect and the 'Born for Style, Born to Ride'
etching on the front. 'It's one of my collection. I've got
loads.'

'Then how about you give one to me, you tight bastard?'

'We don't share. Remember?' I say and we both laugh.

DIRECTOR'S CUT
Aline Templeton

Aline Templeton grew up in the fishing village of Anstruther, on the east coast of Scotland. The memories of beautiful scenery and a close community inspired her to set the Marjory Fleming series in a place very like that – rural Galloway, in the south-west of Scotland. She read English at Cambridge and now lives in Edinburgh.

I saw a ghost today. A ghost in broad daylight on Oxford Street, in the middle of the Saturday crowds. I stepped into his path.

'David!' I cried. 'But you're dead.'

His eyes met mine – those cool eyes, grey-green like the sea, the eyes I remembered so well that even in my dreams I always saw their curious flecks of brown and gold around the iris.

He smiled his mocking smile. 'I know,' he said, then turned away, swallowed up in a moment by the crowd.

I wanted to run after him, take hold of his arm to spin him round and make him face the lies and deceit.

Yet I couldn't move, afraid perhaps that if I caught up with him, if I touched him, my fingers would go straight through the soft tweed of his jacket, straight through flesh and bone to grasp at nothingness.

Because as long as I didn't, I could still tell myself that he was alive and that after all I hadn't killed him, that somewhere all that warmth and charm still existed.

I was only in London at all that day because of a family wedding. I got on to the train back to Edinburgh at King's Cross still shaking, with hours ahead of me to try to make sense of what made no sense at all.

David – had there been a day in the past five years when I hadn't thought of him, five years of guilt? And grief – oh yes, grief too.

As the train picked up speed through the London sprawl I stared out of the window, unseeing, as the life we had known together unfolded in my memory in a series of scenes like a film – a film that began as a romcom and finished as a revenge tragedy.

He came into my life on a spring wind, a wicked little wind that whipped down a corner and snatched my scarf – Ralph Lauren, silk – from round my neck and flew it like a banner down the Royal Mile. With a cry of dismay I ran after it, making futile jumps as the wind played mocking games with me.

A man stepped into my path so that I cannoned into him, a big, solid man. It hurt, but I was angry more than winded.

'What the—' I began, then noticed he was holding my scarf and finished weakly, 'Oh. Sorry.'

He was laughing at my discomfort. 'A simple thank you will suffice,' he said, then as I put out my hand for it he twitched it out of my reach and held it overhead.

'"Here is a thing and a very pretty thing. What must the owner of this thing do?" Did you ever play forfeits?'

I had, as a child, and remembered the silly chant all too well but there are few more irritating things than being put in the wrong and then teased. Ignoring the question, I said stiffly, 'Thank you for catching my scarf. Now, may I have it, please?'

'No, no,' he said with elaborate patience. 'That's not how it works. I'll explain. I have something you want and you have to pay to get it back. I'm just deciding what my price would be.'

He was smiling down at me, his grey-green eyes alive with mischief. He was flirting with me and – well, he was seriously buff.

I said, 'All right – what's it to be? Say a tongue-twister, hop on one leg till you tell me to stop?' As if I didn't know.

Even so, the speed of his response took me by surprise. He cupped my face in his hands and kissed me.

The thing was, it wasn't like kissing a stranger. It felt as if

I'd been kissing him all my life, just not recently, and I'd been missing it.

As he straightened up to an ironic cheer from a passing hoodie, he said, 'Wow! Do you always kiss people like that when you've only just met?'

I blushed. 'Well, not the women,' was the best I could manage by way of reply but he laughed anyway. That was one of the attractive things about David – he was always ready to be amused.

He folded the scarf neatly and handed it to me. 'You've definitely earned your scarf. And an introduction. I'm David Lanson.'

'Jennifer Sandeman.'

He studied my face, eyebrows raised, then shook his head decisively. 'Not Jennifer. Too stiff.'

'I'm Jennie usually. Or Jen.'

'Still a bit prim. Jeff, that's better. I shall call you Jeff.'

Straight out of a movie, right? All the way down to the cute nickname. As Renée Zellweger would put it, he had me at 'hello'. He moved in a fortnight later.

He liked my flat. What wasn't to like about the first floor in Drummond Place with its high-ceilinged Georgian rooms and superb view out to Fife across the Firth of Forth? My parents were dead and I'd been able to buy it outright when I sold the family home in Merchiston, just round the corner from J.K. Rowling and Alexander McCall Smith.

David was renting 'somewhere on the south side' he said, just somewhere temporary. He'd very recently been seconded to Edinburgh from London, working for Standard Life. He told me that with a rueful face and I winced: with the financial crisis, there were rumours about jobs vanishing like snow in sunshine.

It didn't depress us, though. It was a time of enchantment when Edinburgh, the old grey city I'd known all my life, suddenly became a place of stunning beauty – the famous skyline, the romantic cobbled closes, the elegant Georgian squares – suffused with a secret glow invisible to mere mortals who weren't crazily, passionately in love.

We walked the Pentlands, we sailed the little boat I kept

down at Granton on the Firth of Forth. All my friends liked him. 'He's not Mr Right, he's Mr *Perfect*,' one of them said with more than a hint of envy. Oh, and the sun was always shining too.

And despite all that happened afterwards, that's what still seems like the real relationship to me.

What happened afterwards . . .

The northern train was travelling through lush green fields, but I was seeing a different sort of film now, the kind where dark clouds appear in the sky along with threatening mood music.

One night, about a month after he moved in, I got back from work to find him sitting with his head in his hands. I knew at once. 'Oh no!'

His face was ravaged by distress. 'Oh yes,' he said bitterly. 'The next round of cuts. I've lost my job. And now they're even making difficulties about redundancy because I was seconded. They haven't even paid my resettlement allowance – I'm broke.'

His job – that was the one I found out later wasn't so much a figment of his imagination as a plot device, part of the script he had written for me to follow. And I did, as if he'd handed me the lines to say.

'Darling, it doesn't matter! You'll get another job, I know you will, and anyway they pay me a ridiculous amount. It'll give you time to look around, find exactly what you want.'

'No,' he said. 'You're an angel, Jeff, but I can't be the sort of man who takes hand-outs from his partner. Can you imagine? "Can you give me a fiver?" It would be utter humiliation.'

I am an intelligent woman, an accountant. I told him that I would put my bank account in our joint names. I know these statements are mutually contradictory.

But for a bit longer, I didn't hear the eerie shiver of violins in the background. We worked on his CV and he seemed to be as tired as I was at the end of the day from job-hunting. We celebrated when he said he'd got an interview, drowned our sorrows when, yet again, he said he'd failed. I'd offered to see what strings I could pull for him but when I saw his brow darken I realised that this, too, would be an insult to his pride.

'I have to stand on my own feet, be my own man – don't you understand that? It's hard enough already . . .'

He bit his lip and turned away. I apologised, of course, smoothed his ruffled feathers. But I talked to a few useful people anyway and pressed his CV on them, reckoning he'd be so pleased if it came to a job that he'd forgive me.

What was it that first triggered suspicion? I realised his enthusiasm for job-hunting was waning, that he wanted to talk about it less and less, then I came back one day for some papers I'd forgotten and found him lying on the couch watching porn. We were both embarrassed; he was angry. Spying on him, he called it.

Crying, I protested my innocence as if I'd been at fault, and I rationalised it afterwards: it was just an unfortunate fact that men watched porn and as for just dossing about at home, I knew from talking to friends with partners in the same position, and from many magazine articles, that men who lost their jobs got depressed and gave up. So we never mentioned it again and I went out of my way to be particularly sympathetic and understanding.

But after that, I started subconsciously noticing things, things that would come back to me later when the truth started to emerge – like the way the elderly woman who lived in the ground-floor flat behaved towards me. We'd always been friendly in a casual sort of way, stopping for a brief chat when we met in the hallway, doing the odd neighbourly favour for one another.

On a couple of occasions, she'd dived into her flat when I appeared, once when it looked as if she'd been intending to leave it. On the occasion when we met face-to-face she responded only politely, looking embarrassed. I couldn't think of anything I'd done that would have upset her and when I asked David if he knew of anything he looked blank. Very blank.

Then there were the contacts I'd used to ask about a job for David. Nothing came of it; I told myself that it was just the financial climate but hoped that perhaps I might meet one of them at some meeting or other and be able to ask about it casually, without it feeling like pressure. But the time I saw one of them, he was at the other side of the room and by the time I got across to him he'd vanished.

The relationship wasn't quite as idyllic as it had been either. When we were out with friends he was still the David I'd fallen in love with, charming and fun; at home, though we didn't exactly quarrel, I began to have the uncomfortable feeling that the only reason we didn't was because he was keeping his irritation under strict control. I noticed for the first time that he had thin lips and when he folded them into a rigid line, they would disappear completely and his eyes would go cold as steel.

I told myself to grow up, join the real world. The first heady stage of being in love was like drinking champagne and eating caviar – wonderful at the time but sooner or later you had to build a relationship on something closer to a cup of tea and a piece of toast. It took time to adjust for both of you, that was all. And it didn't help that there was still no sign of David finding a job.

So when, at a seminar on tax legislation, I saw Henry Jamieson, one of the people I'd sent David's CV to, I made a beeline for him. He was a friend, not merely a contact, and he owed me a favour anyway from way back so I did wonder why he hadn't so much as called in David for interview, just from social obligation. There was nothing wrong with his CV – he had good qualifications and good experience too.

'Henry!' I hailed him. 'Haven't seen you for ages. How are things?'

He shied like a startled horse. 'Oh – Jennie. Good to see you. How's business?'

'Fine, fine. Look, I just wanted to ask you, did you take a look at David's CV? I know times are tough, but just an interview . . .'

He didn't meet my eyes. 'Well, you know how it is,' he flannelled. 'There wasn't anything going and I didn't want to, well, you know, raise his hopes.'

I felt suddenly cold. 'You're lying, Henry. What is it?'

'No, nothing,' he protested weakly.

I took him by the arm and drew him aside. 'There's something you're not telling me and I'm getting a sort of sick feeling that it's something important. You're my friend, Henry. Tell me.'

He broke into a light sweat but he told me at last. David's CV was bogus throughout, an elaborate fiction that didn't check out at any point. No wonder he hadn't wanted me to pull strings – and I had handed it out to half-a-dozen people who were now either hugely embarrassed or laughing at me. It was probably all round Edinburgh by now.

The film goes blank at this stage. I don't know how I got back home, but when I arrived I rang the doorbell of the flat below.

The owner looked embarrassed when she saw me and it took a few minutes to persuade her to tell me what had been going on. Women going up to the flat, most days. Different women, and a lot of noise.

Somehow I thanked her and got myself up the stairs. I had no idea what I was going to say to David.

He wasn't there – and then I remembered that we were sailing that evening down at Granton, and joining some friends in the local for drinks first. We'd agreed to meet there.

There was something I had to do first, though. I logged on to my bank account.

I had always, I'm afraid, been careless about my own money. I'd never known what it was to be short and money on a small scale bored me so I was delighted when David took that over, making sure the bills were paid and that the balance in the current account was transferred to the deposit if it became too high. There was a lot in there too, since with the state of the markets I'd pulled out of investments.

There *had been* a lot in there. It had been removed cautiously, a bit at a time, nothing to arouse suspicion, and now most of it had gone. When I checked, the credit cards were maxed out as well.

He'd directed every move I had made since the day we met, and this was the nude scene – where I had been presented naked to the world's pity and scorn and stripped of my self-respect.

I felt physically sick, then pure rage took over. I had no legal comeback, of course. I'd handed the keys of the safe to a conman and I couldn't complain that he'd helped himself.

Once he'd cleaned out the lot, was he just planning to disappear? I wasn't going to let that happen. He was going to pay for it and for once it was me in the director's chair. As I drove down to Granton, I didn't know quite what I was going to do, but I was icily determined that he wasn't going to get away with it.

David was in the pub already, propping up the bar with some of his mates – my mates, really; he'd taken over my friends as well as my bank balance. He greeted me with a kiss and put his arm round my shoulders.

I couldn't help but stiffen. He looked down at me quizzically. 'Something the matter?'

'We'll talk later,' I said and pulled away, then struck up a conversation with someone else about the state of the tide, aware that he was watching me. It seemed a long time, though, before we all trooped down to the boats, laughing and talking.

'Are you going to tell me now?' he said lightly as we sailed out of the harbour into the firth. 'Sounded important.'

I glanced at him. He was smiling but it was a smile that didn't reach the eyes – cold eyes. 'Hang on a moment,' I said. 'Wait till we get settled.'

It was a beautiful evening with just the best sort of light wind. As we tacked along towards the two great bridges I took a deep breath.

'I know what you are, David, and I know what you've been doing. You may think you're going to get away with it but you're not. I'm going to come after you.'

It was almost as if he'd been expecting it. I thought he'd bluster, but he didn't. He didn't even try to deny it. He stood up in the boat so that he towered over me, and then he laughed. 'And what do you think you can do, you pathetic fool? The police won't touch it and if you try anything you'll be a laughing-stock.'

The David I knew had vanished and in his place was this evil, cruel man. He was going on, 'Anyway, I reckon it's my wages for putting up with six months of utter tedium with you.'

I lashed out, lashed out in humiliation and fury, with murder in my heart. It wasn't a hard enough blow to do him much damage but at that moment the boat must have pitched a little and then he was in the water.

He scorned life-jackets, mocking those who wore them as landlubbers and wimps, and the water closed over his head. He went under, and he didn't reappear. Alerted by my screams, other boats were around us in minutes but he had gone.

The rest is a blur. I know the search went on for hours – the coastguard, a helicopter, then divers, but they never found him.

I gave carefully doctored evidence at the fatal accident enquiry, bravely biting back my tears. He must have hit his head as he fell, they decided, and it was declared an unfortunate accident and a warning about the dangers of not wearing a life-jacket.

It was an accident, I suppose, in that it must have been a movement of the boat that pitched him into the water; he was a big man and the blow I struck wouldn't have been hard enough to knock him in otherwise. But make no mistake, I had wanted to kill him when I did it. Even afterwards I didn't regret it, though in some twisted way I still loved him. There was guilt, though, that it was my own gullible folly that had caused his death.

And there was certainly grief. The glow of our halcyon days together never quite left me and I feel it even now. But I was free at last, directing my life, no longer just an actor under someone else's control. The revenge tragedy was my own script.

The train was slowing down as it reached the suburbs of Edinburgh. Rain was streaming down the windows, the light was fading and with the gathering darkness came dark thoughts.

What if the director's cut had been not mine, but his? What if David had seen what was coming and prepared himself for it, taunting me precisely so that I would lash out, giving him an excuse to go overboard, to vanish in the most final possible way? He was a powerful swimmer and we weren't that far from the shore.

I had never managed to track down the money either. Languishing useless in some off-shore bank, I had concluded with frustration, but perhaps it had been a nice little nest-egg to fund his lifestyle until he could find another stupid woman to prey on.

Perhaps I'd been only an actor under his direction right up to the end – and beyond. He was still doing it, wasn't he? Haunted by the memory of that original, perfect relationship I'd never found anyone since who measured up. Heartbroken heroine – his new script?

As I gathered up my bags and found a taxi to take me back to my flat in Drummond Place with the beautiful, silent rooms and my comfortable, arid existence, I tried to argue myself out of depression. Perhaps the man in Oxford Street had been a ghost after all, or even just a polite stranger prepared to humour a madwoman.

And yet, and yet . . .

LIKE FATHER, LIKE SON
Ricki Thomas

Ricki Thomas has had five books published and her sixth, *Rings of Death*, is due out this spring. She also has numerous articles, short stories and biographies in magazines and anthologies worldwide. She has lived in many countries throughout the world, and is now enjoying a peaceful life in Yorkshire. Ricki is happily single and has four children.

U ntil yesterday, I hadn't known I had a son, just like I hadn't known I had a father before the age of twelve, when he'd finally found me, having searched for years after my mother had left him. He'd taken me under his wing and I'd felt like I belonged there, but one day I was whisked to a foster home, where they told me that he'd died. I was in my early twenties when I discovered he'd actually been sent to prison for killing my mother; as far as I was concerned it wasn't murder, she'd deserved her comeuppance for having separated the two of us for all those years.

However, having my own boy here with me makes up for any loss or trauma I've ever suffered. Now I can show him the things my father taught me in the brief few days I spent with him before the police – sticking their noses in where they weren't wanted – destroyed my childhood forever.

Gazing at my gorgeous son, I called Nathan over and told him we were going to make a guy to take out to the fireworks display and he giggled, admitting that it would be the first time he'd have made one, despite reaching the grand old age of eight. When my father had showed me how to put one together, he'd involved me in every step, but I thought Nathan was a little young for that, so I'd pre-prepared the body, using my old clothes to cover the limbs and torso, and a Hessian sack as a foundation for the face.

One thing that Dad had insisted was important was having six bottle tops, and he'd forced me to drink one of the beers whilst he'd had the other five. He'd repeated that it was important to steel yourself, to numb any sense of conscience and let the creativity flow. I hadn't understood at the time; it had been tortuous downing the amber liquid – the taste so bitter it had made my mouth twist, the volume so vast it'd made my belly bloat – but now I can appreciate the necessity of not being sober. However, I still thought Nathan needed to be older for alcohol, which is why I'd done the hardest bits without him.

I needed the beer, though.

'You see what I've done, son?' I pointed to the body on the floor of my garage, puffy with the stuffing I'd added under the clothing, the beige sacked head a blank canvas. 'First of all we need to get it into the wheelbarrow, so you take the feet – be careful not to dislodge the shoes – and I'll take the head end because it's heavier.'

With a few grunts and groans, we hoisted the guy from the floor and into place; the arms and lower legs flopped over the sides, and the head fell back. It looked ridiculous, so droopy and lifeless, but we'd soon sort that. I took a cardboard box, dismantled it, and folded it in half to make a stiff base to support the upper half of the body. When I'd neatened the limbs Nathan smiled, and we stepped back to admire our handiwork.

'Now we create the face. One day, when you're older, I'll let you drink one of the beers, in fact, I'll let you help me do the body, but this year –' I passed some bottle tops to him, folding them into his sweet, chubby hand with fatherly love – 'you just make the face. When I've opened the last bottle, you'll have six lids; two for the eyes, one for the nose, and three to make a smiley mouth.'

I forced the lid from the bottle and he caught it as it fell, instantly racing to the dummy to finish it off, but I grasped his shoulder to hold him back. 'Son, you have to be patient. If you want to make the best guy you can, it's important to take your time and attend to detail. First of all, the beer must be finished before we start; my dad said that was essential.' I raised the bottle to my lips and sank the drink that I'd once sworn never to taste again.

Refreshed, I placed the bottle neatly on the shelf to join the other empties, and the light-headedness, the warmth that cascaded through my body, was comforting. 'Is it a he, or a she?'

Nathan drummed his fingers on his lips and it reminded me of his mother. We'd been so in love, Debs and me, but she'd left me all the same, saying she couldn't stand my jealousy any more, and the bitch hadn't considered it important to tell me she was pregnant with my child. When I'd tried to change her mind over the following weeks, she'd moved, with her parents, away from our village, and actually had the audacity to report me to the police for harassment; her spite was pathetic.

Furious, I'd taken every photo of her that I owned and pinned them to a noticeboard as a reminder never to forget. Love letters and poems she'd sent me, little notes she'd left around my bedsit for me to find; they all went into a scrapbook, which had pride of place on the table beneath the pictures. I'd known that one day I'd find her and make her come back to me, it was just a matter of time.

For years I'd keenly searched on the internet for a mention of her name – or her family – and studied the electoral rolls, first nearby, and eventually spreading across the country. It had been a wilderness; it seemed as if they'd disappeared from the face of the planet. But a Facebook account, created by her careless sister, finally rewarded my patience.

Now, I'd already lost Debs once and had no intention of her escaping again, so I'd had to play the game perfectly to avoid her doing anything rash. I'd booked a night in a cheap hotel in the town she'd moved to, and it had been easy to find her sister from her latest status update. I'd gone to the bar she'd mentioned she was meeting her friends in, knowing that, after nearly nine years, Carol would be unlikely to recognise me; I was older, scruffier, and a fair bit chunkier, a result of the heavy drinking sessions that soaked up the tedium, loneliness, and burning anger.

Not wanting to give the game away, I'd driven a discreet distance from the taxi that took her home. I'd parked on the roadside and watched her go inside, and pulled a can from a six-pack, preparing for a long night; after all, I didn't know if Debs still lived with her parents; she could have left home by now. Eventually the alcohol had lulled me to sleep and dawn was breaking when I'd next opened my eyes, momentarily confused by my whereabouts. I'd stepped outside, stretching my aching back after the uncomfortable night cramped in the passenger seat, and clambered back into the camouflage of the car to continue the vigil.

It hadn't taken long in the end; I'd recognised Debs instantly as she came through the door, keys in hand. She'd barely changed over the years – the brunette hair was still long and wavy, her face as pretty as ever – and I'd felt my heart leap disturbingly in my chest. But then the last thing I'd have ever expected happened; a cute boy in school uniform – the image of me at the same age – came trotting through the doorway, and she'd beamed at him with adoration, before taking his hand and leading him onto the street.

At that stage I hadn't known for certain that Nathan was mine, but my suspicions ran deep, and I'd felt a surge of rage towards the callous, thieving bitch; how dare she bear my child and keep him for herself. The temptation to grab them there and then – confront her and take back my own flesh and blood – was incredible, but common sense took over; I didn't want to frighten the boy. Instead, I turned on the engine and shadowed them on the short walk to the primary school; now I knew where to collect him from after I'd dealt with his mother.

'Dad, have you finished the beer yet?'

Startled, I was back in the present, and I apologised. 'I was in a dream world!' He chuckled at the daft grin I gave for his benefit, and I laughed back as I sank to my knees beside him, ready for the next part of his lesson. 'Have you decided whether to make a boy or a girl?'

'A girl, because I want to do lots of hair.'

'Okay. So, you have six bottle tops in your hand and you need to make the face. How do you think we should attach them?'

'Glue, Daddy?'

'That's always an option, but I have a different way, one that will make sure the tops don't get knocked off when you take the guy out on the streets.' His inquisitive expression made me want to hug him close, but cuddles would have to wait. I took a nail and a hammer from the side. 'Put one of the lids here –' I indicated a short length of wood – 'and I'll get a hole started, then you can bang it into place on the head.'

I prepared all six lids, ensuring the holes were loose enough for the nails to move freely, and passed one to him, along with the hammer, before supporting the dummy from behind. He held it where he felt the nose should be and drove the nail in with a hefty swipe. 'Very good, you've got it right in the centre. Do you think you can do the eyes now?'

Again, his placement was perfect, and the two bottle tops that doubled as eyes brought the face to life. All he needed to do now was add a three-lid smile and attach a few tied clumps of brown wool to the head to make the hair, and we'd be ready to go. Fifteen minutes later our guy was finished, and it reminded me so much of the only chance I'd had to do the same with my own dad, although, naturally, I thought Nathan's effort was better than mine had been.

'What are you calling her? Do you have a name in mind?'

'She's called Carol, like Aunty Carol.'

Money had been tight lately, what with not having a job, so I checked the change in my trousers before we left to ensure there was enough to buy Nathan a hot dog and a drink while we were out and, with my son in front of me, his hands underneath mine on the rubber handles, we wheeled our guy into the street, closing the garage door behind us. Strolling through the small village, we soon reached the playing field where the firework display was being held. We'd attracted several compliments for our creativity, my boy and me, mainly about how realistic and well proportioned it was. Nathan was glowing with pride, and so was I.

The evening passed quickly, yet beautifully – the rockets and sparklers banging and crashing, showering the sky with glittering droplets of colour – and I was sure my son was as happy as he'd ever been; a boy needs to be with his father, Debs should have known that. I took his hand protectively in mine, knowing it was time for us to leave for our new lives; we had a long journey ahead. Trying to lead him away, he objected, struggling. 'What's up?'

'We can't leave Carol here.'

'Of course we can, we'll make another one next year.' I smiled brightly and his confidence in me was reassured. He took a final glance at our guy and we trotted home, carried our suitcases to the car and, once I started driving, Nathan was soon asleep in the seat, wrapped in a warm blanket against the wintry chill.

As I drove onto the M1 – and freedom – I thought back to Debs, to our bitter argument when I'd dragged her into my car the previous day after she'd dropped Nathan at school. She'd had fear in her eyes – written across her face – and her body had shaken uncontrollably. She'd begged me to let her go, but I was angry – I still am – that she'd concealed my son from me as if I were nobody.

'You were dangerous,' she'd cried, 'you kept threatening to kill me, and I knew that one day you would.' Her prediction was spot on; alive, she'd always be able to leave me, but dead . . .

Years of bitterness from her abandonment, and the final shock that she'd hidden my son's existence from me, made the job easy. I'd stabbed her, and although I'd felt the life ebb from her body, I did it again, and again, and again – forcing the sharp knife repeatedly through her belly, her chest, wherever it fell. She deserved every blow for what she'd done to me and my boy.

I'd bundled her body into the boot of the car and collected Nathan from school later that day; he'd been unsure at first, but when I'd told him I was his dad he'd come to the hotel with me easily. I'd prepared the body in the darkness of the car park – crudely sewing clothes together to avoid showing the skin underneath – after Nathan had fallen asleep, and the next morning we'd driven back to my village.

I don't have any regrets; a woman should never come between a man and his son, like my mother did to my father and me. It was befitting that Debs should come to the same fate for the same crime, although Nathan doesn't yet realise that it was his mother's face that he'd driven nails into so industriously, just as I had done to my own mother all those years ago. Maybe I'll tell him one day, maybe I won't, but so far he's not asked about Debs. He's quite content with me.

I glance in the mirror at his adorable face – a younger me – and I know the police won't destroy his childhood like they did to mine; my father was stupid enough to get caught, but I'm not. I switch on the radio.

'A body has been found . . .'

GIVING SOMETHING BACK
L.C. Tyler

L.C. Tyler was born in Essex and worked overseas for the British Council before becoming Chief Executive of the Royal College of Paediatrics and Child Health and later a full-time writer. His comic crime series featuring author and agent duo Ethelred Tressider and Elsie Thirkettle has been twice nominated for Edgar Allan Poe awards in the US and won the Goldsboro Last Laugh Award with *Herring in the Library*. His new historical crime series (beginning with *A Cruel Necessity*) features 17th-century lawyer, John Grey. He is Vice Chair of the CWA.

M ichael swallowed hard and tried to look as though having a gun pointed at his chest was no big deal. Which, hopefully, it wouldn't be. These things happened all the time, didn't they? Every day of the week. At his age, it was surprising it had never happened to him before.

The estate was full of guns – Glocks, Baikals, Webleys, Uzis. Yes, really, Uzis. Go and ask the Albanian kids if you don't believe it. Everybody had them. Only the other day, the police had found one in a baby's cot, and had listened unblinking to the father's theory about how the baby had smuggled it into the house.

So the Webley (by the look of it) that was being aimed at him now was pretty much routine. Standard kit. The only thing that was odd in any of this was that the trembling hand holding the gun belonged to his best friend. That was different at least.

'Calum . . . are you crazy or something?'

His best friend considered this carefully, then shook his head in an exaggerated side to side movement that he must be copying from some cop show on TV. 'You disrespected my sister. You shouldn't have said what you said.'

'You call her stuff like that all the time,' Michael pointed out. 'You say she's a slut and a whore and all sorts.'

'I'm allowed to. She's my sister.'

That seemed reasonable.

'OK, sorry then.' Michael half held out his hand, waiting for a matching gesture from his friend. It didn't happen. The gun was somehow in the way.

'That's not good enough. You shouldn't have said it. End of.'

'I'm *very* sorry.' Michael hoped the words sounded more sincere to Calum than they sounded to himself. After all, everybody knew about Calum's sister. 'Slut' was almost a compliment.

Calum again shook his head. Maybe he really was the only one on the estate who genuinely had no idea what she got up to.

There was a strange lull in the conversation, as if Michael had stupidly forgotten his lines and Calum was patiently waiting for him to remember. But no magic words came to Michael that might help him make any sense of what was happening. So, having nothing better to do, he let his gaze travel upwards, away from the gun, skimming the blank concrete wall behind Calum. At the very top of the wall, way above them, he could see pure blue sky. There was always more concrete than sky round here. It was as though, when they designed the crummy estate, somebody had thought: why not put in lots of obscure corners where people can do all sorts of bad stuff without being seen? When he was a little kid he'd rather liked these blind spots, always in the shadows even at midday and well out of the way of adult eyes. Not any more. Not for a long time. The sky, of course, was the same sky that hung above the Georgian terraces over by the Fields, but they seemed to have more of it there. Money could buy you anything. Why not? Go to university. Get a good job. One day he'd have the dosh to buy all the sky he could use.

Michael sighed and dropped his gaze to meet Calum's eyes. 'OK,' he said. 'Just tell me what you want me to do. Then we can both go home.'

'There's nothing you *can* do,' said Calum. 'You can't take the words back. Dead man walking, that's what you are.'

It was odd, Michael thought. Here was Calum, about to shoot him through the head, and his friend looked strangely unworried – strangely, because normally Calum worried about pretty much everything. Being late for school. Being early for school. Kids from other estates. Staffordshire terriers off their leads. Girls who weren't his sister. Social workers. And guns, naturally.

'*What?*' asked Calum. 'Why are you laughing like that?'

'It's not real, is it?' said Michael.

'What's not real?'

They both looked at the heavy gun in Calum's hands. He could scarcely manage its weight, holding it out at arm's length. But it had to be a fake.

'I'm sorry about your sister,' said Michael. 'I didn't mean it. I'm going now. I'll see you tomorrow, maybe.'

'You can't just walk away from this,' Calum insisted. He glanced over his shoulder, as if expecting to see somebody in the shadows, hanging out by the rubbish bins.

'See you, Calum,' said Michael. 'Regards to your mum . . . and your sis.'

Michael sidestepped and Calum sidestepped with him. He placed an open palm firmly against Michael's chest, holding him at arm's length. He could do that, because Michael was just a bit shorter than he was.

'This *is* a real gun,' said Calum. His words spilt out clumsily into the clammy afternoon, as if his tongue had suddenly grown too large for his mouth.

'Yeah sure,' said Michael. 'Like you've got the money to buy a tool.'

'Bennie gave it to me,' said Calum.

'*Bennie?*'

'You don't believe Bennie would give me a gun?'

'I don't believe you would go anywhere near Bennie. He's an arsehole.'

'He's my friend.'

From a long way off, Michael heard a dog yap, then nothing except the distant drone of traffic on the main road. He licked his lip, tasting the salt of his own sweat. How much would it hurt, being shot in the head? And for how long?

'Bennie doesn't *have* any friends,' said Michael, explaining something very simple, very slowly. 'He's crazy. Somebody told me once: he killed a kid. A long time ago.'

'If Bennie killed a kid, why isn't he in prison?'

'He killed him without going near him.'

'Yeah, right. What's that supposed to mean?'

Michael realised he didn't know what it was supposed to mean. It was something he'd overheard – just whispered. Bennie had killed a kid without going anywhere near him. He tried to imagine how you would do that. A rifle with sights on it, maybe, with Bennie up on a roof and the kid walking across the yard below. A really, really accurate rifle with the best and most expensive sights you could buy. And a silencer. *Pfft* and the kid is stretched out on the concrete. But that didn't seem to be the sort of thing they were talking about. Bennie's method, whatever it was, had been strange, underhand, unnatural. And for some reason, nobody was allowed to talk about it. Not ever.

Maybe it was true, maybe not. Either way, it wasn't something you'd care to ask the man himself. Bennie limped around the estate in his dirty peaked cap and tracksuit top, smiling at everyone. Sometimes, if they didn't know him, people half-smiled back. The worst thing about Bennie was that he didn't look evil. Just thin and a bit grubby, with a smooth face and wispy blond hair. That was what gave you the creeps. It was like the bit in a film where you suddenly catch sight of the ghost of a small child, and it's even more frightening because a little girl with blonde ringlets shouldn't be frightening at all. Then you notice the wisp of shroud still clinging to her hair. And the green teeth. You want to yell at the screen that everybody should run away as fast as they can. That was what it was like with Bennie. But Calum hadn't run. He'd walked up to the smiling ghoul and accepted the gun.

'It's just what they say,' said Michael. 'Bennie killed a kid without going near him. But nobody's allowed to say he did it.'

Calum shook his head. 'Bennie says nobody likes him on the estate.'

'Well, they don't, do they?'

'Bennie says they're too stupid to like him.'

'Why does Bennie live here if he's so smart?'

'Why shouldn't he? What's wrong with living here?'

Michael thought again of the stuccoed porches that lined the Fields. They said houses like that cost millions. One day, he'd buy one of those. You just had to work hard enough, earn a million pounds and then go and buy it. Easy.

'Bennie's a dickhead,' he observed.

'Don't say that about my friend.'

'You're going to shoot me for that too?'

'He's my friend.'

'You can't be friends with him and me. If he's your friend, you can't be mine too.'

Calum looked from the gun to Michael and then back again to the gun. That was Calum's problem, thought Michael. It took him a while to work things out. Not a moron like some people said, but not exactly a genius either. In his fantasy about buying a Georgian house, he'd seen Calum coming to live with him in some undefined capacity, with his own sun-bleached room high up in the attic, overlooking the canopy of green chestnut trees. Calum would sit there in his room, listening to Mozart and watching the people playing football and walking their dogs far below. But Michael hadn't thought any of that for some time. Calum would be as happy away from the estate as a butterfly in a jam jar. And anyway Calum didn't like Mozart.

'Maybe I don't want to be your friend,' said Calum.

Michael felt like replying, 'Don't be, then' – inviting 'I won't be', and getting into an endless round of pointless negations and counter-negations. So he didn't say it. 'What's wrong with Bennie's leg?' he asked.

'He was born like that,' said Calum. 'That's why he limps.'

'Does it hurt?'

'What do you care whether it hurts him?'

'I just wondered.'

'I haven't asked him,' said Calum.

'I thought maybe . . .'

'Maybe what?'

'Maybe that's why he's like he is. If his leg hurt all the time . . .'

'He's OK,' said Calum. 'He doesn't want you to care about him.'

'I just thought, maybe he could be helped,' said Michael. 'A doctor or somebody.'

'Just shut up about Bennie,' said Calum. 'He doesn't need anybody to do anything for him. Not a doctor. And certainly not you. He thinks you're a prick.'

Michael looked around the obscure space they were in. Concrete wall on two sides, a row of dustbins protected by a makeshift roof and backed by yet another wall on the third, a narrow passageway to the rest of the estate on the remaining side. He wanted somebody to emerge suddenly round a corner, dragging a large black plastic rubbish sack. Then he'd make a run for it – well, not a run exactly, which might not be safe – but a steady determined walk away from this gun.

'You'd better give that thing back to Bennie,' Michael said.

'Why?'

'Why do you think? Bennie doesn't give guns away as presents. Even to his so-called mates. If he's given it to you, it's because it's hot and he doesn't want it around his own flat.'

Calum now thought about this too. Michael was surprised it hadn't occurred to his friend before. Nobody on the estate kept a gun in their own flat if they could help it – even if it wasn't hot. You never knew when the police might call round. On an estate like this one, the police pretty much had season tickets to search the flats. You didn't want to gift them a charge that they could always make stick. You gave the gun to some little kid you could trust, or who you'd frightened enough to keep quiet about it. Then, when you needed it, you got them to bring it to you. Bennie was crazy enough to leave a gun on top of his telly, along with the remote, so it would be handy for whatever stupid thing he planned to do next. If he'd ditched this one, it had to be so hot it would glow in the dark.

'It isn't hot,' said Calum.

'Just throw it away before somebody catches you with it.'

'I can't do that.'

'Give it to me, then. I'll take it and drop it into the canal – I can do it from the bridge. It's just soft mud there. Nobody would ever find it.'

Michael didn't fancy any part of what he had described – taking the gun, carrying it through the streets wrapped in his hoodie, waiting until nobody was watching, then letting the gun fall agonisingly slowly into the still water. Cold steel almost floating in the air. Then the splash. Somebody would be bound to hear that splash. Then it was a toss-up whether the police or Bennie got him first. Still, he'd do it for Calum.

'What would I tell Bennie?' asked Calum.

'Tell him it's no business of his,' said Michael with no more confidence than he felt.

'It might be his business.'

Well, yes, obviously.

'So, he's only lending it to you, then?'

'No . . . it's mine. But he could ask me where it was.'

'Lie to him.'

'Yeah, right. Lie to Bennie? Like I'd do that.'

Michael said nothing. He didn't doubt that Bennie would ask for it back some day – when the police were no longer looking for it. And Bennie probably wouldn't want to have to dive into the canal to get it. He didn't look like somebody who did a lot of swimming.

'Say somebody nicked it off you.'

Calum said nothing. Only an idiot would imagine a story like that would save you from a beating. On the other hand only an idiot would trust Calum with a gun. Waving it around like this was not the best way to keep it a secret. As for actually firing it . . . Michael imagined the sound reverberating around this enclosed space. It would be deafening. Not even Bennie would risk doing something that stupid.

'I'm going home,' said Michael. 'See you tomorrow.'

As he walked away he heard Calum shout some sort of final warning. Then he was flung forward as if his friend had pushed him suddenly from behind and his face smashed onto the concrete path. Then, or perhaps a little after that, he died.

*   *   *

Bennie stepped out from the shadows of the bin shed. It stank in there on a hot day like this one, but bad smells didn't bother him the way they apparently bothered some people. Smells couldn't hurt you.

The scene in front of him was not entirely without interest, though. A small kid – couldn't be more than nine or ten by the look of him – was standing holding a gun in his hand. His friend was lying on his face, arms flung out in front of him and very, very still. The back of the friend's shirt had a ragged hole in it and was now almost entirely red, as was the ground around him. The kid with the gun was called Calum. A bit dim, but nicely brought up by his mum. Everyone on the estate said what a well-behaved boy he was. They wouldn't say that any more, of course, but they'd said it in the past. The other one – the dead one – had been called Michael. Bright. Very bright. They reckoned he'd go to university. Become a lawyer or a doctor or something. Well, that just showed how wrong people could be, because he obviously wouldn't become either of those things.

Bennie noticed that the kid with the gun was staring at him. Bennie cocked his head on one side and smiled in a friendly way.

'You said it would be OK,' said the kid. 'You said they weren't real bullets.'

Bennie considered. 'Did I?'

'When you gave me the gun. You said it would be a joke. I could frighten him.'

'I don't think you did frighten him, Calum. If you wanted him to be frightened, you shouldn't have shot him in the back.'

Calum was fighting back the tears. He knew that he'd done it all wrong. He just wasn't sure what he'd done. Bennie was a grown up. He was his friend. He'd said it would be OK. But it wasn't.

'Is he dead?' asked Calum.

Bennie glanced again at the body. 'What do *you* think?' he asked.

'Maybe if we got him a doctor . . .?'

'You could, if you like,' said Bennie very reasonably. 'You dial 999. Have you got a mobile?' He heard Calum give a choking sob, then another.

Bennie looked away, as if to save Calum some minor embarrassment. He should probably be going, he told himself. The shot would have been heard all over the estate. Not that that meant anyone would come here any time soon to find out what had happened. Round here, if you heard a shot, you didn't necessarily run towards the sound of firing. Few people wished to become collateral damage in a turf war between two of the ephemeral gangs that strutted their stuff on the estate. One solitary shot might not even be enough for most people to think it worth a phone call to the police, depending a bit on what was on television at that moment. When the police finally did come, they'd all say what a nice kid Calum was – thick as a plank but kind to his old gran. Their memories wouldn't stretch to much more than that. 'Yes, inspector, we do know somebody called Bennie – by sight anyway. No, we've never seen him with a gun, have we, Jim? We definitely didn't see him down by the bins earlier. I haven't been down there all day of course. Jim hasn't either. We don't get out much. Not at our age.'

Calum saw, through his tears, Bennie turn slowly and deliberately, as if to leave him. Calum held out the gun, silently imploring him to take it. Bennie was a grown-up. He'd know what to do. Even now, Calum expected Bennie to reach out, gently remove the gun from his hands and say, 'Run along, kid, I'll deal with this.' Because that was what grown-ups did. And Calum would sprint home and bury himself under the duvet and not come out until they had taken Michael away and cleaned up the blood and everything back to how it was before. Because that was what grown-ups did too.

But Bennie simply shook his head.

'It's your gun,' he said, generously. 'I told you that. Yours to keep. You look after it now.'

'Will they make me go to prison?'

'I imagine so,' said Bennie. 'You've just killed your best friend. But they'll have to let you out eventually because you're also only a kid. Probably give you a whole new identity. It's what they did for me. It worked out fine.'

'I don't want to go to prison,' said Calum.

Bennie shrugged. 'Why don't you tell the police that? See what they say. Maybe they'll just let you off with a warning.'

'Really?' said Calum.

'No,' said Bennie. 'Not really.'

Bennie walked cautiously, almost sideways, down the narrow passageway and out in the light. He paused and lifted his head, as if to sniff the air. He was not especially surprised that nobody was risking coming out and checking who had been shot, but he knew curtains would be twitching all over the estate. Let them twitch. He had carefully wiped the gun clean before handing it over to the child. There couldn't be any doubt who had actually shot Michael. Bennie hadn't gone anywhere near him. As for who had supplied the weapon – well, that would be Calum's word against his.

And maybe Calum wouldn't try to grass him up anyway because Calum was, at the end of the day, a decent kid. Straight as an arrow. Kind to his gran. A young offenders' institution would toughen him up and teach him some useful skills – give him a proper career. Car crime, for example. Or drug dealing. In the long run, he'd probably be grateful.

As for Michael, the estate wouldn't miss that stuck-up little jerk. Listening to Mozart and that sort of shite on his iPod. Looking down his nose at everybody. The tosser wasn't even properly frightened of him. When you thought about it, Bennie had done society a favour by squashing him under his foot before he could become a politician or a judge or a psychiatrist or a probation officer.

And why shouldn't he offer society a helping hand now and then? Society had been good to Bennie, in its way. It had fed him, clothed him and accommodated him for much of his life. It had made him what he was today. He was only too pleased to give something back from time to time.

Bennie stepped out of the estate and onto the main road. One of the other residents, a widower who lived alone in a top floor flat, was returning, laden with four orange plastic bags bulging with shopping. Somebody ought to be helping him with stuff like that. At his age.

'Hi, pal! How's it going?' said Bennie.

The old man gave him a wary nod, and gulped silently. Then he quickened his pace. A few minutes later, he would stumble over a child's body, with a single bullet hole in the back. But he didn't know that yet.

'Suit yourself, dickhead,' said Bennie cheerfully. And he set off down the road, dragging his left foot slightly, jingling the coins in his pocket.

THE ART OF OLD AGE
Yvonne Eve Walus

Yvonne Eve Walus lives in New Zealand. She is a doctor of Mathematics, wife, mother as well as a poet, novelist and writer of short stories. She wrote her first poem when she was four and her first short story when she was nine. Her first publishing success (a short story in a local magazine) came when she was 22. Yvonne has lived on three continents and her work reflects the range of her cultural background. Her latest thriller, *Operation*: *Genocide*, is published by Stairway Press.

New Zealand Herald
21 June 2013

<u>**Robber raids elderly victims**</u>

Police are warning the elderly in Auckland to be wary after several were confronted by a robber – in some cases while he was lying in ambush awaiting their return home.
There have been eight incidents in recent days where people have been challenged and robbed while they were at home. In all cases the victims were elderly.

Sometimes I wonder who these people used to be, the ones I rob. They all look the same, dotted with freckles of old age, their skin leathered and thinned and in urgent need of ironing. Their shoulders are always caved in, their backs rounded like tortoiseshell, and their eyes emit that switched-off look even when they stare right at you from above the gag.

Sometimes I wonder whether it's an ex-model I'm tying to her dining-room chair, as rickety as her own eighty-year-old frame. Whether the old man who's pissed his pants in fear used to swish – immortal and forever young – in his sports car. Whether this couple, holding hands as they shuffle hand-in-hand into their golden-years cottage where I lie in wait, used to bicker the way my parents did. Have they ever been unfaithful? Felt tempted to throttle the living daylights out of one another? Is the hand-in-hand shuffle a bluff? Usually I can tell as soon as they see me. It's whether they choose to protect themselves or the spouse.

The old rimu wood floor looks like solid honey but it's hell on my elbows. Give me a carpet over wooden planks any day.

With single old folks, I knock on the door and pretend to sell vacuums or cheaper electricity plans. Sometimes I'm a gas inspector or a police officer. Starved for company and for something to do with their infinitely long day, they usually let me in.

Couples are trickier. That's why I wait for them inside.

Here they come now. The garden gate squeaks on its slanted hinges. I part the slats of the venetian blind. The old woman has her thin arm zigzagged through his, the Louis Vuitton handbag hanging off the other arm for counterbalance. Against all odds, she's wearing high heels. Not stilettos, granted, but still about a metre too high for an old bird like her.

The old geezer is carrying a plastic bag from the local electronic shop. Oh, good. Normally, I take what's in their houses and wallets, which doesn't amount to a lot. A brand new gadget, still in its box and with a receipt attached is a bonus.

Old age is a nuisance, I think, as my wife switches her bag to the other hand and weaves her arm through mine to steady herself. Anybody who's experienced the aches, the insomnia, the shortness of breath, can tell you that old age sucks. For me, though, old age is more than a nuisance. It's a nightmare.

I used to run ten kilometres every morning to stay fit. My handgun would find its target within a hundred metres. I was a wizard with explosives. The perfect spheres of my biceps could lift a woman and throw her onto a bed. I used to do a

fair amount of that back in Russia, before I met my wife. And
after, if truth be told. What can I say? The times were tough,
the future uncertain. Under Stalin and under those who came
after him, we learnt to take life one day at a time, one pleasure
at a time, one enemy at a time.

Back then, we knew the meaning of the word 'fear'. Fear
made me fake and kill friends and brown-nose my way out
of trouble.

And now? Now I'm holding a new laptop computer a thousand times more powerful than Stalin ever was. Now my
greatest problem is that the footpath between our garden gate
and the front door is strewn with brown leaves, as ugly as the
face I see in the mirror when shaving.

Old age is more than a nuisance and a nightmare. It's also
unsightly.

My wife lets go of my arm, pokes the key into the lock and
turns the handle. 'Tea with jam?' she asks.

She used to offer blowjobs in that tempting tone. Now it's
tea. Old age, I tell you, it's worse than death.

'Tea with jam?' I ask.

My husband has no time to reply. A shadow detaches itself
from the window and pins him to the floor. Isn't it the other
way round, I wonder, aren't you supposed to pin your shadow
down? I'm sure there was a story like that.

I used to like stories, back when I was young. Younger.
Back then my husband was a great storyteller, able to explain
every smear of lipstick on his collar, every bundle of hundred-
rouble notes hidden under the mattress, every visit from grey-
suited officials. I ooh-ed and aah-ed and nodded. Knew better
than to believe a single word.

While my husband played soldier-spy, I tinker-tailored our
existence from a room shared with two other couples into our
own luxurious villa on the peripheries of Moscow and a palace-
like dacha on the pebbly beach of the Black Sea. I had the body
and the brain to achieve it. I had the cunning and the KGB
training to hold onto what I'd achieved, and once the system
had crumbled, I had the foresight to flee to New Zealand.

While my husband is flailing on the beautiful wooden floor,

in vain trying to force his muscles to remember how to be the James Bond of the Eastern Block, I swing my designer handbag. The weight of make-up, hand cream, hairbrush, coins for the parking meter, three pens, a book and everything else we women carry around, makes contact with the intruder's skull.

Before he has time to recover, I yank off one of my shoes and aim its heel at his temple. It's not my first time. It's why I always wear heels, even on days when my lower back is demanding slippers.

The beauty of old age is that nobody ever expects it to fight back.

'You get rid of the body,' I tell my husband. 'Like in the old days. Meanwhile, I'll make the tea.'

I feel half a century younger. Perhaps we should do this again. Soon.

New Zealand Herald
21 December 2013

Christmas For Cops

The last six months saw a sudden plunge of burglary statistics across Auckland. But the real Christmas gift for our police force came when they entered twenty-five abandoned premises, each full of stolen goods.

'It's like Christmas has come early,' says Detective Ian Macdonald. 'We got this anonymous letter with the addresses. Had no idea what we'd find.'

The police are still looking for the owners or lapsed tenants of the properties, but word on the street is, they're not looking too hard.

THE MAN IN THE NEXT BED
Laura Wilson

Laura Wilson was brought up in London and has degrees in English literature from Somerville College, Oxford, and UCL, London. She lives in Islington, London, where she is currently working on her twelfth novel. She is the crime fiction reviewer for the *Guardian* newspaper, and teaches on the City University Crime Thriller Novel Creative Writing MA course.

'. . . all these poor bastards, and they keep on finding 'em dead. Months go by, and there's more and more of 'em, always in this one room that's off the main ward, and no one knows why. Then they've only realised–' Spicer gave a phlegmy chuckle '– they've only realised it's always on a Friday this happens, and that's when the cleaner goes in, see? She don't speak a word of English and she's been plugging in the hoover or whatever – only to do that she has to unplug this other thing, and it's only—'

'The life support system,' Nick finished, eyeing the scratched plastic side of the jug on his bedside locker. The water looked grey, and there were specks of something floating in it.

'You've heard it before,' Spicer wheezed, disappointed.

'I guessed.' Nick pressed the buzzer or bell or whatever it was, but the nurse at the station at the end of the ward didn't look up from her computer screen. He'd assumed that a light must come on to indicate when a patient needed something, but if it had she wasn't heeding it. It wasn't just the water. He wanted to know what was going on. The brisk efficiency of his admission that morning had subsided, after half an hour or so, into unfocussed uncertainty, with talk of procedures being 'put back' and notes misplaced. A nurse – the previous one, not the current screen-gazer – had said she'd find out, but that was over four hours ago. Four hours during which he'd had no choice but to receive a thorough grounding in the life and opinions of Tommy Spicer, up to and including his age: 50, three years younger than Nick, although he definitely looked older; his height: 1.82m 'or 6ft 1 in old money', the same as Nick; and his current weight: 238kg or 'down to 17 stone now'. That was about four stone more than Nick, at least at the moment. Before the diagnosis, he'd been pleased to be losing weight. Now, it worried him.

He'd seen quite a bit of Spicer's 238kg during a display of his children's names, which were tattooed on his arms and chest. Ryan ('I was only 18, so he'd be over 30 now') and Amber ('always my princess') on his biceps, Ashley ('Should be *ee* at the end, but the muppet got it wrong') and Briana ('Different, innit? Brian's my middle name, see, after my Dad') above his nipples. Slightly further down, the names of the three mothers of these four had been buried under arrangements of crosses and roses. Judging from his remark about Ryan, Nick suspected that Spicer hardly ever saw his children, much less paid maintenance. Perhaps he thought that having their names engraved on his body was commitment enough. *Briana*. God Almighty.

Listening to Spicer was worse than being in the back of a cab. At least then you were going somewhere and you knew it would soon be over – and taxi drivers didn't insist on showing you their body art. He'd seen a photograph of Amber, too, on Spicer's phone: orange and laminated, with tits out to here. ('Sent that to me at Christmas. Only run off to Huddersfield or some fucking place with her mum's new bloke, hadn't she? Real chip off the old block, she is.'). Not that Nick could afford cabs nowadays. He couldn't actually remember the last time he'd taken one.

Spicer probably earned far more than he did. Cash only, of course. As he'd talked, Nick had imagined him, a cheerful bodger, causing more damage than he ever repaired and pulling all sorts of strokes on the side – nicked copper, pilfered lead, half-inched garden ornaments. He'd obviously got form. 'I asked them to give me treatment for it when I was in there, but they never. But it was just, like, normal burglaries,' he'd added, virtuously. 'I've never took from old people or kids or if they was poor or nothing.'

Presumably, thought Nick, a 'normal burglary' meant robbing someone like him. Spicer appeared to think that this was not only all right but actually praiseworthy, which was ironic, given their respective circumstances. Spicer was a council tenant. He rented the house his mum had lived in for £85 a week, and it was secure for the rest of his life. Nick knew the estate. It was one of the older ones, with most of the houses – semi-detached boxes in two-tone pebble dash – sold off to private owners.

They were probably worth a bit, too, because of the location. Nick wondered whether, if push came to shove, if he and Cath could afford one. They still had a mortgage of over £100,000 on their four-bed Victorian terrace, and keeping up with the payments was a struggle nowadays. Christ knew what they'd do when interest rates went up, although that wasn't supposed to happen for a couple of years. Would he even be around when it did?

Spicer was still talking. Something about unjust persecution by the police for something he couldn't help (the stealing, presumably). 'Always at my door, when I ain't done nothing. I mean, for fuck's sake, look at me.' Nick was tempted to comment that perhaps the coppers couldn't help it, either, but of course he didn't.

He'd tried to get stuck into the Booker prize winner he'd brought along, but it was impossible. Not that he actually wanted to read the bloody thing, but Cath had been going on about it after her book group and he'd thought it would be nice to show willing. He imagined the two of them talking about it. It would be a topic of conversation that wasn't how his work had dried up almost completely or how they couldn't downsize because Holly and Josh were coming back to live at home or why they weren't talking anymore, just arguing, or where the bloody hell had he been this time or what are we going to do if. That was the worst, because it was blindingly obvious what *he* was going to do if. He was going to fucking *die*, wasn't he? It was also the worst having to listen to Cath oscillating between the pointless recital of 'potential scenarios' and bracing statistics accompanied by anecdotal evidence about somebody's friend or brother or aunt who'd had what he'd got ten years ago and was now completely cured and running marathons or swimming the channel or about to be launched into space. Or something. And then he'd get the of-course-if-you-hadn't-gone-freelance-we'd-still-have-private-healthcare speech. She'd been all for it at the time – but this was revised, now, to 'going along with it for your sake.'

What was he lying here pressing the stupid buzzer for, anyway? He wasn't immobile. Hating himself for being so quickly reduced to querulous dependency, he pushed back the covers and swung his legs out of the bed. He could perfectly well walk down the ward, take the jug thing with him for a refill and ask the nurse what was happening.

'Don't worry, mate. She'll be back.'

'Who?'

'You know, the one with the arse. That nurse who said she'd find out what was going on.'

'She's probably gone off duty.'

'Well, you're here now, aren't you? They'll have to do something. You're entitled.'

'I'm going to find out.' Nick reached for his robe. 'I can't use my phone in here anyway.'

'Or,' Spicer grinned, revealing teeth like rotten fenceposts, 'is it that girl brought you in this morning?' His rasping laugh turned into a fit of liquid coughing. 'Your face!'

'How . . .?'

'Obvious, mate. Give us a minute, and I'll come with you. I could do with a fag, as it goes.'

'A fag? You told me you'd got—'

'Won't make no difference now, will it?'

'They're taking half your—'

'I'll still have one, won't I? That's all you need. My Dad, he was on the oxygen at the finish. Used to sit there – one puff of that and a puff on the roll up – all day, doing that. And it don't make no difference. When all this started I told the doctor I'd give up, and every time he's seen me, he's only said he can see the improvement now I've stopped, so what do they know? Anyway,' he added, fatalistic, 'my mum had emphysema, too, so it runs in the family, dunnit?'

'Did she smoke?'

'Yeah, course.' Spicer shook his head at the stupidity of the question. 'Like a chimney. Mind you, that was my dad. The stress of living with him. Until he done a runner, that is. Come on, give us a hand. And don't worry about the bird –' Spicer's leery, exaggerated wink hailed him as a fellow member of the fraternity of middle-aged adulterers '– I won't tell if you won't.'

Nick hadn't intended to go outside the hospital, but found himself standing, slippered, in front of the litter-strewn car park trying to call Cath while Spicer, propped against a bollard, sucked on a Mayfair Kingsize. Cath wasn't picking up. The meeting, which was the reason why she hadn't given him a lift to the hospital, was an important one about a new contract – 'one of us has to earn something' – and, now he thought about it, she'd said something about lunch afterwards, hadn't she? No message from her, but a text from Holly wishing him good luck with a line of kisses, and three texts from Natalie as well as four messages. He started listening to the first one – 'Darling, I haven't been able to concentrate on anything, I'm so worried for you . . .' and then deleted it, and the ones that followed, unheard.

He didn't want to talk to Nat. He hadn't wanted her to bring him here this morning, either, but she'd insisted on meeting him outside the tube station in her car. She'd been so tearful and needy when they'd talked about it that he'd agreed, fearing that if he didn't she might actually turn up at his house. No, he wouldn't call her. What was there to say? Nothing had happened, and he didn't have the energy to console her about her feelings when he was the one with the potentially fatal illness.

It was all to do with mortality, of course, even before the diagnosis and before he'd started feeling generally under the weather with the collection of minor symptoms that had given rise to it. Although not, probably, before the cancer itself – Dr Gomberts had told him it could take as much as three years before a single cancer cell divided and divided again until it grew to a noticeable size. If that was right – he thought that was what Dr Gomberts had said, but those first meetings, he hadn't taken much in beyond the word itself – then that made it around the time he'd noticed his pubes were starting to turn white. He'd been lying in the bath and when he looked down, there it was, a single hair, gleaming palely in the sunlight.

Now, he wondered if his body, knowing that it was not only getting old but also had cancer, had impelled him into Nat's bed. It certainly hadn't been a conscious decision, a line deliberately crossed for the first time. Proximity, opportunity, and, yes, quite a few drinks – and it had just sort of . . . happened. The sex had been mind-blowing, and he'd become a walking, talking, breathing (at least for the time being) cliché: a middle-aged married man having an affair with a woman over twenty years younger than he was, and who had introduced him to moisturiser. A couple of months ago, Nat had started asking when he was going to tell Cath so they could get a divorce. Nick couldn't afford a divorce even if he wanted one, which he was 99 per cent sure that he didn't. He'd never seriously contemplated Nat's proposal that he move in with her and start all over again, whereas she'd begun to talk as though it wasn't a matter of if, but when. Even breaking the bad news hadn't stopped her. She'd talked about how they'd 'get through it together' and 'beating it' and 'positive thinking', as though it were a test of character.

At least Cath hadn't come out with any of that stuff – probably because she thought his character wasn't up to being tested by anything. This morning, Nat had been coming out with crap about how the stress of his marriage had caused the cancer in the first place. She'd made it sound as if asking Cath for a divorce would cure him. Couldn't she see he could do without it? After all, he'd played fair with her, hadn't he? He'd never lied – she'd known he was married from the off. He shoved the phone irritably into the pocket of his robe.

'Didn't phone the girlfriend, then?' Spicer flicked his dog end into the gutter.

'No.'

'Left you a few messages though, didn't she?'

'A couple.'

'You like to live dangerously.' Spicer paused to give a light to a hefty woman in a towelling robe who was hitched up to a drip on a stand. 'She didn't look like a bunny boiler to me.' He wagged his head judiciously. 'Not that you can always tell, of course. I had a girl once, a real psycho, she . . .' Hanging onto Nick's arm as they walked back inside, he began a complicated narrative about how some woman had slashed his tyres and waylaid Ashlee and Briana's mum at the school gates to tell her what a shit the twins' father was, which had led to a cat fight. 'Wish I'd seen it, though,' Spicer added wistfully and then, as they were passing the hospital shop, 'Couldn't get us a paper, could you? Left me change upstairs, didn't I?'

'Look at that.' Nick didn't want to look. He didn't want to look at the rows of cheerful, pastel-coloured cards bookended with buckets of cellophane-wrapped flowers and teddy bears with satin hearts on their chests, or at the headlines. Property prices, fracking, illegal immigrants, more property prices and the one Spicer was pointing at, a tabloid with 'FOUND DEAD AFTER NINE MONTHS' on the front in 24-point capital letters beside a headshot of a smiling woman in a party hat captioned 'Tragic Valerie Wiseman'. 'Fucking disgrace, that is.'

As they waited for a dishevelled-looking young guy in scrubs to pay for a Mars bar, Nick stared through the reinforced glass partition at the people milling about in the lobby: young mothers trying to pacify shrieking toddlers with junk food, a bloke with a bandage round his head flailing, drunk, between the rows of seats, a scabby-pated tramp arguing with the receptionist and a monstrously overweight man beached in the corner. If he'd still had private healthcare, Nick would be being tended to by sleek nurses in designer uniforms in a tasteful haven of tranquillity. None of these people, Spicer very much included, would be allowed through the door.

'Poor cow.' Spicer brandished the paper as they made their slow way to the lifts. 'It's not right, her being left like that. Nine fucking months – you've got to wonder what the world's coming to. Where was the social services? Too busy finding homes for all them illegals, that's where.'

'How old was she?' asked Nick.

'Sixty-nine.'

'No family?'

'Don't look like it.' Spicer scanned the two short columns of type beneath the headline while they waited for the lift, before grubbing over the page with his thumb and forefinger. 'Says here it was the housing charity people found her when they come to repossess the place. The telly was still on, though, and the heating.'

'Jesus.'

'Yeah, well. Would have been back in November, wouldn't it?'

'But surely, if she hadn't paid the bills . . .'

'If it was all direct debit, though,' said Spicer, 'then the pension goes in, the bills come out, and she's not spending it on anything else if she's dead, is she? So there'd be enough in there. Perhaps she done the rent by cheque or something, and she never answered their letters, so then they've sent the bailiffs in.'

'I suppose so. Is that how she died, watching television?' Nick imagined the flat: junk mail piling up on the mat, the washing up, never to be done, in the sink, the food, long past its sell-by-date, mouldering in the fridge, the television flickering its way through months of news, soap operas and chat shows in front of Valerie Wiseman's unseeing eyes until . . . until what? What did happen to your eyes after you were dead? Did they liquefy entirely before decomposing, or harden and shrink in their sockets, or . . . For God's sake, he told himself. Stop it.

'Yeah . . .' Spicer frowned, scanning the rest of the article. 'They don't know what killed her, though. Too far gone an' that. Nine months, Jesus.'

'Did she have any cats?'

'Cats? Nah.'

'Just, you hear those stories . . . You'd think someone would have noticed the smell, though.'

'Depends on the neighbours. Their sort–' Spicer nodded towards the brightly dressed black family emerging from the lift, arguing in some African language or other '– they wouldn't notice nothing. Just think it was normal, wouldn't they?'

The pretty Asian nurse who'd arrived just in time to hear this raised her eyebrows before following them into the lift. Inside, Nick, not wanting to be bracketed with Spicer as an ageing racist, put as much distance between the two of them as could be managed in thirty square feet. 'Even if they did notice,' Spicer continued, 'them lot don't bother to learn English so they couldn't tell no one, could they?' The nurse's face twitched. Nick willed her to look at him, so that he could signal his lack of sympathy for this view, but she was staring at the floor. *Briana*, for fuck's sake. Spicer was about to enlarge on his previous point when Nick's phone rang.

It was Cath. 'I'd have left you a message, love, but there's been a bit of a mix-up and I'm still not sure what's—'

'Nick, shut up. Josh has been arrested.'

'What?'

'He's been dealing drugs.'

'I can't eat this, it's fucking cold.' Spicer gestured at the tray on the over-bed table.

'We should have waited.' Perhaps there'd been a mistake, although Cath had been pretty definite about it. The charge was possession with intent to supply, and Josh had been found with five grams of cocaine as well as 'a massive amount' of dope. When Nick had told Cath he'd discharge himself and come straight to the police station, she'd snapped that she'd got enough on her plate without having to look after him as well. When the children were little they'd faced things together – Holly's meningitis, various issues that had cropped up at the children's schools, structural problems with the house – and she'd been glad of him. Now, he'd gone from being the main breadwinner, a reliable, solid part of a team, to a dependent, even an encumbrance. It hadn't happened just now, of course, or even all at once, but gradually, over the last few years.

'They should have waited till we come back. This is the last meal I'll get till after my op tomorrow – and you haven't got nothing.'

'I'm not supposed to have anything except water.' What did Josh think he was playing at? Dealing could get you a prison sentence. A proper one, and not a borstal or whatever it was called nowadays, because Josh was twenty-one.

'Yeah, but if they're not going to do anything to you today, they've got to give you something to eat, haven't they?'

'I'm not hungry. Anyway, I don't know they're not going to do it.' The nurses' station was deserted, and there was no one around to ask. 'It doesn't matter.'

'Course it bleeding matters.' Spicer jabbed an angry finger at the buzzer and held it there. 'Hey! Where the fuck is everybody?'

The other patients looked up from their meals. As far as Nick could see, nobody had eaten much. Perhaps Josh would only get a fine. After all, it was a first offence, and prisons were overcrowded, weren't they? 'It's OK.' He sank onto his bed. 'I'm not bothered. Honestly.' Josh would still have a conviction, though, wouldn't he? Surely you didn't have to include that on your CV? They might ask specifically, if there was a questionnaire or something – which there probably would be, even for an internship like the ones Josh had been talking about applying for, where they didn't give you a salary, just travel expenses.

'Well, I'm bleeding bothered. I mean, look at it! I wouldn't give that to my dog. Hallo! Nurse!' Spicer stopped, grasping at breath. 'Fuck's sake,' he wheezed. 'You have a go.'

'What's your dog's name?' asked Nick, hoping to distract him.

'Bronson. Jesus, I can't fucking breathe.'

'Why don't you get into bed?' Christ, he felt shattered. If Josh got a fine, that could come out of his savings, the money Cath's mum had left him. Assuming he hadn't spent it all since his twenty-first birthday, of course. Assuming he hadn't used it to buy the drugs.

'What,' gasped Spicer, 'about, my, fucking, dinner? And what's my dog's name got to do with it?'

'Who's looking after him while you're in here?'

'Neighbour. Why?'

'Just interested.'

'He's fine, mate. Good as gold.'

Nick pictured a snarling status dog with a studded collar.

What if Josh couldn't pay the fine? Would they send him to prison? Or would they fine him and imprison him? What if he couldn't get a job and ended up . . .

'Fuck's sake!' Spicer gave the over-bed table a shove, so that it skidded away, plates clattering as it crashed into the wall, and fell back on his bed.

'Look,' said Nick, 'why don't I go and find someone?' He was exhausted, but clearly Spicer wasn't going to be deflected, and trailing up and down corridors was preferable to being stuck here next to him.

'It's their job, not yours. Hey! Nurse!'

'They're probably overstretched.' Nick had just levered himself off the bed when the Asian nurse who'd been in the lift appeared and told Spicer that there wasn't any more food. Nick, imagining Spicer telling her to fuck off back to Pakistan and take the grub with her, winced in anticipation.

'What do you mean, no food? This is a hospital, for fuck's sake. It's got a fucking kitchen, hasn't it? And what about him?'

Great, now he'd be bracketed with Spicer as an overly-entitled chav as well as a racist. Nick smiled weakly as the nurse turned to him, her face carefully neutral. 'I'm fine, honestly. I don't think I'm meant to eat anything.'

'Did you fill in your form?'

'Form?'

'To choose your meals.'

'I'm sorry – I might be wrong, but I don't think I was given one. I was meant to be having a procedure but there was some—'

'Excuse me!' said Spicer. 'I'm still here, you know, and if you can't get me anything else, this food's not going to warm itself up, is it?'

'I'm afraid we can't re-heat meals.'

'Why not? Stick it in a microwave, job done.'

The nurse explained about health and safety regulations and Spicer swore at her. Nick wanted to tell Spicer to shut up, but was afraid of incurring his hostility. Why was he scared of him? The man was about to have half his breathing apparatus removed, for God's sake. What could he possibly *do*? Other than spend the next few hours – or as much of it as they were both, simultaneously, conscious – swearing at him, of course.

After several minutes' circular explanation and recrimination, the nurse turned to leave. 'I'm sorry,' said Nick, 'but would you mind finding out what's supposed to be happening to me?'

'They haven't told us,' said the nurse. 'We can't do anything unless they tell us.'

'I'm not asking you to do anything,' said Nick. 'I don't want any lunch. I'd just like to know what's going on.'

The nurse, sounding as though she were humouring the whim of a madman, said that she'd try, and left.

'What a fucking shambles,' said Spicer. 'I bet if I'd wanted halal or one of them things, they'd be straight onto it, but heat a bit of food up? No mate, too much bother. Got trouble at home, have you?'

Nick stared at him.

'That phone call, before. Your missus, wasn't it?'

'Yes, but—'

'Not found out about the girlfriend, has she?'

Nick shook his head.

'One of the kids, then?'

'It was work. We work together.'

'Oh.'

Nick could imagine, all too clearly, Spicer's 'Welcome to the club, mate,' and the subsequent advice about doing your bird. Or maybe – assuming the man actually knew anything at all about any of his children apart from their names – he'd regale him about when Ryan or Amber or possibly even the eight-year-old twins Ashlee and Briana (God) had got into trouble with the law. He'd almost certainly know all about probable fines and sentences and whether you had to disclose a conviction to a prospective employer, as well.

Nick went and hid in the loo, which was quiet and reasonably clean. He sat down and leant sideways to rest his head on the tiled wall. His phone rang and he answered, assuming it was Cath. It was Natalie.

'Didn't you get my messages?'

'Messages? No. I mean, I didn't . . . I had to turn the phone off,' he lied.

'So you didn't hear them? I sent you a couple of texts, too.'

'I'm sorry. Look, Nat, I'm going to have to cut this short because I've got to—'

'Nick, I'm pregnant.'

Spicer talked all afternoon, various grievances. His bad luck in being easily led, so that he'd skipped school, his bad luck in getting in with the wrong crowd, in not being nabbed earlier, which might have scared him onto the right track, in not finding the right woman . . .

Had Nat done it deliberately, Nick wondered for the umpteenth time. When he'd hinted at this she'd become tearful and said she thought he'd be pleased. *Pleased!* Unbelievable . . . They'd had a row, of course. She'd threatened to ring Cath if he didn't tell her himself, today. He'd hesitated just a second too long when she'd asked if he loved her, which had made her start crying again. He didn't love her. He'd never loved her – surely she knew that saying it in bed didn't count? He just wished she'd go away.

No chance. Her last words, after he'd managed to mollify her, were that he wasn't to worry because no one would ever love him as much as she did and she and the baby would always be there for him. Remembering this, Nick only just managed to restrain himself from groaning aloud.

This wasn't how his life was supposed to be. He could cope with the slackening of ambition, the knowledge that his career had already peaked and he'd not been half – well, OK, maybe not half, maybe a third – as successful as he'd hoped, but for Christ's sake! He'd kept his part of the bargain, hadn't he? Worked hard at school, and later at his job, saved, got married, bought a house. He was supposed to do better than his parents, and his children, in their turn, better than him and Cath: that was the deal. Except, apparently, it wasn't. As for the cancer, that was a trick, too. He'd been watching his diet and taking regular exercise since the age of thirty, when he'd also given up smoking and started following the government guidelines on booze. Unlike Spicer, who was even now talking about an almighty piss up in his local when he got out – although that was obviously bravado because the guy had *lung cancer*, for Christ's sake – Nick had done nothing to deserve any of this, so why was it happening?

He'd always imagined that, by this point, he'd have made his pile. He'd have the London house, all paid for, and perhaps a country place, too – nothing grand, just the cottage. The children would be successfully launched into the world, and he'd be contemplating early retirement. Nick thought of the adverts showing bright-eyed pensioner couples, always with plenty of silver hair for the wind to ruffle as they stood on the decks of ocean liners and pointed at things on the horizon and smiled with perfect teeth. The way things were going, the only thing he'd be pointing at on the horizon was the bloke in the cloak with the scythe.

His eyes fell on the newspaper on Spicer's bed. 'Tragic Valerie Wiseman'. There she was, grinning in a party hat, with no idea that she'd end up dying alone and rotting for nine months before anyone noticed. What a colossal fucking mess. He couldn't tell Cath. He'd have to persuade Nat. Supposing he couldn't? Nat might be phoning her right now! Nick imagined his wife picking up the phone in the kitchen, elbows on the butcher block then springing upright as she realised what was being said to her. Except that Cath would still be at the police station trying to sort Josh out, wouldn't she? Oh, God, Josh . . .

There was no way Nat would have Cath's mobile number, was there? She'd had plenty of chances to get it off his phone if she'd wanted to. Cath being at the police station also meant, now he thought about it properly, that she must have missed her meeting this morning, or had to leave it almost as soon as she'd arrived, which in turn meant that the new contract – and, let's face it, their main source of income for the next two years – had, in all likelihood, gone up in smoke.

Not that Nat knew anything about any of *that*, of course. He'd always been careful to give the impression that he was, if not exactly flush, then comfortably off. There were two credit cards that Cath, who was in charge of the paperwork, knew nothing about. Then there was Holly, expecting them to finance her while she did an MA in journalism, as if there was any point in that. The fact was, there were more places on journalism courses than jobs in the profession – all of which were, in any case, already filled.

This thing with Nat couldn't happen. Surely she'd see that. Wouldn't she? What if . . . He couldn't think about it. Any of it. He shouldn't have to, not now. For Christ's sake, he was ill, wasn't he? Probably dying. Why couldn't he do it in peace?

'You all right?'

'Yes, fine.'

'Just, you looked . . . Wouldn't blame you if you was scared, mate.'

'Are you scared?'

'Yeah. Yeah, I am, as it goes.' Spicer leant towards him. 'I'm fucking terrified.'

'Me too.' But, Nick thought, right now, I'm more afraid of living than of dying.

The luminous display on the clock read 02.14. Nick had had the procedure, a day later than scheduled, and the various tissues were now awaiting analysis in the lab. By the time it was finished it had been too late to send him home, so he'd been returned to the ward until the consultant could discharge him – assuming all was well – in the morning. Nick felt physically fine – surprisingly good, in fact – but he didn't want to be discharged. He'd rather stay here, even with Spicer, who, having had his lung removed first thing yesterday, was now back in the next bed.

He didn't want to go home. In fact, he no longer had a home to go to. Despite his efforts to dissuade her, Nat had turned up the previous evening, and so, fifteen minutes later, had Cath. The ensuing showdown, which had taken approximately three minutes and during which he had spoken no more than ten words, had resulted in Cath saying that if that was the case then Nat was welcome to him and she'd be in touch via her solicitor. Then she'd left, impervious to Nick's pleas as he sat in bed, trapped, with Nat clinging onto his arm and Spicer lapping it up from his ringside seat.

He'd always imagined that, in the event of a situation like this one, Cath would fight tooth and nail to keep him. Now, he wondered why he'd thought that. She'd seemed almost relieved, as if he were an item that could now be crossed off one of her to-do lists. She hadn't even paused long enough to give him an update on Josh's situation.

Everything was conspiring to push him to the margins of his own life. Natalie's flat was a few scruffy, boxy rented rooms above a fish and chip shop. She shared it with another twenty-something, who worked in PR and who Nick had only ever seen preparing to go out partying or nursing a hangover. He'd be living – aged 53 and with more than likely terminal cancer – a version of his children's lives, if they could have afforded the rent. Surely Cath wouldn't actually start divorce proceedings? After all, if he died, she wouldn't have to sell the light-filled home they'd spent so long doing up, but if they had to split the proceeds, they'd be lucky if they could each afford something as big as Nat's place. And what about the children? They could hardly expect Holly and Josh to share a divorce-regulation IKEA bunk bed, could they? And what about when Nat's baby arrived? After Cath had gone, she'd kept on saying how happy she was and how it was all she'd ever wanted. He hadn't had the heart – and certainly not the energy – to tell her that he had no money and no prospect of getting any and that the last thing he wanted was another child and as he was probably dying would she please just bugger off.

He sat up, feeling as though he were suffocating. After he'd finally got rid of Nat by making God knows what promises, Spicer had been surprisingly tactful. 'Don't worry, your missus'll come round. You're a sick man – ain't going to leave you in the lurch, is she?' Nick wasn't at all sure about that. What had he been thinking of? He and Cath had been together for over twenty years. Nick remembered Spicer's words, 'Mind you, she's a good-looking woman, your wife. Don't mind my saying, she must have been a real knockout when she was that other one's age.' That was true. Cath had been a knockout – much better looking than Nat. Christ! Did *she* have someone else? Was that why she'd told Nat she was welcome to him?

He hadn't thought of that. All this time, while he'd been
worrying and feeling guilty, she might have been having an
affair of her own. Just because he no longer looked at her that
way – or not very often – it didn't mean . . . If only there was
someone – a friend, a bloke – that he could talk to. As Cath
had pointed out a couple of weeks ago, he didn't have any
friends any more. He'd drifted away from people he'd known
since school and university because they no longer had
anything in common or they'd moved abroad or got too rich
or something, and – as Cath had also pointed out – having a
bunch of people you kept meaning to have a drink with wasn't
the same thing.

He looked over at the curtains enclosing Spicer's bed.
They'd been like that since he'd been wheeled back at around
ten o'clock. Now, there was a faint noise coming from behind
them. It sounded like speech, but Nick couldn't make out any
words. Perhaps Cath was even now spending the first night
in his – OK, their – house with her lover, who would move
in, putting his things in Nick's drawers and on Nick's shelves,
while his own belongings were stuffed into bin liners and left
in the hallway for him to collect 'at a convenient time' (the
locks having been changed). She couldn't fucking do this to
him! She couldn't!

Spicer must be awake. Nick could ask him if that was what
he'd been hinting. The ward was quiet, and there didn't seem
to be anyone at the nurses' station. Energised by the injustice
of it all, Nick peeled back the bedcovers and swung his legs
over the side. He felt a bit wobbly, but he was OK. He could
stand all right, and walk. He let go of the bedside locker and
poked his head round the end of Spicer's curtain.

Spicer was lying on his back, his eyes open but unfocussed,
spittle at the corners of his mouth.

'It's me. Nick,' he whispered.

Spicer turned his head towards him. He looked confused,
and Nick wondered if he remembered who he was. 'I never
meant it,' he murmured, hoarsely.

'I didn't mind. You're probably right – what you were getting
at, I mean.'

'She wasn't meant to be there, was she?'

'Nat? No. I told her not to come. It couldn't believe it when she—'

'I didn't know she was there.'

'I don't understand. She was sitting on the bed, right beside me, so—'

'I thought it was empty.'

'What?'

'When I went in. I didn't think there was anyone there.'

'Where?'

'I'm in the middle of it when suddenly she's standing there. I never had time to think. She was going to phone the police. I couldn't have that, could I?'

'What are you talking about?'

Spicer ignored the question. 'Just get in and out as quick as I can. If it looks like trouble, I don't want nothing to do with it – if I'd thought she was there . . .'

'Who?'

'That woman.'

'*What* woman?'

'In the paper.'

'What? You mean yesterday? The woman they found?'

'She wasn't supposed to be there, was she?'

'Wasn't she?'

'No. On my life . . . One minute I'm by myself, next minute she's there saying she's calling the police, and my head just went. Next thing I know, the knife's gone in.'

'You killed Valerie Wiseman?'

'I never meant to. It's like it wasn't me. After it happened, I just scarpered, and the next thing I know I'm reading about it in the paper, aren't I?'

'You were turning over her flat and she surprised you and you killed her?'

'It's like I said, I didn't know what I was doing, did I? I told you, when I was in the nick I asked them to give me some help, but they never. I only ever done normal burglaries, on my life. It wasn't my fault. I told you, she wasn't supposed to be there.'

'So it was *her* fault?' Nick felt as if his head were about to burst. He must have raised his voice, because Spicer's eyes widened in recognition. He had the look of someone who'd been submerged and had just broken up through the surface. Nick wondered who he thought he'd been talking to – a ghost, perhaps, a dream? 'No,' Spicer said now, 'but it wasn't the real me. Just bad luck, that's all. It wasn't supposed to happen.'

This wasn't supposed to happen to me, either, thought Nick, but it did. He was vibrating, now, gripped by his fury. Spicer went to lay his left hand, drip taped in place, on his arm, but he jerked it away. 'I'm only what society's made me,' Spicer whined. 'One mistake, I get fucked off to borstal, and all I learnt there was how to commit more crimes. Well, they got what they wanted, didn't they?'

Nick stared down at the close-cropped head, the glittering eyes. 'It happens to all of us, mate,' continued Spicer. 'Life. You get fucking ambushed.'

How dare you, thought Nick. You're a murderer. I'm nothing like you. Nothing at all.

'Women,' said Spicer. He was wheezing badly now, clutching at breath between the words. 'Kids. Cancer. Every fucking thing. Load of shit. I tell you, mate, it wasn't the real me done that. It just happened before I could stop it. If they'd just give me some help when I'd asked. You know what it's like – things get away from you.'

I don't know, thought Nick. I'm not like you.

'You can't help it. Like you and your missus and that –' Nick turned away for a moment, re-traced the two steps to his bed, then back again – 'and before you know it, you're fucked, aren't you? And you never meant none of it . . .'

Spicer's chest heaved as he tried to refill his remaining lung. Nat had said she wanted to call the baby Willow if it was a girl. In another burst of fury, Nick suddenly imagined the word tattooed on his own chest, the letters in slightly gothic script, curving over one nipple, as Spicer had Ashlee, complete with spelling mistake, and – Christ All Fucking Mighty – *Briana*.

Nick could never entirely explain it afterwards, but he always told himself – the only person who knew – that *that* was what had tipped him over. That that was when, as Spicer himself would have said, his head just went. *Briana*. 'I'm not like you,' he'd said to Spicer. 'Don't you understand? I. Am. Nothing. Like. You. At. All.' Then, holding the pillow he'd taken from his own bed over Spicer's face, he pressed down hard until the struggling stopped.